T0067911

THE
HEART
OF A
WRESTLER

DANIELLE C. AUCOIN

authorHOUSE·

AuthorHouse™
1663 Liberty Drive
Bloomington, IN 47403
www.authorhouse.com
Phone: 833-262-8899

Published by AuthorHouse 08/16/2022

ISBN: 978-1-6655-6878-4 (sc)
ISBN: 978-1-6655-6877-7 (e)

CONTENTS

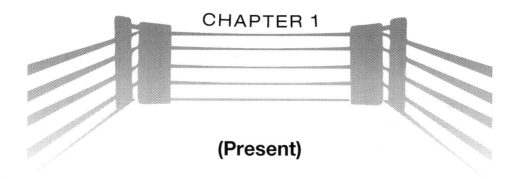

CHAPTER 1

(Present)

A s I stood there in the backstage area of the arena lacing up my knee-high neon green leather wrestling boots it felt as if the hustle and bustle around me was moving in slow motion, and it could all come to a halt in with the blink of an eye. Taking a deep breath in I could practically taste the electricity that loomed in the air as my body buzzed with a nervous energy and a hint of fear deep within my gut. I always begin my transformation by getting ready with my routine of oiling up my long lightly trembling spray tanned legs, that lead to my ring gear of high cut-off denim short and a vintage rock n' roll t-shirt cropped just right to show-off my toned abs and moderate bosom that brushed against my brown hippie hair topped off with a band of flowers in my straight strand. My excitement built as I keenly watched all the seasoned pros going on about their business at hand of metamorphosing themselves into their own personal wrestling creations. I was still trying to wrap my head around the fact that after everything I have been through, I had beaten the odds by finally making it here that it still felt so bizarre, I needed to pinch myself to make sure this just was not some façade.

"Do not get nervous now Cammie" I quietly reminded myself to keep my composure "this is not the time to freak out"

I just could not understand how apprehensive I suddenly was, after all this certainly was not my first performance, I have done this thousands of times before. Having slaved my entire career working to attain this and to be right here, right now in this moment being aware of how high the stakes were for me on this night. Knowing comes easy and but staying was not it was a fight to be here, so I knew I had to be on my A game while putting on the act of a lifetime so not to let all my efforts be in vain. From the moment my feet touched that mat in the ring it was as if I was meant to be there learning the business, the people, and continually revamping this new version of me to keep up with the times.

In the beginning I began working the independent circles appearing for several small locally known companies with quite scarce audiences taking advantage of this time to learn as much as possible and getting to know the tricks of the trade. With further experience and exposure came the offers to work for bigger promotions where I could work my way up the ladder of success. With each step higher my name went further up the card and my picture was even placed on the publicity poster which all felt so surreal that I had to look twice just to be sure my eyes were not just playing tricks on me. With these changes came things like larger audiences, bigger venues, and more time to spend in the squared circle. It started with entertaining a scant amount of people but with lots of determination and grit I was able to ascend here going on to amuse hundreds, then thousands of fans, and now tonight I will be on cable television put on display for millions of people to watch around the world.

Everything seemed unreal like I was seeing all my dreams coming true in front of my eyes. I know this may not be for everyone, some of my friends have told me as much, but it is 100% for me. Nothing can compare to the rush you feel when your theme song hits causing your heart rate to increase as you burst through the entrance then set off down the ramp and into the ring which is simply glorious. That exhilaration you feel while the fans are going wild, jumping out their seats, and the roar of the crowd deafening yet magnificent, if adrenaline were a drug, I would be addicted a certified adrenaline junkie. I am part dreamer and part realist I do not know how they both live together in my head. However, I somehow seem to manage it while staying sane doing it. The dreamer in me believes in fairytales and happy ending yet the realist side understands this is a tough business, you must always be at your best, not to complain about bumps and bruises, and know with a doubt that the show will go on with or without you. And Rule #1: Everyone is expendable.

The harsh truth is no one was here to see me, well not the real me at least, they wanted to see my alter ego Miss Penny Lane the free-spirited, peace, love, and rock n' roll persona I had created and carefully crafted with my distinctly unique artistry. But it does not bother me although perhaps how it should. I think I am just more comfortable being Penny than myself sometimes. Penny was a huge part of me, she was everything I thrived to be, she was confident, engaging, tough, comfortable in her skin, and adored. I smiled blissfully at the thought that I had finally gotten everything I wished to have; success, the perfect career, and most of all a chance to become someone else even if it is just for a little while. But the most important thing I have is the Heart of a wrestler which among other things is Fragile, Intimate, Loyal, Strong, and Brave!

Because of my passion I play Penny Lane with such conviction that most people think we are one in the same. The fans do not know my name they all call me Penny or Miss Penny, so I wear it is as a badge of honor. The positive point is if they know my stage name, they at least know who I am which means I must be doing something right. And for them to want a picture or autograph from me is extremely flattering. The audience pays money to come see all of us play our roles, enjoy a show, and to be entertained. They do not need to know me or my life if they know my character than I am one happy hippie. People do not come here to see Camille "Cammie" McEnrowe from nowhere Louisiana that lived a chaotic existence marked by tragedy so dark that it would threaten to take down even the most hardened of souls. Yet, it did not manage to get me down, no sir, not me I have overcome everything life has thrown my way and now I am only looking up. And

I am certainly on my way there just look at me now only mere minutes from debuting on the Worlds Grandest Wrestling Stage!

Becoming an official Total Wrestling Entertainment (TWE) Goddess was even more electrifying than I imagined filled inside with pleasure astounded by the most magically mystical moment of my calling. At last, I had made it here, and there was no one who could steal this feeling away from me this was my time to revel in the glory of what every drop of my blood, sweat, and tears had ultimately consigned me to. Suddenly, the music blared catching me off guard causing me to jump as fireworks exploded in my ears announcing the arrival of a Totalstar who was making his way to the ring. The shriek of the crowd instantly snapped me away from the tranquility of my mind bringing me back down to earth where I was still in disbelief of being here in the TWE and knowing I had earned this all. A bolt rushed through me, and the energy was palpable as I wished that this short flash in time could somehow last forever. This picture-perfect memory will now be permanently branded into my subconscious where it could be held and cherished for eternity never to be forgotten. I desperately needed to remember this feeling because no matter how much I wanted or how hard I wished today would soon be history and reality would once again sink its cruel icy fangs deep into my warm sumptuous skin foreboding the inescapable face-to-face with him after all these years. It was just a matter of time he would find me soon enough.

Am I ready for him to appear? What will I say? I have conditioned myself for that consequence, but all the preparations cannot equip me for the unknown. Will he be happy to see me, will he be mad, or will he simply ignore me and shew me to the side? Do not psych yourself out I reminded myself. I dare not speak his name not even in my mind because it makes me weak. After so much time am I ready to see him? The him I have spent the last few years trying to forget, the face that still haunts my dreams at night, the one I had tattooed on my body and whose kisses still stained my lips, the man I hated as much as I loved, and the only person capable of breaking me and mending me both at the same time. He was the only other human on this earth that could understand my messed-up mind because he is just as beautifully damaged as I am and had walked through the flames beside me. Lord, I hope we do not combust.

The very thought of seeing him again sent chills down my spine as my heart begin to race. It is incredible how after so long my body still automatically reacts to nothing more than sheer pondering. This could be fantasy, or it could be a nightmare we will have to wait and see since I currently did not have the luxury of worrying or trying to figure it out, I had to shake these feeling off and regain my wits about me because my performance is priority. Right now, I am in high spirits and no one, and I mean no one, is going to pop my bubble. I heard my song hit and I was off to the races. It is SHOWTIME baby let me do this!

"Hello world here I come, the one you want, the one, the only Miss Penny Lane!"

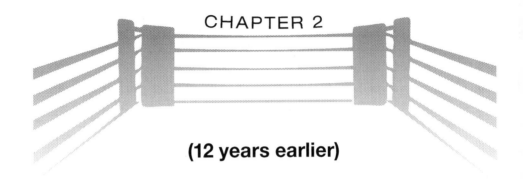

CHAPTER 2

(12 years earlier)

I t does not seem that it was all that long ago when I would never dare allow myself to dream big because I knew it would bring nothing more than another disappointment. And even though I still logically knew that my dreams will probably never come true, I learned to allow myself to dream because dreaming was my one and only escape from the world in which I was unfortunately got stuck in. I realized a while ago that I was different and not like my classmates, yet I never let it bother me much, although being the outcast was lonely at times. I thought being normal was overrated anyways beside what was the fun in being like everyone else. I was quite a quirky girl and could not tell you why since it totally came naturally to me and was just in my nature to be a bit strange or abnormal. Perhaps I was a product of my upbringing, maybe I was unbalanced, or just maybe it was a little bit of both. I suppose that I will never really know since the past is nothing more than yesterday and the future is yet to come. But at this point I do not care to know any longer I would rather just roll with the punches and keep on living.

I was born to a set of loving parents until I was four and they started dabbling in this and that. I went from a wonderful happy home to having a drug addicted mother and well-meaning yet equally disturbed father. Although the outside world classified us as nothing more than poor white trash the world looked much different through my innocent eyes seeing us as just another normal family since did not have any friends, I did not know what other people's homes were like. I spent my days running around town on my pink Huffy Mountain bike that I received from the lady down the street, but I was happy it was perfectly new to me. While we were living in poverty, I went on acting as if I was the queen of my small south Louisiana town rushing to beat the heat, exploring things around me, and living purely in the moment.

I had a feeling that some changes would be coming, and my life would be transforming. Maybe I will make a friend or maybe my parents will clean up their act or it could be something I never even thought of. It was a hot day in May when I was 12 years old that I first laid eyes on the boys that maybe be at the center of this life-changing event. I watched with excitement as the big U-Haul truck pulled into the driveway of a neighboring home while I wondered who could possibly be popping out. Mostly I wished for another kid in the neighborhood, so I would have someone to play with and share adventures plus having a friend right next door would be awesome.

Holding onto hope I watched as a tall man in his thirties with disheveled short light hair and an unshaven face stumbled getting out of the truck and cursed furiously. Then to my delight a young boy around my age with long dark hair, an angelic face, and piercing blue eyes jumped from the truck and ran to help support his bumbling father.

"Please do not embarrass us" the young boy pleaded "We just got here"

The ungrateful father thanked his son by knocking him forcefully to the ground in a fit of anger.

"Shut up kid" he shouted with slurred speech "When you start paying the bills then you can tell me what to do"

He was even worse than my parents, which is saying a lot. How could this man be so cruel? The boy on the ground seemed resigned to his fate as he picked himself up off the ground and dusted his jeans off with a look of defeat covering his face. I could only stand there monitoring the scene that was playing out straight in front of me as my heart broke for this lad I did not even know. Before I could wrap my head around what was happening another young male emerged from the truck appearing to be a carbon copy of the first boy The only difference was this one had shorter hair that touched the tops of his ears. I did a doubletake to make sure my eyes were not playing tricks on me and confirm that I was really seeing my first set of twins. Even though, the two were mirror images of each other there was something different more distinct and edgier with this second one. Oh my, I already feel it, here comes trouble I thought.

My heart fluttered slightly as I felt a strange sensation inside my stomach that I had never encountered until now. Suddenly, one of the twins looked my way and I swiftly turned my head while my cheeks flushed with a red heat as my heart jumped.

"What is going on with me?" I questioned myself quietly trying to understand these completely unfamiliar feeling that I was experiencing.

"Drew, why do you even try?" the second boy narrowed his eyes scolding his brother "It is pointless, he's nothing but a drunk"

"Just leave me alone Joey" the first boy yelled back upset with his twins chastising.

I smiled so wide I probably resembled a cartoon character totally mesmerized by my new neighbors. I see what being nosey gets me.

"Take a picture it last longer" Joey shouted in my direction after catching me staring their way "Girls, huh"

I was filled with dread straightaway as the tingling in my tummy turned to nausea. I had never been so embarrassed in my entire life as I instantaneously turned to run inside wanting to disappear into the safety of my bedroom.

"I am sorry my brothers a jerk" Drew called out to me then was rewarded with a swift punch in the arm from his brother.

"Dang, that hurt Joey" Drew said while I ran to hide away "Why do you have to be so mean?"

All I heard after that was silence as I entered the sanctity of my room. I threw myself on the bed and buried my face in my pillow beginning to feel the tears building behind my brown eyes.

"Way to go Cammie" I berated myself "Now you look like total dork"

I let my tears flow freely down my face soaking my pillowcase as I tried to erase this humiliating day from my mind.

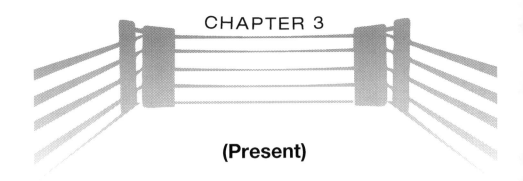

CHAPTER 3

(Present)

"**G**reat Job!" Barb E. Dahl yelled to me from the backstage corridor "Loved your intro"

"You looked great out there!" Sarah said leaning in giving me a big hug.

I was literally beaming with rejoicing feeling every possible human emotion running up and down my body. I was extremely pleased yet also relieved to have finally been given the chance to debut Miss Penny Lane on the world's most famous wrestling stage of all times. Additionally, not many Goddesses get to debut with a one-on-one, so I felt honored to do so. And even though I got pinned and technically lost my first official match in my opinion just getting to be part of Monday Night Wild made me a winner. With a little time and practice I would soon become a winner in the ring as well. I cannot way it for the chance to feel the glory of having my hand raised in victory after the count of three, I imagine victory taste sweet.

"Damn girl, you looked seriously hot in that ring" Sarah complimented genuinely happy for me.

Me and Sarah came up around the same time in TWE's Developmental Program and became remarkably close working most preshow, charity events, and meet and greets together. Before long we were training side-by-side nearly every day growing into workout partners and best friends. Sarah was the actual definition of a blonde bombshell, tall, with her long golden hair, blue eyes, and never-ending long legs. She was perfectly tanned, toned, and had a personality to match her sunny looks. We were complete opposites but somehow managed to hit it off and became instant friends. She was the Ying to my Yang when you saw one of us you saw the other, well as much as our growing schedules allowed. I could not have picked a better friend if I tried, and she had become an expert at breaking me out of my shell which was certainly a unique skill.

"Drinks on me tonight" Sarah commanded "Time to catch up"

It had been a while since we have seen each other because of TWE's very demanding schedule with all the various appearances and shows so it would be nice to enjoy some girl time alone.

"Sounds good to me" I told her with a wink "And I want details about your new man"

"Of course," Sarah giggled "But my priority tonight is getting you over your ex and under a new man"

"Hey, not so fast I just had my premiere" I recanted with a smile "And it may just shake some folks up"

I knew that once he saw me on live television there was no going back and no ignoring our situation or me any longer. The time had come for us to meet once again I was just waiting on him, the ball was in his court now. No matter what the outcome might be we for once could receive the closure we both deserved and the long and winding road we have been on for so long needs to come to an end.

"Whoo! Shake it up girl!" Sarah nudged my shoulder "I cannot wait to feel those tremors"

We left the stadium arm in arm relishing what time we did get to share with one another. Sarah had debuted a few days ahead of me on Thursday Night Knockdown and we were considered the official fresh meat of the company therefore we had to watch ourselves because the sharks do come out. As we headed to our rental car, we could hear a group of fans behind the barrier yelling our names and it felt spectacular.

"What do you think autograph time?" she asked looking at me

I nodded my head yes with a smile so big it hurt my face these were the times I would forever remember. TWE fans were the most loyal of any fans and it was great to get to show my gratitude for them. It was amazing seeing the admiration on their faces and hearing the excitement they had in meeting us. The two of us signed some autographs and posed for some pictures while basking in our new-found fame. The fans were over the moon that we would come out and talk to them, but I figured it's the least I could do for them.

Once done we made it into the vehicle, I finally could release the breath I had been holding in as my mind spun from tonight's introduction of Miss Penny Lane. With the exhaustion of the day starting to settle in there were few words as the radio filled the silence that fell between us. I was ready to hit the hay, but Sarah had other plans as she pulled into a crowded parking lot where I could hear loud music exuding from the building and observed a neon sign sitting atop blinking Broken Spoke Lounge.

As we entered the bar a cloud of smoke and stench of cigarettes hit me in the face and the sound of country music filled my ears as I gazed at a group of girl's line dancing in sync on the dancefloor.

"Sarah where the hell did you bring me?" I asked over the music "Country is not my scene"

"Just thought a change would be nice" she replied with a devilish smile "And you may even find a nice cowboy to take home"

Making our way to the main bar I noticed that we had attracted a few admirers and had a good laugh when I saw one girl hit her boyfriend with her purse when she caught him drooling a bit. Although I stuck out like a sore thumb, I still felt rather confident with my long straight hair dangling down, in my Lynyrd Skynyrd crop top tee, ripped skinny jeans, and red high heels and all I can say about Sarah was she looks hot in her mini back dress and matching black heels. As we had a seat at the main bar and ordered some drinks Sarah began to drill me.

"Get real Cammie your can have any man you want so what is the problem... How long has it been?" she pried

I let out a sigh knowing this was a touchy subject for me, but Sarah was not one to give up easily. Maybe it was time to talk to someone about it all and who better to confide in than my best friend.

"Truthfully, it has been two years but its more complicated than that..." I took a deep breath "We are married"

"Hold up, your married and have been celibate for two years?" she said in disbelief and shock "Your still in love with him, are you not?"

Sarah had hit the nail on the head. I was still madly in love with him no matter how fiercely I denied it or tried to ignore my feeling after what he has done nothing ever seemed to work. But life was different for me now and maybe I could find a way finally move on.

"That is enough about me" I said changing the subject "I want to hear about your new guy"

"Where do I begin, he is gorgeous, tall, tan, built and has a body you just want to rub up and down" Sarah began to explain describing half of the men we worked with when we were interrupted by the bartender.

He placed two shot glasses on the bar in front of us and filled them with some Jack Daniels.

"These are from those guys down there" he said pointing at two young men in cowboy hats who I mouthed a kind thank you to.

"Bottoms up!" we raised our glasses clinking them together with a cheer then threw back the whiskey and slammed the glasses back down on the bar.

I could feel the warmth of the whiskey going down my throat heating up my body as we ordered more drinks for ourselves. I really hope I do not wake to regret this in the morning. However, before we could finish our drinks a petite redhead in bedazzled cowboy boots and matching shirt approached us with her companion by her side.

"Excuse me, are you two Sensational Sarah and Miss Penny Lane?" the lady asked

We shook our heads confirming she was correct even though at this moment we were just trying to be plain ole Sarah and Cammie. But I suppose having our personal time disrupted was the price we pay for celebrity.

"I am a huge fan been watching you since Next Wrestling Star" the redhead gushed

The both of us of course agreed posing for the snapshot with happy smiles. I had to admit that it felt strange being noticed in public yet also felt great at the same time. It appeared that our picture taking attracted some attention and soon more fans approached squashing any girl time we had left but who am I to complain this is what I signed up for and this was now my crazy life. Time ticked by while I signed autographs and took photos when out of the blue a handsome dark-haired man in his early thirties with some stubble on his face took me by surprise when he walked up and with a quiet confidence extending his hand out towards me.

"Looks like you could use a break" the good-looking stranger said, "Care to dance?"

I did not reply only took his hand as I let the liquor running through my veins lead me out onto the dancefloor. The man pulled me closely as we swayed slowly to the mellow melody playing on the jukebox as I closed my eyes allowing myself to relax in his arms until I felt his hand slide down my side and gently caress my left side where the tattoo for my husband sat underneath my shirt instantly causing me to tense up.

"Miss Penny Lane you sure can dance" he said with a southern drawl.

"Thanks" I replied to the kind man

I lectured myself on how I weakened and allowed one blip in time to temporarily warm my soul, but it was nothing more than a foolish disguise letting me believe that for a moment I could just let go. The truth is that I am lonely, and the most embarrassing part is that this gentleman was not even dancing with me he was dancing with Penny Lane.

"Thank you for the dance" I smiled pleasantly as the song ended and I escaped his grasp.

There was only one man's embrace I longed for and whose touch I wanted to feel, and he was not some stranger in a bar. Worn out and ready to go home I made my way over to Sarah who was in the corner flirting with a cute cowboy a little too closely making me nervous considering we had reputations to hold up and a boss to answer to if we did not.

"Sarah, we need to go your boyfriend should be missing you" I urged her as I stepped between her and her new friend.

"Come on Ice Queen I am just having fun and my so-called boyfriend is probably with the chick he is hung up on" she stammered from one-to-many drinks "Sounds familiar perhaps you two should meet"

Hurt by her words without thinking I yanked her arm and lead her straight out the lounge. She put up no resistance sensing my anger realizing she had crossed the line.

"Is that what you really think of me?" I asked furiously once we arrived at the car "I wish I were an Ice Queen it would make my life much easier"

"I did not mean it; it is not what I think" she apologized her eyes watering with sincerity "I am so sorry"

I pulled her in giving her a hug she was my best friend after all, even if she tended to say harsh things sometimes. I knew that we had both been under a ton of stress the last few weeks and at times I could come off as frigid but that was my go-to defense mechanism to save myself from the heartache and hurt this world could deliver us.

"I cannot stay mad at you, sometimes the past is just hard to overcome when you've lost the one you love the most…" I took a breath trying to compose myself before driving off "…More than once"

One the drive home I could not control all the thoughts swimming through my head. He was like poison running in my blood, yet he was the only one who held the antidote. It would be so easy to claim it was all his fault but how could I lay the blame wholly at his feet when we both played our parts. A chill ran down my spine causing a me an unanticipated physical reaction to my thoughts of him.

Sarah and I entered the hotel lobby walking towards our rooms with shoes in hand moving like two zombies in the night. We arrived at our neighboring rooms when Sarah hugged me once again.

"You are my best friend; I am sorry about what I said" she apologized again "I love you"

"I know you are I love you too, night" I responded with a tired yawn.

I plopped down on the bed which had never felt better as I wrapped my body in the warmth of the covers and laid my head on the soft feather pillows which felt like heaven. I then said the same prayers I have said my entire life and ended with a more recent prayer of my own.

"Dear God, help me stop loving him just let me let go"

I fell quickly to sleep where all my worries were gone, and dreams of a life passed reigned supreme. Opening my eyes, the next morning I instantly realized that my prayers remained unanswered when I woke up loving him as I have every morning before and probably would for many more mornings to come. God works on his own time not ours.

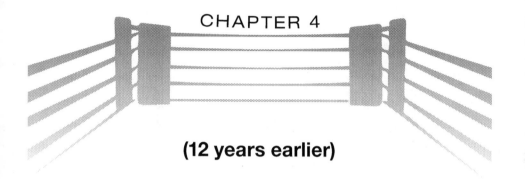

CHAPTER 4

(12 years earlier)

I t was a hot summer day where the humidity seemed to surround and cover you like a blanket as I walked gingerly around my backyard picking blueberries for an afternoon snack. When I heard a sweet voice, I did not recognize and turned to see Drew standing at the fence.

"Hey pretty girl, what is your name?" he asked with the sweetest eyes I had ever seen

"I am Camille, but everyone calls me Cammie. What is yours?" I asked already knowing the answer from peeping

"It is Andrew, but I go by Drew" He replied with a smile.

"Do you have a brother?" I inquired about the new duo on the block.

"Yeah, he is my twin Joseph or Joey sorry he can be an ass" He apologized for his brother which I sensed was not the first time.

Just as we finished our introductions Drews counterpart walked out back and joined us at the fence.

"Hey, it is the spy" Joey said rather cocky looking straight at me.

"I am just curious" I defended myself as I rolled my eyes trying to hide my embarrassment and aggravation.

Joey laughed seeing my red face which infuriated me. I could not understand how someone could make you mad yet make your heart flutter at the same time.

"Hold on seriously, I do not want a bad start in a new place" He said then extended me his hand "How about a truce?" he asked catching me off guard with his unexpected proposition

"Truce" I said wearily shaking his hand.

Drew had a wide smile on his face pleased with the truce. He then threw his hand up waving it back towards him signaling me to join them in their yard.

"Come on" Drew encouraged me.

I quickly jumped the fence hopping down into their yard where I introduced myself to Joey "I am Cammie by the way"

"Joey" he responded with a boyish smile and shrug.

There was something about him that piqued my interest although I could not entirely put my finger on exactly what it was. Of course, it was just like me to take an interest in the rebel twin if I did not know better, I would think I was a glutton for punishment since I was not one to do things the easy way.

"So, what now?" I questioned

"Want to show us around the neighborhood" Joey suggested "But first I need shoes" He looked down wiggling his bare toes in the overgrown grass.

"Cool" I agreed excited to go on my first adventure as a threesome I smiled.

I followed the boys to the single-story wooden house like my own as we entered through the back door that opened into the laundry room where clothes were thrown in stacks near the washing machine. When we got to the kitchen Drew looked back at me putting his finger over his lips signaling me to keep silent while we crept across the kitchen passing dirty dishes in the sink and beer bottles lining the counter making it appear unkept. The three of us then tiptoed down a small hallway where we came to a door with Keep Out written in big red letters taped on it. Joey reached for the knob just as a big shadow overtook us in the dimly lit hall.

I felt like my heart was going to leap from my chest when a deep voice shouted from the darkness "What are you little brats doing?"

"Well...umm..." Drew tried to explain with a trembling voice.

While I stood there frozen in place the man I recognized as their father stepped under the light dirty with filth and smelling so strong of booze it was as if it were seeping from his skin. The disgusting man raised his drunken hand towards Drew and judging by the healing bruise above his left eye this would not be the first. Despite my overwhelming fright a feeling of protectiveness took over and I could not bear the guilt of being the reason for any new bruises.

Refusing to let the fear win a sudden burst of adrenaline shot through me grabbing control of my movement as I watched the scene unfold in front of my eyes as though I was viewing it from outside my body. Without a thought I jumped between Drew and his dad bracing myself for the blow but lucky for me he stopped only inches from my face with the breeze from his hand passing my cheek.

"Stupid girl!" he yelled angrily.

What in the hell did I get myself into here? I wondered completely shocked by the situation I found myself in. At this point I would be happy to just make it out of here alive.

"Hurry Cammie" Joey called with urgency "Let us go!"

This all seemed bizarre in my adrenaline filled haze when Joey promptly pushed me through the, now open, Keep Out sign door immediately slamming it and locking it behind him while Drew was on the opposite side of the room working to open the window. I heard a pounding coming from the other side of the of the door along with the wrathful voice of the twin is father. I was grateful for the small barrier between us and hoped that once he passed out in his drunken stupor that he would not remember any of this tomorrow.

Scanning the boy's room in this chaos, I saw a set of wooden bunks with unmade beds and clothing on the floor along with a couple soda cans and dirty dishes. Wow, boys could certainly be gross I thought. On the wall was a poster of a rock band and another of a big breasted blonde in an itsy-bitsy bikini. The sight of the girl plastered on the wall brought my insecurities to the surface about my barely budding body which resembles nothing close to the bikini model whom I aspired to look like but with brown hair one of these days.

"Are you crazy?" Joey said swinging me around to look at him eye-to-eye "Or do you have a death wish?" the shock was clear on his face.

"I…" I shook my head realizing the danger "I do not know"

"I am sorry you had to see that but thanks for helping my brother" his face turned soft "But you are no doubt a homicidal maniac"

I shrugged my shoulders I have been called worse. Then he gave me a quick unexpected peck on the cheek turning my face rouge. That seemingly simple gesture made my heart flutter I was almost positive that he was my first ever crush. I found my mind, body and, emotions all scattered while encountering things I had never felt before.

"Come on you two" Drew implored holding up the window "We have to go"

I was the first out of the window sliding onto the plush grass glad it was nothing more than a short fall as the twins followed directly behind me. Before our feet could get a firm hold on the ground, we sprinted out the yard as quick as our legs would take us to escape the clutches of that evil man. A sense of relief came over me as we reached the street until I heard screaming coming from the house, we barely managed to escape this time.

"I am go getting to you two" the father yelled increasing my heartbeat "And your girlfriend too"

"This is our life" Joey admitted "I understand if you do not want to be friends"

"We are friends" I told them "My life is pretty bad to"

It upsets me thinking of what the boys may have to face once they returned home. But for the mean time we are at the safety of my home where no one had ever put their hands on me, even though I still had my own very personal demons to contend with in my own private hell.

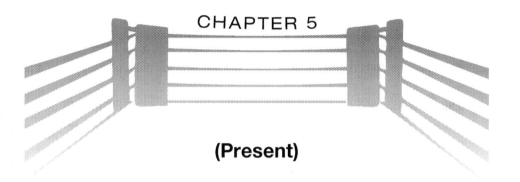

CHAPTER 5

(Present)

Dear Diary,

Wow! There truly is never a dull moment here at TWE, who knew it could be this much fun? I really enjoy the spontaneity of not knowing what is coming next, getting to travel the world, and all the beautiful relationships you make along the way. It was nice getting to spend some time with Sarah last night until she called me out on still loving my husband, but I could not be mad because it is hard to argue with the truth. Once I said my last good-bye to him that should have been the end however nothing is ever that easy and as terrible as this is going to sound, I hope this has been just as hard on him. More than once, I have dreamt of creating a magic potion to save us as I clung to the hope that we were not already beyond repair. The longing to be held in his arms and to feel his love surround me is incredibly stronger than my will. Does hope still draw breath or has all the oxygen escaped me? Should I just give up and move on? I am so confused but always optimistic. Well old friend until next time. Peace Out!

"**W**riting again?" Sarah asked trying to sneak an innocent peek at my private thoughts.

"That thing looks ancient" She commented eyeballing my irreplaceable keepsake "How long have you had it?"

"Ever since I learned how to write" I told her "It holds all my deepest secrets"

As childish as it may be my diary was my one priceless and most treasured item. It had been there when I needed to vent or wanted someone to listen. It was a friend when I was friendless and never abandoned me keeping all my thoughts and dreams safe within its pages. It also documented every victory and hardship I have been through thus far. I slipped my dairy back into the nightstand of my temporary home before joining Sarah on the living room couch.

The two of us recently rented a modest two-bedroom apartment here in Miami, Florida where we could be close to the TWE Performance Complex where we did most of our training and were taught the ends and outs of the business by the best coaches' money could buy. This place was just what we needed not too much, not too little, and in our price range.

"So, you and your man have any plans this evening" I asked but the look on her face told me there was trouble brewing.

"What Happened?" I pressed "I will kick his ass if he hurt you Sarah"

I could feel my blood beginning to boil with disgust for a man I did not even the name of. She has not seemed to want to talk about him and I am not one to pry. But the warning signs are certainly there.

She replied with a saddened expression "He has not really done anything and that is the problem." She sighed "Maybe it is just me"

"That is a bunch of bull" I remarked as my anger increased with each word "He is here in Miami, no excuses"

Who did this loser think he was treating my friend with such disrespect? Sarah was a prize, and any man would be proud to have her on his arm. She absolutely deserved better than the treatment she was receiving now, she deserves to be someone's queen.

"He gave me some lame excuse before cancelling, you warned me wrestlers were heartbreakers" she said holding back tears that filled her beautiful blue eyes "I feel like a fool"

"You are no one fool" I assured her "Let us get your mind off him and go get a bite to eat"

"I suppose it truly is like you always say" Sarah commented forcing a smile "Being happy and looking good is the best revenge"

"Damn straight girlfriend" I added with a cheerful wink.

Sarah was my best friend and an all-around great person so seeing her this way hurt me. Having her in my life has been a blessing and I probably could not have survived this wild ride without her. And what a wild ride has it been! So, anything I can do to help her out of this funk I will do.

We freshened up a bit before leaving for Calvin's Cabana a great little restaurant and sports bar that many pro wrestlers in the area liked to frequent. The wrestling community was a small tight knit circle since it was hard for outsiders and sometimes even spouses to understand our hectic schedule, determination, life on the road, and the emotional and physical demands that came along with this line of work. Due to these issues, it was natural for us to gravitate towards each other for support, friendship, relationships, and the occasional one-night stand. Although, we had each other's back for the most part we would on the other hand compete for camera time, for the spotlight, and most importantly to get that championship gold around our waist.

Coming into the front door of the cabana I quickly spotted some usual faces in the crowd two of whom noticed us and moved our way. I was dressed in my typical casual attire of a Beatles tee tied up in a knot, jean shorts, and some Doc Martins with my hair hanging loosely down while Sarah heated things up in a tight fitting little black dress that displayed her long legs in her dark stiletto heels and blonde hair put up in a messy bun. Any man foolish enough to push her aside is undeserving of a chick as classy as she was.

Two of our co-workers Braedon aka King Braedon and Steve "The Bullet" walked up and greeted us.

"Care to join us?" Braedon asked gesturing his hands towards the table.

Considering the men's veteran status, I would be lying if I said the offer was not flattering. I looked to Sarah to see if she was up for it and the grin on her face was saying yes.

"Sounds good" I answered with a friendly nod.

The four of us sat down at a quiet table in the corner where we rattled off our orders to the young waiter while we made small talk. It pleased me to see Sarah smiling after how down she was earlier. I watched as she grinned happily at Steve with a spark of interest in her eyes and who could blame her Steve was quite the hunk with chin length wavy dirty blonde hair that matched hers and hazel eyes that twinkled as they spoke. Steve was built like a machine with humongous muscles and the sheer size of his arms showed how much time he spent at the gym. Braedon was not as big as Steve but certainly a beautiful specimen none the less with closely cut black hair that complimented his brown eyes and golden skin. We unquestionably worked with some of the sexiest men and women in the world therefore I could see how Sarah could fall for any one of them.

"How is TWE treating you girls?" Steve asked in his deep voice.

"It is great!" Sarah answered for us as I wasted no time digging into my perfectly cooked steak "It is more amazing than expected"

"So, Sarah are you still dating that douche?" Braedon boldly asked catching me completely off guard.

I slightly choked on my steak hearing the unexpected question then gave him a swift vengeful kick under the table leaving a lasting sting from my boot.

"Ouch" he exclaimed eyeing me with amusement "Do not bruise the merchandise"

"Sorry" Sarah giggled "She is just a bit protective"

"I see that" Braedon grinned at me "It was oddly arousing"

All I could do was roll my eyes at his comment not letting on that I found his reaction oddly arousing as well. Stop it Cammie now is not the time I prompted myself. For now, I will focus on Sarah and Steve's mutual attraction which was evident to anyone with eyes. Whereas me and Braedon were attracted to each other's flesh more like impulsive bodily cravings. But I had to be stronger than my lust I had to many complications in my life right now and do not need one more. I was glad for Sarah but could not say I was exactly thrilled he was a wrestler but who am I to judge considering I was in love with one.

"To answer your question, I do not know where we stand" Sarah explained as Steve's eyes lit up "And really do not care"

"Glad to hear that" Steve hinted

"Cammie, what is your status?" Braedon asked curiously

Unsure of the correct response I answered "It is complicated"

Braedon seemed visibly disappointed with my answer leaving me feeling somewhat foolish. He was gorgeous, blunt, and weirdly charming yet I still pass up a possibility of happiness for someone I was not sure even knew I still existed. What is wrong with me? I have waited this long what is a little more time going to hurt.

We continued talking as our conversation flowed as freely as the wine. Braedon scooted closer to me and casually put his hand on my legs sending a shiver through me and instead of pushing his hand away I pulled it closer. He looked me in the face and smiled at me which I returned with a sideways smile. He was rather enticing, and I was allowing him to believe that I was falling for it and maybe I was just a little. I was having such a wonderful time that I could have stayed there all night chatting it up however it was getting late, and I was becoming tipsy, so we decided to call it a night and stood to leave. I gave Steve a friendly hug then left him and Sarah to talk privately as Braedon walked up beside me with a warm look.

He then gave me a hug and whispered in my ear "If it ever gets uncomplicated, I am easy to find"

"I will keep that in mind" I said gently kissing his cheek.

Braedon was undeniably a great charmer, but could he ever be my lover? Could his kisses taste as sweet, or his touch linger the way it should? The possibilities frightened and excited me causing my stomach to tingle in ways I had not felt for some time. But I still find myself stuck in the vicious cycle of doubting everything I saw, sensed, and experienced never giving myself the break I very much deserved. Would I ever allow myself to find a new love, or shall I go to the grave with his name fresh on my lips? There must be life after him, does there not? Those thoughts were quickly swept away when Sarah sprinted up to me.

"Steve asked me to go have a drink" she fished for my approval "What do you think?"

"Sounds like a good idea" I gave her the confirmation she was seeking.

"You sure?" she asked looking for an out I would not give her "You will be, okay?"

"Do not worry about me" I assured her "Now get out of here"

"Thank you, Cammie" she hugged me before rejoining Steve.

We watched the two of them walk off into the distance then Braedon asked, "May I walk you out?"

"Sure" I accepted "Why not?"

He put his arm around my waist escorting me to my car and politely opening the door for me.

"Who knew you were such a gentleman?" I teased with a giggle.

"Shhh..." he spoke lively "You will ruin my reputation"

I should have gotten in my car right then and made a fast escape, but I was engrossed in his unwavering gaze feeling a static charge between us. Without warning Braedon boldly brought his lips to mine for a warming kiss I returned. I could hardly believe what had just transpired, I had not been kissed in such a long time. I swiftly turned my face towards the ground shyly trying to hide my blushing cheeks.

"Goodnight beautiful" he said turning with his hand sliding in mine.

Screw it! Cammie, you deserve to live I told myself in that moment. Before Braedon could leave, I impulsively gripped his hand and pulled him to me pressing my body to his chest as we kissed once again this time with more of a lust and craving. As we finished, he pressed his forehead softly to mine.

"Wow, your amazing" Braedon commented "Do you know that?"

I smiled up at him then ran my hand down his chest feeling the sculpt of his muscles beneath his shirt while avoiding his question.

"Goodnight handsome" I replied "Sometimes I wish I was that kind of girl"

Finally finding my way to the driver's seat then closing the door as Braedon watched me with amazement. It was a solemn ride home just me and a mellow song on the stereo while I prepared myself for another lonely night. My emotions were all over the place with thoughts flashing through my mind of my work, my absent husband and of that breathtaking kiss. Tonight, has been a good night maybe that kiss was exactly what I needed to finally move on I pondered as I pulled into the driveway. Stepping out the vehicle the night air was nice as it blew across my skin making my hair prickle at its touch. I looked up to the star filled sky admiring its twinkling magnificence and soon found myself wondering if he was looking up upon the same night sky the way we always use to look at it in each other's arms. I let out a solitary sigh as I turned my key in the lock and stepped into my empty apartment letting the door close behind me. Will tonight be the night? I wondered aloud.

As I walked inside my quiet apartment, I let a lonesome sigh out readying myself for another lonely night when I was startled by a loud abrupt thud coming from behind me. I turned swiftly on my heel to see a man's black Doc Martin boot stopping the door from closing. My heart skipped a beat when a hauntingly familiar voice from the past came from behind the door.

"Hey pretty girl"

And with those three simple words I knew the answer to the question I asked myself each night "Will I finally stop loving him?"

I closed my eyes gently one part of me wanting to slam the door and lock it but the other part of me wanted to throw that door open and jump into his arms. However, I did not know what he wanted, what his motivations were, I should just see how this will this go? It was too late to run away now so I answered my last question and stood statuesque there with compressed breath as my anxiety headed towards high.

"Stop loving him tonight huh? I told myself "Cammie not this night or any soon to come"

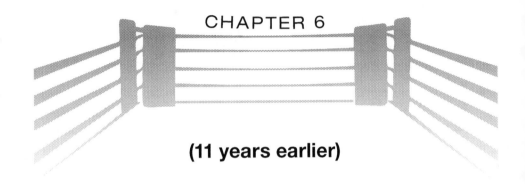

CHAPTER 6

(11 years earlier)

Dear Diary,

Today is a special day because I just turned 14 years old today and can see and feel all the physical and emotional changes happening within my body. My parents have been missing most of the day and I am almost positive that they unsurprisingly forgot today was my birthday. However, there was no way I was going to let that get me down because it was my special day, and my friends have plans on taking me down to the pond or as we like to call it our special spot to celebrate. The twins and I have become practically inseparable, and the locals dubbed us The Three Amigos. I can barely even remember what life was like before they came into the picture. By the way, just a quick update, I still have a huge crush on Joey although the probability of him feeling the same is way is bleak. Oh well, here is to dreams! Peace Out!!

I tucked my diary beneath the socks in my drawer before flopping down on my bean bag in my jean shorts, black tank top, red flannel shirt, and bare feet getting comfy while waiting on the boys to show up. I hastily flipped through the few channels we had until I reached my favorite music video station and sang along to the rock song just when I heard the secret knock on the glass.

"Yeah, yeah, I hear you" I fussed lightheartedly raising the window expecting to see the twins.

Confused by the sight of Joey standing there alone I inquired "Where is Drew?"

I was legitimately concerned by his absence knowing the dangers they faced at the hands of their father.

"He is fine" He explained expelling my fears "I asked him to head to the pond, I wanted to give you your present in private"

"Alright come in" I conceded while giggling as he clumsily stumbled through my window.

I was a little perplexed and unsure of what to think but I knew that Joey had something up his sleeve as I surveyed his face of any hint of what was to come. While looking into his face I noticed how much he had sprouted up since our first meeting. He appeared more grown now and his maturing face was as handsome as ever. He kept his hair unchanged still ear length allowing it to blow across those hypnotizing blue eyes that always pulled me in. Joey walked over to me taking a seat on the carpet in front of me looking straight into my eyes.

He leaned forward coming closer to me as our stare remained unbroken "Tell me Cammie, why do we play these games?"

Puzzled by his question I responded, "And what games do we play?"

"You know" he answered "The I do not like you, you do not like me, but we secretly do game"

Be still, my heart! I was shaken and taken completely off guard by his response. Never in a million years did I expect to hear those words come from his lips. Did he just say what I thought he did? Could he really have liked me this entire time and I was oblivious to it? Or was I being pranked? What do I say? I was the one who usually never shuts up but now found myself struck mute. I had seen Joey smile a million times before but there was something different in his smile tonight. I felt fuzzy as if I had entered the twilight zone.

Then he asked me "Do you have any feelings for Drew?"

"Really, is that what this is about?" I asked sort of irritated "Did Drew put you up to this?"

It is an open secret that Drew has a crush on me so Drew getting Joey to do his dirty work is in his wheelhouse. I put nothing past those two.

"No, that is not it I swear" he shook his head "I wanted to make sure I would be your number one guy" He confessed turning his head to the floor.

Joey looked adorable when he was embarrassed although it was something that I did not see often. I brought my face near his and softly swept the hair away from his eyes as he sat quietly awaiting my words.

"You will always be my number one" I assured him.

Raising his head Joey caressed my face as I closed my eyes getting lost in his touch. He then ran the tips of his fingers though my hair and grasped the back of neck pulling me in his heated lips melded into mine creating a breathtaking kiss. My pulse raced tantalized by his luscious lips and the sweet taste on my tongue caused my body to tremble with a nervous satisfaction. I had dreamt of this exact moment a million times before, yet it was even better than I ever could have imagined. I had no idea it was possible to feel this way.

"Look who is speechless now" he teased with a charming smile.

I blushed in response still attempting to catch the breath Joey had taken from me with our first kiss. I was walking on clouds in a state of euphoria the whole world could come tumbling down around me and I would have not even noticed.

"I took a big risk you know" he boasted confidently smiling like Cheshire Cat "You could have shot me down"

"Yeah right" I laughed "It was obvious to everyone that I liked you from day one" I threw a pillow at him telling my not so well-kept secret.

I looked deep into his blue eyes, brushed his hair back, and gave him a sweet kiss that left me with goosebumps from head to toe.

"I can get use to this" Joey smirked "But Drew is waiting on us and he is going to be mad that you are my girl now"

I could have stayed there for hours but our friends were patiently awaiting our arrival, so we swiftly jumped out my window and raced on down to our special spot. When we arrived at the pond, I found my usual sitting spot on the bank where I dipped my naked feet in the pond wiggling my toes as the cool water traveled around my skin. Joey took a seat beside me, rolled up his jeans, and put his feet in the water touching them to mine then playfully splashed me as we innocently laughed and joked.

"What is up with the two of you?" Drew observed eyeing us closely "You two are never this friendly"

We were totally busted. I felt terrible because this was not the way I wanted Drew to find out. I was racked with guilt knowing how much Drew liked me, but I could not pretend to have feeling that just were not there.

"Drew you are my brother, and nothing will ever change that" Joey tried to explain "But I honestly like her"

The disappointment on Drews face hurt my heart and I knew he realized exactly what was going on. I instinctually ran to his side where he stood stunned placing my hand gently on his shoulder, I only wanted to bring him comfort even though I was the one at the cause of his pain.

"I never wanted to hurt you" I said honestly "You are my best friend, and nothing is going to change that"

Drew was without a doubt my best friend and the last thing I ever wanted to do was hurt him. I would be completely lost without him since Drew and Joey were like family to me and pretty much all I had in this world. I would never purposefully jeopardize my friendship with Drew but on the other hand it was virtually impossible to deny the feeling I had Joey.

"Is this what you really want?" He questioned squeezing my hand.

"Not if it means losing you" I admitted wanting his blessing.

"Camille, there is nothing you can do to lose me" he said sincerely "No matter how many jerks you date" he smiled over at his brother.

Then Drew reached into his pocket pulling out a paper rose he had made and handed it to me. Opening the rose I found a silver charm bracelet with a charm in the shape of a peace sign dangling from it.

"Happy Birthday" he smiled sweetly as he put the bracelet securely around my wrist.

"Thank you, sweet boy" I responded kissing his cheek.

I blinked back the happy tears as my heartbeat with joy from the beautiful gesture. I owed a lot to those two for teaching me what real love should be like and I honestly loved them both but in two separate ways. Drew slide his hand back in his pocket, gave us a nod of approval, and turned to walk away giving me and Joey some time alone as we watched him fade into the night.

Joey wrapped his arms around my waist pulling me in close "You can still catch him if you want"

"I am exactly where I want to be" I assured him as I turned to face him.

"I am glad to hear that" he responded grabbing me for an impassioned kiss.

His kisses made my body ache with a power that ran through me like lightning as his body was snuggly against mine. I was now entering uncharted territory and knew I should move cautiously as I navigated the waters of this developing relationship. Yet, what I should do and what I will do could be two totally different things. Only time shall tell.

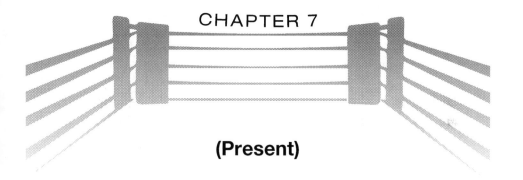

CHAPTER 7

(Present)

My heart raced feverishly as I watched him step across the threshold in a dreamlike fog, I finally laid my eyes on the man my heart continually ached for. I could barely contain myself after seeing the face I had loved for so very long, the face that awaited me in my dreams, the most stunning face I have ever seen. Then it was as if all the air escaped my lungs, and it became hard to breath.

"Andrew" I somehow managed to speak his name aloud.

I fought in vain to hold back my tears as they rushed out leaving a trail of black tears staining my face. Drew stepped towards me as my breath quickened while he wiped the tears tenderly away causing my body to tremble beneath his touch.

"How can you not hate me?" I asked fearful of his answer.

He scooped me into a tight embrace saying "Camille, how could I hate the only woman I ever loved?"

I buried my face in the safety of his chest taking in his alluring aroma that had remained unchanged. I fell into his orbit allowing myself to release all the emotions I had pent up inside.

"I only wanted the best for you" I sobbed "then you disappeared no calls no visits I figured you did not want me any more"

Pleading for his understanding I tried to explain

"I waited by the window positive you would figure it out and come home and get me but... you never did"

There was so much I wanted and needed to say but had no idea where to start. My nerves were raw, my body numb, and my mind twisted it is a sheer miracle that I have not unraveled yet. Only he can help if I come undone.

"I am here now" he said with glassy eyes "And that is all that matters"

I stood there spellbound by the blue eyes of the boy I fell in love with who was now a strong handsome man that still possessed my heart in the palm of his hand. His eyes still glycine as they always did, the stubble on his face made him appear more rugged and mature, and his long dark hair still looked as if it spun of silk.

As I reached out touching his face my fingers trembling then Drew placed his hand atop mine to calm the shaking. The memories of us and our life together came flowing back burning in my mind like a flame I could not put out. Why had he come to me? If this goes wrong, I do not think I would recover however at this point I had nothing left to lose and was ready to take the chance. I was completely prepared to dive into him and the hurt that may accompany it because I could not bear living without him even one more day.

"I am not here to hurt you Cammie" he said as if he could hear the dialogue in my head.

He kissed me sweeping me off my feet with lustrous lips that still tasted sweet as a I remembered. I was not innocent by any means and every short coming and each mistake has built my character and made me into the strong woman I have become. And now my strength was being tested because I was fed up with running and had no place left to hide. At this point feeling hurt was better than not feeling anything at all.

"Promise you will never let me go" I begged of Drew with my heart hanging on the line.

"I promise" Drew whispered in my ear "I love you Camille"

Those words were like magic on his tongue for I have yearned to hear those words again for some time.

"My hearts pounding right now" he admitted

I calmly placed my hand on top of his heart where I could feel the thuds of its rapid beat. This was the same heart that belonged with mine and filled me full of love.

"I love you too" I kissed him back "That has never changed"

I thought beyond a shadow of a doubt that Drew was indeed my soulmate. He was one of the few people who could always see through my character and see the real me instead of who I was pretending to be. It felt fabulous to be seen once again. I was tired of the blame game and no longer cared about who was right or wrong I just wanted him to hold me until the heartache was gone. Here we were united again and given a second chance at life and love that I would not let slip away from me. A love that burns as bright as ours did was almost impossible to snub out and we somehow always seemed to manage to find our way back to each other.

I silently took him by the hand leading him to my bedroom. Let them judge us and talk if they want because consequences be damned, I wanted and needed him like never before. I sat at the foot of my bed engrossed in his gaze feeling my pulse growing as he locked the door behind him.

"You are more magnificent than ever" Drew told me with a fiery desire in his eyes that had reached a flash point.

Reaching out he ran his fingers through my hair getting my sensual juices circulating. He then twirled my hair in his hand tugging my hair backwards tilting my head to face him as I let out a lustful sigh. Drew moved in closer kissing me deeply while he laid me back onto my bed his body pressed snuggly to mine. He pushed up my shirt exposing my tattoo of a M entangled in an infinity sign of thorns to symbolize no matter how prickly the path got our lives were eternally intertwined. He then kissed our intimate insignia sending chills rushing across my skin as I pulled his shirt over his head tossing it hastily to the floor which was quickly becoming scattered with clothes. Running my lips tenderly over the tattoo placed above his heart, that mirrored mine, I moved my hand across the silkiness of his chest before running my fingertips down his stomach listening as he let out a long deep breath as we both pulsed with an undeniably intense hunger that begged to be fulfilled. It Has been way to long for me.

Lying in the stillness of the night staring into the face of the man I loved had me captured in the moment wanting to feel his lips on every part of me and leave no piece of me untouched. Taking unabridged advantage of every second together we wasted no time feverishly undressing one another as we kissed with an animalistic passion freely indulging in the desires we had suppressed for far too long. We brought our pulsating bodies together crashing into each other like waves breaking on the shore losing myself in his abyss. The sweat dripping from his skin tasted salty on my tongue while his moistened mouth nibbled softly on my neck. I laid back with bated breath absorbing every sultry touch as if it were the last. Letting go unreservedly I held nothing back releasing myself to him I cried out in erotic pleasure as the sounds of ecstasy brushed Drews lips at the same time. Wrapping my body snuggly around his I gripped his back with my fingers digging into his skin as each thrusting move revitalized me. I finally began to become whole again feeling Drews as he is exploring all the parts of me. The hedonistic gratification merged us together making us no longer two halves but one once again. The tenderness of his touch lingered on my skin making me tingle from head to toe erasing any remaining doubts as we filled each other with a love rejuvenated.

Each kiss we shared encircled me in the ambience of an affair of the heart, body, and soul. Giving ourselves to each other in every way influenced us to get lost in time as the world falls away and we land in a universe that only the two of us inhabit. Feeling the electric waves running inside made me shudder in pleasure captivated by his blue eyes that stared into my soul echoing with love. During our impassioned romance I felt during our intimate encounter enamored me as I was swept from my feet by the uncensored tenderness and adoration shown to me by my beloved paramour.

With every touch I sensed myself being rebuilt as the shattered pieces of me were put back together leaving only scars behind to remind me that it happened. The trials and tribulations I have overcome taught me to focus on what I had right in front of me and not to dwell on days gone by because all we have is the present, so we must appreciate what we have for the time that we have it.

Totally spent from our liaison I rested my head on Drews chest listening to the rhythm of his heartbeat which had a soothing effect on my fatigued body. At last, the worst was over, and I could breathe again. I honestly believed this day would never come yet here I was, and it was such a great relief I could not be happier.

"I love you Camille" he said those deeply touching words that danced in my ears "I never stopped"

I responded back genuinely "I love you too sweet boy"

I took in every vivid moment not wanting tonight to end as I daintily rubbed his stomach while he ran his fingertips up and down my side putting me at peace as we laid their skin on skin. Fully relaxed I closed my eyes wanting the night would go on forever.

Drowsily Drew asked, "Can I stay?"

"I want you to stay" I admitted "But you terrify me"

"I promise to keep your love safe" he assured me kissing me sweetly on the forehead "I got you now and forever"

"Forever sounds good" I commented in almost a whisper before drifting off to sleep secure in the arms of my beautiful lover.

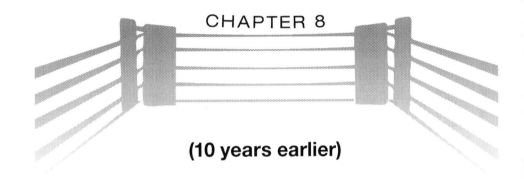

CHAPTER 8

(10 years earlier)

As quietly as possible I slid open my bedroom window before snatching my currently neglected diary and sneaking out to meet my friends at our special spot. Soon as my feet hit the ground, I sprinted down the road, across the field, and through a patch of woods that lead directly to the pond.

Joey caught me off guard as I exited the woods

"Hey babe" he said as I jump slightly.

"Hello, my love" I greeted him with a smooch.

Joey was a distinguishable character who did not care what others thought and lived life at his own pace. My peers often gave me a hard time for dating Joey and questioned why I would be with someone like him who tended to rub people the wrong way but with me he was kind, sweet, protective, and loving. Drew liked to tease that I put a spell on his brother or bewitched him however I like to believe that I just brought out the best in him.

Joey pointed to the diary in my hand "What did you bring that for?" he asked.

"Thought I would catch up on some writing" I explained.

He looked at me with his cute boyish smile "Cool baby doll I will leave you to it." He said sending me off with a slap on my butt.

I turned back playfully looking at Joey in pretend shock as I rubbed my rear with a grin before finding my sitting spot and began to write an entry.

Dear Diary,

Well old friend it seems like we have some catching up to do since I have been busy dealing with the hectic business of starting my sophomore year and trying to kick myself back into school mode. So now where do I start? I suppose my love life is as good as any plus it is my favorite topic. Today makes a year and two months that me and Joey have been a couple and as lame as this is going to sound, I love him more and more each day. We are a teenage love story. This past November for our first anniversary Joey allowed his romantic side show when he brought me out on a date to a clearing in the sugarcane field where he had laid a blanket across the ground and set out a picnic basket complete with strawberries, chocolate, and a dozen beautiful red roses. No one had ever done anything so sweet for me and the genuine joy on his face made me smile inside and out. It was perfect there beneath the starry sky only the two of us surrounded by rows of sugarcane when for the first time he told me that he loved me. Those were the absolute most valuable words to ever grace my ears. I thought my heart would explode with jubilation and I did not hesitate in expressing my mutual feeling for him then sealed our love with an electric kiss. Without a single word there was a presence in the air telling us that this magical evening was not over and now would be the right time to move our relationship to the next level and give the gift of ourselves to one another. Enraptured in the moment we allowed our hearts to lead the way giving into carnal desire leaving our innocence behind in the clearing. Man, love is grand!! ` Peace Out!

After finishing my confessional, I placed my diary inside the hollow of the tree near where I was sitting for safe keeping when I heard Drew come up behind me.

"What is up pretty girl?" he greeted me.

I stood up dusting the dirt from my raggedy jeans then gave him a hug catching a whiff of Joeys Calvin Klein "CK" Cologne that struck me a little odd since I never knew Drew to wear cologne before.

"Smelling good, sweet boy" I complimented

"Thanks Cammie" he said just as an unfamiliar face stepped forward "There is someone I want you to meet"

The wholesome appearing girl came closer and joined Drews side.

"Cammie this is Ginny" he introduced us "Ginny this is Cammie"

Ginny was a pretty country girl with teased bleach blonde hair, a tied-up plaid shirt with tassels, bedazzled boots, jeans, and dark green eyes.

"Cool to meet you" I welcomed her with a hug.

"I have heard tons about you" she said with a cute southern twang "Nice to put a face to the name"

When Joey heard the chatter, he came around the tree to join us and meet Ginny. Joey responded with a confused smile that he tried to conceal as we exchanged amused glances. He then wrapped his arms around my waist putting his hands over mine while he cuddled against me on this chilly night.

Perplexed by the situation he leaned in and whispered a question in my ear "What is going on? Seriously, am I being pranked?"

I could certainly relate to Joey's surprise since Ginny looked like an all-American girl who made good grades, cheered, played sports, and was proper. Whereas our crew was the troublemakers, skaters, rockers, not at all proper, more like all-American rejects. So those two together made an unusual coupling but if she made Drew happy that was all that mattered to me. Looking over at Joey I could practically see the wheels turning in his head and knew he had a bad habit of speaking without thinking.

"Be nice baby, your brother seems to really like here" I warned before he put his foot in his mouth.

"Okay, okay" he replied rubbing my hand "But only because you asked me to"

I always felt right at home in the depths of Joeys arms which made standing here under the moonlit sky that reflected in the pond on such a gorgeous night even more spectacular. Suddenly Joey leads me into the woods and out of earshot of the newly formed couple.

"I have a present for you" Joey spoke nervously "I just do not want you to think its cheesy or anything"

This was indeed a rare moment to see Joey nervous. Personally, I think it was adorable and it also filled me with joy because his nervous demeanor showed that it was something he cared about.

"Anything from you is priceless never cheesy" I responded.

I watched his confidence grow as he reached in his pocket placing a small item in the palm of his hand. When he opened his hand, I saw a dazzling silver mood ring, that I had been admiring for some time now, in his hand which brought a smile to my face pleasantly surprised. He knew me so well this was the ideal present. He took my right hand and slid the ring on my middle finger.

"This symbolizes my devotion and unwavering love for you" he proclaimed.

I believed him because I knew he had to cut quite a few yards for this. I smiled at Joey lovingly it never failed to amaze me how such a rough and tumble guy could be so sweet and good to me speaking the language of love into my heart. I have never felt this secure and cared for by anyone in my life as I twirled the ring around my finger admiring my priceless gift.

"Forever and always" I agreed with a jubilant heart.

I watched while the ring turned from black to a dark shade of blue before my eyes which was said to indicate love and to my joyful surprise it was right on point.

I raised my hand pointing at my ring "Love" I smile showing Joey.

"Well, we know it works" he grinned giving me a short kiss.

I felt like I was glowing we were young, in love, and had the rest of our lives ahead of us it did not get better than this. In my juvenile mind I thought we were indestructible; nothing could stop us or tear us apart. Me and Joey walked back to rejoin the group just as Laura and

Billy arrived. The six of us walked down to the gathering spot where the music was blasting from our battery powered radio. We sat around the small fire conversating and goofing off simply enjoying the night and the company.

Ginny dug in her purse searching for something then pulled an item out catching us all off guard with an unexpected offer "Want to smoke?" she asked us.

I glanced up to focus on what she was holding up when I saw the joint in her hand. I chuckled to myself this was the perfect proof that you should not judge a book by its cover. For instance, we were the crazy rock kids who had a reputation for being bad asses and troublemakers, yet we had never actually broken the law before. Then this sweet-faced country girl comes in to corrupt us if that is not ironic, I do not know what is.

Billy was the first to accept her proposition "Sure" he said.

With a few gestures the rest of us came to an unspoken agreement to give it a try. Drew looked at me with uncertainty, so I gave him a quick wink and nod of assurance as he took a few puffs then passed it to me. I hesitated for a split second unsure of what to expect however I figured that your only young and fearless once therefore the time was ripe for experimentation.

The harshness of the smoke that hit my throat made me cough, but I got it under control as we freely passed it among ourselves. Soon my body became light and floaty while a wave of happiness and giggles followed as we made random small talk, laughed out loud, and carried on like the bunch of silly teens we were. I glimpsed down at my hand and noticed that my ring had changed to yellowing showing my mellow mood that caused me to smile in satisfaction. I leaned into Joey snuggling against him as he put his arm around my neck and covered my face with tiny smooches.

Joey stood up extending his hand out "Come see I want to show you something" he said

I followed him into a patch of trees a few feet from our special spot. He placed his hand on one of the tree trunks drawing my eyes to a carefully carved heart that decorated the bark of the tree. Then he took out his Swiss army knife from his back pocket and carved his initials JM and a plus sign inside the heart flashing me his charming boyish smile.

"You should finish it" he said hand me his knife.

Taking the pocketknife, I carved my initials CL on the opposite side of the heart and blew the dust away. I ran my fingers across the rough surface in pure delight of our handy work. I was proud to know there an icon of our devotion will stand, even after we were gone, a living tribute to the bond we shared forever sculpted in the wood of this old oak tree for all eternity. Joey moved his hand over mine as together we touched the beautiful heart we created while he stared deep into my soul.

"You look stunning under the moonlight" he complimented.

"And your crazy" I shook my head with a shy smile.

He pointed to the twinkling stars in the night sky beaming "You give the stars a run for their money"

I turned my head to the side attempting to hide my blushing cheeks. It really must be love that had him seeing me in such a warm shimmering light. Comparing me to the stars was a bid corny yet nonetheless flattering.

I stared into the face that had me so infatuated and teased "Must be blinded by love"

Leaning against our tree we locked lips with an authentic unadulterated feel, and I had never felt more alive in my entire life, and nothing compared to the haze he put me in when we touched. How does he make bad seem so good with such ease? I hope I survive this fever he has given me because I have never seen my future quite so clearly.

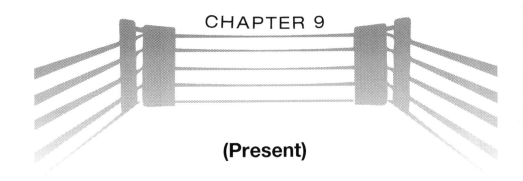

CHAPTER 9

(Present)

I slowly blinked my eyes open clearing my vision as the early morning sunlight crept through the window brushing my cheek when I felt the warmth of the body lying next to me. I was in no rush to leave the bed watching Drew beginning to wake from his peaceful slumber stirring around while rubbing his eyes and stretching his beautifully sculpted nude body.

"Good pretty girl" he said softly opening his eyes looking over at me.

"Morning sweet boy" I replied pulling him closer never wanting to let him go again.

For a long time, I believed that moments like these had completely passed me by for good, so I am not willing to take our second chance for granted. I felt like Drew breathed life into my failing lungs saving my life and it boggles my mind how one person, out of millions, could be that important that without him life seems meaningless, and everything just feels wrong. But for now, my world was right once again, the earth could continue spinning. I could stay here in this room forever and never be unhappy if he was with me, I was thinking when I was disrupted by a tapping on the door and jiggling of my locked doorknob.

"What is up? You never lock the door" Sarah inquired excitedly from outside my room "Did you finally take my advice and bring Braedon home?"

Oh, my goodness! Really, did she just blurt that out? Drew looked at me in amusement while I pulled the sheet over my head sinking into the bed fully embarrassed.

"Nope" I said from beneath the sheets "Not Braedon"

"Ops sorry" she pressed "The anonymous husband?"

You could not ask for a better friend than Sarah, but she was also extremely nosy. I knew her well enough to know she was not going to leave my door without some sort of answers.

I gave in confirming her suspicions "Well if it was not this would be even more awkward than it already is"

After receiving a satisfactory answer, she relented leaving my door and finding her way back to her own.

"Braedon? Seriously?" Drew teased uncovering my head "I cannot picture that"

"Hey, it is not my fault if I am a wanted woman" I laughed as I went to get up.

Before I could get a firm footing on the floor Drew yanked me by my waist pulling me back down against him and landed a kiss that put my soul at ease. It is incredible how a mere touch of his lips could transport me to the clouds.

"Damn straight my wife is smoking" he grinned tossing me his shirt.

I caught the shirt and hurriedly threw it on as I have hundreds of times before. I recognized the scent of the CK cologne he always wore and found it comforting how somethings never change. Pressing the shirt to my nose I took a whiff of his sweet fragrance before starting my daily routine. Drew pulled on his blue jeans that sat loosely around his hips leaving his chest bare and hair unbrushed which was a very sexy look indeed. I had hung my hopes of a real future on a thin thread that was becoming stronger, and I could finally see a light at the end of the tunnel. I prayed Drew wanted the same thing because if not it would be a crushing blow. I was hesitant at first but took a stabilizing breath fully prepared to tell him exactly how I feel consequences be damned.

"I love you Andrew" I said nervously "I hope we can focus on the future, not dwell on the past…"

"That is if we have a future I mean" I second-guessed my confession.

I got a warm fuzzy inkling inside as he stared at me with those baby blues saying "Whenever I picture my future, you are always there as of last night it is the future anything before that is the past and that is where it stays"

"I see you too" I admitted unable and unwilling to imagine a future without him.

"But there are some things you should know" he informed me.

At this point I was not quite ready to hear any of the sordid details of our time apart and wanted to concentrate on today not letting anything ruin this memory of us because now we had the rest of lives.

"Shhh… sweet boy" I said placing my finger over his freshly kissed lips "No one taught us how to love yet together we figured it out and found happiness in the most hopeless of situations"

We were both raised absent of affection and attention having only each other to lean on. However, we had defied our upbringing and look where we had landed. Nobody expected two kids from the wrong side of the tracks bore by addicted neglectful parents to do anything with their lives, yet we proved them wrong. We allowed their doubts to become our motivation literally rising from absolutely nothing to celebrity status it was truly a rag to riches story if there ever was one.

"How about some Cajun Eggs for my Crazy Cajun lover?" I asked poking a little fun at his stage name as we walked into the kitchen.

He rubbed his belly with a goofy grin "Drooling just thinking about it""

I prepared breakfast carefully seasoning the eggs just right while Drew stood behind me inhaling the delicious aroma in the air. Cajun Eggs has been Drews favorite food for as long as I could remember but only, I knew the recipe that I kept filed safely in my mind.

"This smell and watching you at the stove bring back many memories" Drew kissed my neck as he reminisced.

I turned my head slickly to catch one of his kisses before plating our food which Drew wasted no time digging into not saying a word as he enjoyed a taste of home. Afterwards without me having to ask he politely washed the dishes as I hopped up on the counter peering at Drew while he finished up then walked towards me placing his body between my thighs kissing me warm and wildly. The two of us were acting like a pair of schoolkids unable to keep our hands off each other and it was phenomenal.

"Oh, hell no!" Sarah hollered catching me by surprise when she entered the kitchen "No! No! No!"

We swiftly turned our heads to face Sarah who was standing there with a look of pure horror on her face.

"Cajun, what the hell is going on?" she screamed angrily at Drew.

As tensions built, I shook my head in denial beginning to put the pieces together and not liking the image that was starting to appear. I felt as if I had just plummeted into an alternate universe where I did not belong.

"It was never my intention to hurt you Sarah "he tried to explain unsuccessfully "When I found out about you and Cammie's friendship I acted like a jerk, I did not know what to do, what to say because I love her, I have always loved her"

This was downright unbelievable I could not wrap my mind around what was happening it was like I was in a living nightmare. The thought of my best friend and my husband together cuts deep add it to my other scars.

Sarah looked at me with sad eyes "Cammie, please tell me this is some kind of cruel joke"

"It is not a joke Sarah" I admitted "I am so sorry if I would have known things might have turned out different"

I lowered my head confirming her fears once I could find my voice. I felt a huge lump in my throat and tears burned me eyelids that I fought to hold back. I hoped beyond hope that this was a huge misunderstanding yet not even I was that naive.

Drew firmly grabbed my hands pressing his forehead to mine pleading "The past is the past, remember"

Regardless of how messed up the current circumstances I was not ready to just give upon him. I mean how could I expect him to be faithful when it has been two years. I do not know what happened and I do not want to. So, I am going to turn the page, and this is a brand-new chapter for us. Drew raised his hand to my face tenderly wiping my runaway tears and kissed my lips.

"This is pure madness" Sarah said red with rage "How could I have dated my best friend's husband?"

"I am sorry there is no defense for my actions, I am the only one to blame" he apologized but the words seemed to fall on deaf ears "When I lost everything, I spiraled out of control taking my hurt out on others and I am truly sorry"

I closed my eyes exhaling deeply ashamed of my contributing to his pain which inadvertently hurt Sarah as well. Can we get past this? I had no idea what to say and the words were not coming easily. In my head I could hear myself screaming although I remained quiet.

"I know this is messed up Sarah" I said searching for the right words "But I am in love with him even you know that"

"He knew" she replied as a vail of sadness fell over her face "He does not deserve you"

My mind ached bewildered by the turn of events. What had started as a perfect day suddenly took a nosedive before I even knew what was happening. I loved Sarah as a sister and would never intentionally want to hurt her, but she did not know our story and she did not know his heart the way I did. He was ingrained in every part of my being I had let him sink into my veins, becoming part of my soul, entangled in me. All that we were and could still be played in my mind as clearly as a movie. I have tried to shake him off, but it seemed mission impossible. I knew without question he was my sweetest addiction.

"If he loved you then why did I hear you crying every single night" she continued "You are special Cammie make him treat you like you are."

"I never want to make you cry again" he said falling to his knees

"Sarah, I have some really tough things you need to know about me when we get a chance, then you will see it through my eyes" I made an emotional appeal for understanding and compassion. "I have loved him my whole life"

Feeling a bit overwhelmed I sat down on the couch as my vision became blurry and I could not see nor think clearly. I tried but could not comprehend how this happened because Drew had always been my sweet boy so loving and caring but now, he was the bad buy, and I was having a hard time grasping what was going on around me. Has he really changed?" If so, how much?" Could he have in truth changed so much that he is beyond repair? No! I would never except that. I was willing to do whatever it took to rescue him and find my sweet boy again.

"I hated the man that caused you such grief making you cry every night" Sarah said in a hauntingly mellow tone "But now I feel nothing for him because he is not even worth my hatred"

"I am sincerely sorry" he apologized again

"Do not waste your breath apologizing to me I could care less, apologize to your wife" she snapped always wanting to have the last word "Besides I am fine me and Steve had a wonderful time last night"

I sat there numb watching my best friend walkaway hoping I had made the right choice. Why does love to hurt? This was the most awfully sickening pain anyone could live through. Yet I knew the pain was only temporary, there was no way I could fathom losing Drew all over again. I treasured our shared history, be it good or bad, he undoubtedly owned my heart. I loved the boy I met and fell madly in love with on the verge of adulthood and was currently prepared to love the man he was and the future we could still create together.

Wanting to console me he stepped up close sweeping me into his arms, where I felt unconditionally at ease, I asserted that it was easy to get lost in his arms where I fit so perfectly as if they were made specifically for me. Since the day we parted ways I missed his loving presence, craved his touch, and wanted to take it all back. There were many reasons for why I loved Drew and why I still loved him after all the hard knocks we had taken.

"Camille, I am sorry, I do not even know how to convey my love for you it is that strong" he begged for my mercy with the tears visible in his eyes "I cannot bear to lose you for a second time"

Standing there looking into those ocean eyes tearing up I could feel that he was being truthful. And I could not bear to lose him again either therefore I am all in.

"You will not have to" I vowed earnestly

Staring intensely into his eyes I rubbed his soft face in the palm of my hands giving him a long loving kiss to reaffirm that I was in this with him for the duration. I had faith that we could move passed this and come out on the other side and I hoped that my friendship with Sarah would too. The only thing I knew for certain is that with Drew by my side nothing was impossible. No more tears.

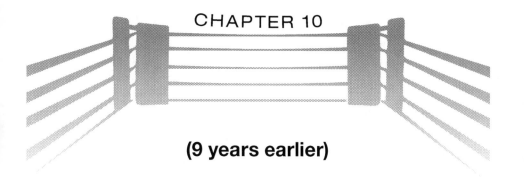

CHAPTER 10

(9 years earlier)

Dear Diary,

I am totally psyched that Joey and Drew have finally turned 16 and earned their license which means FREEDOM awaits us! Tonight, my crew plans on going out to a bonfire behind the levee that some classmates organized, we should have tons of fun. Recently me and Joey hit a rough patch in our relationship over something so petty and stupid that it is not worth mentioning. We worked everything out and now we are closer than ever before. The stress of my home life seems to just get worse and worse. Its already a widely known fact that my parents have always been dysfunctional but lately they have spiraled utterly out of control staying higher than ever which I did not even think was possible. I am thankful to have a partner like Joey who helps me hold myself together when I am about to come unglued and fall to pieces. I am also really blessed to have great friends, who are more like family to me, whom are always there when I need them. Well, got to go suns going down its almost time to go. Here is to the good times!!! Peace Out!

I heard the distinct clunk of the old Chevy truck pulling into my drive as I quickly ran out the door and hopped in. I kissed Joey hello then lightly rubbed my fingers across the fresh bruise above his left cheek.

"Damn him to hell" I cursed his father for putting his violent hands on my beautiful boy.

He just shrugged it off in typical fashion, but I found it tremendously infuriating. What made his father think he had the right to put his hands on any child in a drunken rage. I know that Joey usually tried to take the brunt of his dads' fury but Drew still showed up regularly with black and blue marks as well.

Ginny greeted me sliding onto the seat between me and Drew "Hey Cammie" I smiled back

Those two made such a cute couple I thought seeing Drews arm draped around her shoulder. However, I had to admit initially I was a little jealous since I was accustomed to having the twins all to myself but after getting to know Ginny it was much easier to accept and despite all our outer differences, we managed to become good friends. Ginny loved country, I loved rock, she wore cowboy boots, and I wore combat boots but somehow it weirdly worked and if Drew was content then that was good enough for me.

We made small talk on the short drive to the levee all of us brimming with energy looking forward to the party scene. You could feel the heat from the blazing bonfire before even stepping out of the vehicle on the already hot May night. Once we were all out of the truck, we noticed Billy and Laura near the fire and made our way to them passing some mutual school acquaintances who we greeted with a friendly hello then continued walking. We were not exactly "The Cool Kids" so they did not care if we were there or not. Do not threaten us with a good time because we will take your offer.

"Head's up!" Billy hollered throwing us a cold beer from the ice chest.

Catching a can, I popped the top sipping the beer as I swayed back and forth to the mix of music coming from one of the vehicles. I was doing all my favorite things catching a buzz, jamming to good music, and hanging out with my friends, just typical teen things. But I learned from my parents' have fun and make mistakes while you are young and get it out of your system because who wants to still be out partying trying to preserve your youth once you get older. I have plans for a future, I will not be a mess, this is only fun for a little while like now. Joey then lit a cigarette taking a few puffs before pressing the filter to my lips for me to take a couple drags.

"Thanks babe" I said giving him a sweet peck on the cheek.

I loved the way Joey thought of me, never forgetting about me, and always looked out for me. Pulling him in to me I wrapped my arms around his neck making him dance with me to the mellow rock ballad playing.

"Have I told you I love you today" Joey asked

I light-heartedly responded "Nope, not yet"

"Well then I love you" he said kissing me as I kissed him back.

The intimacy between me and Joey was breathtaking we must be under a spell. I could sense the love in the air tonight while Joey held me from behind tickling my neck with his lips and just growing in facial hair.

"Cammie, there you are finally" Laura interrupted us sounding a little intoxicated.

Then Ginny chimed in assisting Laura in pulling me away "Okay enough love birds"

I managed to get in one last kiss before we were torn apart. Joey laughed then gave me a charming wink as he joined the guys. The three of us girls walked to the other side of the fire where we carried on, having fun, not caring about feeling foolish as we drank, smoked, and danced under the clear night sky when one of the girls we often partied with, Christie, walked up and joined our conversation.

"Stick out you tongues girls" she politely commanded "I have a surprise"

We did as she asked without a second thought then Christie placed a tiny square of paper with some sort of symbol imprinted on it on each of our tongues.

"No swallowing it let it dissolve" she instructed "It should hit you in about an hour"

"What is it?" Laura asked

Ok that was not smart however we did catch it as an afterthought which made it to late, perhaps we were not the brightest, but we were the most fun and closest crew in town. No breaking our bonds the rumor mill meant nil to us.

"Purple Haze LSD" she answered casually then returned to her usual group of friends.

We exchanged smiles and prepared ourselves for the new experience that was soon coming our way. This was going to be a first for all of us, but it was nice to know I was not alone in it. We carried on normally until some random guy at the party inserted himself into our girl time.

"Hey girl you fine" the boy said grabbing my waist making me incredibly uncomfortable.

I instantly pulled away getting out of his reach. Who is this dude? Whoever he is he certainly has no self-control whatsoever. I mean who in hell just walks up to a stranger and starts touching and grabbing them?

Unamused I asserted "Thanks but no thanks"

"Come on baby" he continued as if he did not hear me as he crept closer.

"I am not your baby" I shoved him away furious with the nuisance.

This guy sure had some nerve and did not know when to quit. I had never seen him before tonight and never cared too again. He needs to take a hint, so he can move on and find his new prey.

"Is there a problem here?" Joey unexpectantly popped up putting his arm around me and I have never been happier to see my great protector.

He ogled the strange boy with an expression of anger. Me and my girls were just trying to have a goodtime until this idiot showed up trying to stir up trouble. I wish he would just disappear at this point freeing me from having to deal with him any further.

"Hey, do not blame me" the ignorant partygoer remarked "She is a hot"

"I dare you to disrespect my girl again" Joey warned his eyes full of rage "I will give you something you will never forget!"

Hearing the commotion Drew and Billy joined Joey for backup incase anything was to go down. Knowing Joey was never one to back down from a fight and sensing the rising tension I gripped Joeys shoulders bringing him back to me trying to calm him some. Then at the worst possible time the effects of the acid I had taken earlier began to hit me. I watched the world around me turn bright and colorful with the flames of the fire licking the sky as music pulsed through the air and over vibrant patterns covered the ground. Wow this was insane.

Joeys' threats seemed to have fallen on deaf ears because the guy just kept on running his mouth "I am going to give your girl something she will never forget"

I saw Joey ball his fist up tightly ready to charge when I accidently let out a sudden burst of laughter caused by vision of dancing trees. He instantly halted his attack turning to look at me in confusion.

"Sorry babe I am tripping'" I admitted not wanting him to think I was laughing at his defense of me.

The jerk took advantage of Joeys distraction and wasted no time disappearing into the crowd, but Joey had already lost interest in him and turned his full attention to me.

He worriedly asked before checking my pupils "What did you take?"

"Christie gave us some acid" Ginny readily admitted.

I waved my hand in front of my face watching the vivid tracers following my every move. Joey just smiled as he led me back to the truck with Drew and Ginny in tow. I was entertained by the neon trees putting on a special show for my eyes only I giggled at my visions.

"You two are in no shape to go home" Drew told us as we pulled into the driveway.

We snuck passed their drunken father passed out in the recliner as usual making it undetected to the twin's room. I laid back on Joeys bed with my hands behind my head while Drew flipped the lights off and turned on the blacklight illuminating the psychedelic posters hanging on the wall helping to focus the hallucination. Joey then laid beside me wispily running his fingers up and down my stomach. His fingers felt like clay molding his skin to mine. It was an awesome transforming encounter, all my senses were heightened but also weird, something you cannot put in words it is a whole experience.

"Do not worry baby I gotcha" He said sweetly "Enjoy your trip but do not do it again it can be dangerous"

"I promise" I said

I smiled up at him feeling totally safe while being delighted in the brilliant colors swirling around me. The hours sped by and before long my visions began to subside with the rising of the early morning sun. Drew quickly grabbed the keys off the chest of drawers cutting it close to leaving to bring Ginny home before her parents noticed she was gone.

"I will be back" Drew informed us as him and Ginny rushed out.

Now we could have some quality time together. We can sit together in total silence and never be bothered or bored. But we did talk a lot about everything our day, parents, school, feelings, and what is it going to be like when we finally escape this town.

"Thanks for taking such good care of me" I said showing my appreciation with an amorous kiss.

He gave me that beautiful boyish grin I adored "That is what I am here for"

I was in no hurry to leave and since my parents never noticed whether I was home or not I could practically do whatever I pleased and what pleased my right now was being with my best friend, my protector, and my lover.

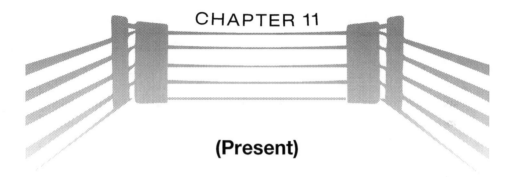

CHAPTER 11

(Present)

"Do not worry bae" Drew reassured me trying to calm me down after seeing the distress on my face "It will all work out"

The sheer thought of facing my boss Dallas was enough to put terror in me. My nerves were on edge which was made worse by knowing I had just started here so I was expendable and could easily be replaced at any time. Being replaced was my worst fear because although I had only been with TWE for a short time my life already revolved around it plus my love was here as well. I tried but could not reconcile the thought of having worked this darn hard literally leaving my blood, sweat, and tears in the ring. I imagine it would be like having the rug pulled out from under me just as I was putting the pieces of my life back together. In this line of work there is always someone prettier and equally as talented just waiting for you to mess up, so they can step right into your place. However, I was a born fighter and if they were in line behind me, they better have a lot of patience because I fought for this spot on the roster and was not planning on going anywhere, anytime soon without one a hell of a bout.

"I did tell them I was married" I commented with the gravity of the situation weighing me down "I just did not say who to"

Then expressed in an ultimate panic "I am really freaking out"

"Calm down baby" Drew said soothingly "Remember if you go, I go"

Drews character "The Crazy Cajun" was a fast fan favorite with his quintessential combination of good looks, a glowing smile, and outrageous antics made him a superb entertainer. Last week he proved he belonged there by earning the number one contender spot for The Shining Star Belt which was only second to The Heavyweight Championship that every Totalstar aspired to have around their waist. Drew was headed straight to the top and there was no way on God's green heart I would let him give that up for me. He has worked too hard and come too far to simply just throw his dreams away that easily. Did not let it happen the first time and I am hopeful there will not be a second. I desperately wished that everything would work out in our favor.

At a hotel in Nashville, we prepared to head to the stadium where we were supposed to perform and where we were also meeting with management before the nights event. My mind was reeling with various scenarios that may happen, but I needed to clear my mind, stop worrying, and focus on what is ahead of me before I drive myself insane. I walked to the room adjacent to ours and knocked on the door which Sarah answered with damp hair and a towel wrapped around her body. I waved at Steve, who was relaxing on the bed watching television, and he politely smiled waving back.

"We are finished" I informed Sarah since we were carpooling to work "When are you going be ready"

"Give me 20" she answered

"You are such a diva" I teased

"Not a diva, a Goddess" she corrected me as we laughed.

Once me and Sarah got a chance to sit down and hash it all out privately, I laid my entire life out on the table for her to see. Leaving nothing out I confessed the good, the bad, and the ugly in hopes she could then understand why I was so hung up on Drew. Lucky for me I have world's greatest best friend who decided to forgive and attempt to forget even if she still did not like Drew much. Sarah was the very first person I felt close enough to tell my story to from beginning to end which really got deep at some points. After releasing that heavy burden, I had been carrying off my chest I felt much lighter and freer. We laughed, hugged, and cried while we talked bringing us even closer than we were before.

Having a friend of that caliber whom I could trust with my life was something special and only comes around every so often. Since this week's unpredictable turn of events, I was glad to see that Sarah and Steve had become an official item because I think she deserved happiness more than anyone else I knew. Sarah had never looked more radiant than she did when Steve was around, and they made quite an impeccable couple. Crazy as it may appear to the outside world me, Drew, Sarah, and Steve have been together a good while this week and have developed an unlikely friendship. A week ago, I never would have predicted this outcome, but people work in mysterious ways.

Back in my room I found a peaceful corner where I sat comfortably on a pillow and took full advantage of this rare downtime to do a little writing.

Dear Diary,

It is beyond words how amazing it is having Andrew back in my life. At one time I thought having him back was impossible therefore I will never take even small things in my life for granted. The connection and desire we shared years before came back to us so naturally it is as if it never left. But today we must reveal our marriage to the bosses, and I am terribly nervous of what backlash may be. Sarah being a fabulous friend has been a comfort through this trying time and has been surprisingly accepting of me and Drew's relationship. I found myself constantly looking over my shoulder waiting on a bomb to drop but soon realized that worrying about that would get me nowhere and would not stop anything from happening. I decided to finally embrace this life while I have it let the rest of the pieces fall where it may. I learned at the tender age of 16 that life is too short to wallow in regret or attempt to change things beyond our control. Like my Joey once said, "All you can do is live in the moment" and that is exactly what I plan on doing. Got to go! Peace!

Drew walked to where I was sitting and kissed me on the forehead "Ready love"

"I can do this" I said attempting to build my confidence.

We walked to the car to meet Sarah and Steve then headed to the stadium. I could literally feel my heart pounding in my chest as we entered the makeshift office where we sat opposite of my boss Dallas and Drews Boss Tyson.

"So, what is this about?" Tyson asked getting straight to the point

Frozen I tried to figure out the words to use scared I might say the wrong thing.

"Well, Camille's my wife" Drew blurted out taking the pressure off me "We just thought you should know"

"Come on Cajun you know better than this" Tyson fussed "you are supposed to get permission to elope"

The tone of his voice was clearly unhappy which put my nerves further on edge. I hope my presence here was not a huge mistake that would jeopardize Drews future. Should I have just left good enough alone?

"We got married seven years ago way before TWE" he explained

"You should have disclosed this to us" Dallas scolded me "This could be considered a breach of contract"

My heart feel into my stomach and I could feel a lump in my throat Dallas was unquestionably an intimidating tough chick, when she talked, we all listened. She was a former Goddess Champion who paved the way for other female wrestlers. She commanded respect wherever she went and any Goddess that claims not to admire or aspire to be like her is either out right lying or not passionate about their career.

Tyson and Dallas sat back perplexed by our unusual situation wondering what to do with us. Their silence frightened me much more than their griping.

"I am sorry, I own my mistake" I apologized "I have no excuse, I should have told you"

The management duo stared at us for a while, and you could almost see the wheels turning in their heads. What could they be thinking? Drew reached over squeezing my hands showing a united front.

"Alright here is what we are going to do" Dallas said with her creative juices flowing "I recently received a request for you by a Totalstar and I can throw in the marriage for some good ole drama and betrayal"

A request for me? This is a little weird, but I had a sneaking suspicion who this Totalstar was.

"You will be King Braedon's new servant and Cajun here can fight for your honor; I will work out the details" Tyson announced before shooing us away "Dismissed"

There it was just as I suspected no big surprise there. Braedon's character took whichever Goddess he fancied at the time then brainwashed them into being his servant until he tired of them and let them leave. The upside of being partnered with him is I would gain exposure escorting him to the ring on Monday Night Wild and Thursday Night Knockdown. My worry was that Drew would find out about the kiss I shared with Braedon. Although I considered it no big deal, Drew may not take as lightly. I hope this innocent omission does not come back to bite me.

"This could be a good jumpstart for you" he said amiably before giving a warning "But he better keep his hands to himself"

"I can handle myself Mister" I assured him pressing my hands on his chest "But none of that even matters can I only want you bae" I finished then pulled him back to me.

Sarah and Steve were waiting eagerly to hear how the meeting went. Drew filled them in on the details as Steve gave me an all-knowing glance when he heard about Braedon request. He was Braedon's closest friend, so I am positive he knew the true motives plus Braedon made no secret of his dislike of Drew. Did Braedon really want to fight for me or just to get at Drew?

Drew leaned in giving me a quick kiss before heading to the locker room while me and Sarah left to wait in hair and make-up. Standing around talking we noticed a few girls snickering after watching the kiss from Drew who last they knew was Sarah's boyfriend. We looked at each other with a grin then burst out laughing.

"It is okay girls" Sarah loudly commented stopping them cold in their tracks "We share everything"

We laughed even harder at their shocked expression and gaped mouths. It was nice to have some comic relief in this high stress situation. There were only a handful of people who knew the facts leaving everyone else guessing and confused. Therefore, it was somewhat humorous to us as me and Sarah giggled when Braedon butted in interrupting our laughter.

"Hello beautiful" he said, "Can I borrow you a minute?"

"Sure, but just one" I agreed reluctantly

I can already see that me and Braedon talking privately was going to put the rumor mill into overdrive for sure. Although I did find it all kind of entertaining hearing the absurd and twisted stories they can come up with. I followed Braedon to a semi-private corner to talk as Tweety watched us intensely. I had heard that Braedon had dated her, and they had a history together, but they split up for reasons I was not aware of. However, it was obvious she was not over him yet and her obsession gave me the creeps like she was going to slip my throat in the middle of the night. Man, she is giving me the evil eye as if she does not look evil enough with her normal face.

Braedon boasted "I take it you heard the good news"

"Yes, I have" I said arrogantly "And I am sure you heard my good news as well"

"I can care less about Cajun" he said with a slick smile "There is a connection between us even if you refuse to admit it"

Braedon is without a doubt a master charmer which is what pulled me in but most like most men he could also be a sweet talker. I had a suspicion that he was accustomed to getting what he wanted and did not give us very easily. He honestly believed that he could somehow lure me into his arms. But if he knew me, he would realize that he was on an impossible mission because Drew kept my heart beating and no matter the time or distance, we always found our way back to each other. The ridiculous rivalry between the two left a visible hostility lingering about and I did not want to get stuck in the middle of their brewing war.

"Do not be ridiculous" I snipped back defending my relationship "Remember I am a good actress"

"We will just see about that" he said pecking my cheek as I rolled my eyes then watched him walk confidently away

I went back to make-up and hopped up in the chair with several variables of how this could play out running ramped in my head. However, this was not the place nor time to think about this because it was time to send Camille back to the shadows and transform into Miss Penny Lane once again. I just hope this whole thing does not turn into a disaster.

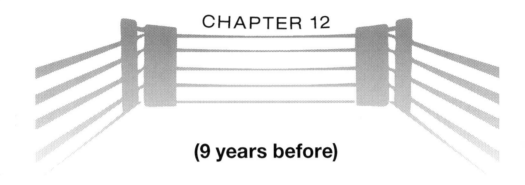

CHAPTER 12

(9 years before)

Dear Diary,

Last month I celebrated my sweet 16 and can hardly believe it. Where have the years gone? Time seems to be flying by and I will be an adult before I know it. Scary, right? But unlike some people I am in no hurry to grow up because I am enjoying my childhood and young love. Right now, I am happy to be on Christmas break giving me more time to spend with Joey and the rest of the gang. Tonight, we are going to sneak out to our special spot find a little fun and do some night swimming. The air outside may be a bit chilly, but the water always feels nice. Cannot wait to see my love later. Talk again soon. Peace out!

"I love this place" I said as me and Joey arrived at the pond "I always feel so free here"

"That is why it is called our special spot" he commented

The sun was just beginning to go down and I loved watching the sunset over the pond it was incredibly breathtaking. We were prepared to have a goodtime having brought all our favorite party favors as well as an ice chest full of beer to loosen us up. I fiddled with the radio going through the static until I found a good rock station to keep us entertained. Then I stripped down to my underwear and jumped into the pond hand in hand with Joey for a little innocent night swimming leaving the others chit chatting on the bank. I laid back under the night sky chilling on my raft singing along to the Pearl Jam song on the stereo when Joey snuck up behind me flipping the raft and sending me plummeting into the cool water. I laughed coming up for air then dunked him in the water for retaliation.

"You are a son of a bitch" I grinned watching him shake the water from his hair "I should have saw that coming"

"Awe, I am sorry love" he smiled pulling me into him "Come here baby"

I wrapped my legs around him as we waded together in the water and shared a few kisses. My heart danced jovially floating in the moonlight with my forever love. I closed my eyes allowing myself to fall deep into his gravity dreaming of our future and the day we can finally get out of this good-bye town.

"So, tell me" He asked, "What does my baby want for Christmas?"

"I already have everything I could want" I answered honestly

He looked absolutely dashing as he smiled at me with the water dripping from his face glistening in the light of the moonlit sky.

"Life may never be perfect but with you I am always perfectly happy" I told him sincerely

Joey meant the world to me, and I felt like the luckiest girl on earth because he chose me. There was nowhere else I would rather be than right here with him.

"Well, I hope that never changes" he said spinning me in the water "Because now you are stuck with me"

"Promise?" I asked unable to envision my life without him.

"I promise" he assured me with an unbreakable gaze

"I get scared you will bore of me" I admitted "or find someone prettier"

"First, you are the most interesting person I know" he responded brushing back my dampened hair "And finally you are the most beautiful creature in the universe"

It is beyond my comprehension how two people can find their way to each other in this gigantic sea of life. And there is not one thing you can put your finger on to say this is how I knew; it was just an undeniable feeling saying that they are the one for you. Everyone has that person, and I am sure that Joey is mine.

"I love you baby" I said with my eyes tearing up

"I love you to the moon and back" he reiterated "I never want to lose this feeling"

And neither did I. With him I found my harmony when the world was beating down on me, I could turn to him and find peace in a crowd of madness. Love is majestic.

"Shame, shame, shame" Drew teased snapping a shot of us with his camera "I know your name"

"How rude" I hollered splashing him then laughed at the expression on his face as he jumped backwards.

"Alright pervert" Joey told Drew "Make yourself useful and toss me another beer"

Drew did as commanded digging into the ice chest and throwing Joey a beer. He swiftly popped the top, guzzled it down, then crushed the can and tossed it to the garbage.

"Now, where were we" Joey asked tickling me with his smooth puckered lips.

"Bombs away!" Ginny shouted as she and Drew jumped into the water making a huge splash with Laura and Billy following right behind them.

We all messed around a while racing, splashing, and playing games as we do. My friends are considered as family since we had chosen to replace the dysfunctional families, we all had back home. We were the outcast, the misfits but I would not trade them for all the money in the world. Money cannot buy me love, money cannot buy me happiness, and I am already rich in both so what good does money do me? At school we were the freaks and most people steered clear of us but on the Brightside at least we had one another and were not alone in this hell we called high school.

"What time is it?" Laura inquired

"12:30" Billy answered

"We better go" Laura warned "We do not want to get busted after curfew"

The curfew reminder combined with the alcohol in our body made leaving a good idea. Joey climbed behind the wheel as I took my place beside him while the other four hopped in the bed of the old truck.

"To the moon and back" Joey said giving me a sweet kiss before taking off.

"To the moon and back baby" I smiled awash in all his tender affection.

We bopped to the beat of the music as we made our way down the desolate backroads lit only by the headlights just as we have done hundreds of times before. I glanced over admiring Joeys youthfully alluring face in the shadows as he squeezed my hand lovingly when I was suddenly distracted by the headlights of and oncoming vehicle shining through the windshield. I closed my eyes and put my arm up trying to avoid the glare of the high beams coming towards us when instantly everything got blurry pulling me from my love story into a real horror story. There were a few brief moments jumbled up like snapshots in my head replaying the horrible crash.

My ears still rung with the sounds of squealing tires, shattering glass, and the painful screams of my friends in the distance. I cried out but cannot be sure if any sound came out as I tried to grasp the magnitude of what was really happening. I could feel the warmth of my blood flowing down blurring my vision while the numbness of my body began to wear off and the overwhelming reality of our circumstances sent me into a panic. Oh God, where is Joey? My heartbeat rapidly in my chest as I frantically searched blindly for Joey in the wreckage. Our hands managed to find each other in the chaos as we desperately clung to each other trapped in the warped metal of the truck. But it was some relief to me knowing he was beside me.

"Joey" I said in confusion

"I am here baby" he responded sounding weak "Are you okay?"

"I am okay, do not worry about me" I told him worried more about him than myself at this point.

"Camille, remember I love you to the moon and back" he said letting out a painful cough and squeezing my hand tightly "Forever and always but if...find love again"

"To the moon and back" I cried letting my tears flow the blood "You are my forever love"

"My forever love" he said as I felt him softly kiss my hand

We need to get out of here I tried pushing the door, but it would not budge. The smell of gasoline filled my nose making me cough as I began to grow frantic with fear. I knew Joey sounded bad and needed help. God, I know I am not much of the praying type, but I am begging for you to save Joey please do not take him away from me take us together. The anguish would be sweeping. I cannot make any sense out of any of this we were just a bunch of misfit kids. Why us? I sobbed deeply from my soul.

My pulse raced as the blinding lights of ambulance and cop cars brightened the pitch-black sky. Suddenly the beam of a paramedic's flashlight hit my bloodied face as he attempted to rescue me from the mangled vehicle.

"Joey, we have to go" I tried pulling him to me, but he would not move "I will not leave you I promised"

"Camille, my love I am trapped please go" he pleaded "I am begging you"

I pushed the paramedic away with my feet determined to save Joey. How could I possibly leave him in his time of need? We have so much life left together.

"Mam, you are injured we have to go" the paramedic tried reasoning with me

"I love you baby... now go" Joey reached up pushing me towards the man with all the strength he had.

"No" I screamed grabbing his hand one last time.

Please do not leave me here alone, Joey you are my person I whispered to myself.

"To the moon and back" I heard those beautiful words leave his lips

"To the moon and back" I said with my last conscience breath before it all faded to black.

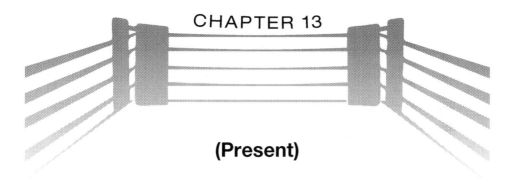

CHAPTER 13

(Present)

"In this corner standing 6'7" 255 pounds from Pittsburg, Pennsylvania King Braedon" I acted as the announcer trying to break the ice at our first practice session with Braedon at the TWE Training Center "And his opponent from New Orleans, Louisiana standing 6'5" 246 pounds The Crazy Cajun"

Although me and Drew were from a pretty much unknown small town in South Louisiana, we claimed New Orleans as our hometown because of the cities colorful character, charming tones, cool vibes, and its reputation giving our alter egos a bustling background and added the excitement of the Big Easy. We live about an hour and half west of their which made it less of a lie and more of an embellishment.

I looked down at my left hand and turned my mood ring around my finger letting Joey know that I know he is still with me as I always have whether for a real fight or just a practice. I watched on as the two locked up to start the match. I could not help but appreciate the sight of my husband in the ring watching his beautiful physic and how his muscled flexed when he grabbed Braedon's arm and twisted it. I saw the beads of sweat bubbling on Drews skin while they exchanged blows making my body flush with warmth. I could watch this all day long sexy sells and it does not get much hotter than the TWE roster. I was positive the audience would enjoy the match as much as I did.

It is a primal instinct to take pleasure in observing two men competing against each other. As far back as you can go in history people have used the sport of fighting as entertainment it is built into our DNA. We are like the modern-day gladiators who enjoyed the art of wrestling and put our bodies on the line to amuse others. I knew there were many women lusting after my husband but who could blame them, he is tall, tanned, and chiseled with long dark silky hair and dazzling blue eyes. It was an incredible feeling knowing he belonged to me. The thought made me grin as I bit my lower lip.

Come one Cammie, time to quit daydreaming and get to work becoming Penny Lane. I went to Braedon corner banging on the mat and cheering him like a good servant should. To make it in this business not only did you have to be a talented wrestler, but you also had to have the ability to act and convince the crowd that it was all real to draw them into our world. It was like a sport soap opera full of drama, craziness, fighting, and you never know what is coming next. Someone may even get possessed!

Drew put Braedon in the Voodoo Vice then gave me our secret signal to reach in the ring and pull him out breaking his grasp and distracting him long enough for Braedon to gain the upper hand allowing him to steal the win cementing my villain status. This was going to be fun to act out live I was psyched about it.

"Good job bae" Drew said happily

"Thanks" I responded giving him a helping hand up.

"You like hearing your wife scream my name" Braedon commented attempt to antagonize Drew.

"Only in your dreams" Drew said coldly

"Every night" he kept on

"That is enough boys" I stepped between them trying to cool things off.

I kissed Drews cheek wanting to give him a sense of security which seemed to work as I felt his body relax and his face turn soft again. He understood how important this opportunity was for us and would not jeopardize that no matter how hard he was pushed. Many would assume that being cast as Braedon's servant did not sound glamorous however being paired with one of the companies most popular villains certainly had its perks. This meant that Miss Penny Lane would be noticed, I would gain experience, get camera time, plus playing the bad girl could be fun. On the flipside Drews character The Crazy Cajun was the exact opposite of King Braedon. The Crazy Cajun was a babyface wrestler with tons of charisma and thrilling to watch in contrast to heel wrestlers like Braedon the rule breaker who people love to hate, and which makes this match sure to bring in big ratings. Plus, I would get a chance to show off a few skills although I will be booed for just for being Braedon's arm candy. But wrestling fans were thankfully adaptable and may love you one day then hate you the next. Got to love it or leave it.

This occupation was not for the weak at heart you had to have thick skin because things could turn on a dime depending on the creative powers that be. Fame is a fickle friend one day you are in the spotlight the next day no one knows your name. That is why it is important to have a special love and passion for what you do to make it believable, to give you the power to press on even when you are exhausted, to go out there and put on a show no matter how you are feeling, and to keep the fans wanting more because they are the lifeblood of the company and my career. The fans could make you or break you and you can never forget that there is always someone just waiting on you to fail so they swoop into your place.

"Want to go a few rounds" Drew asked when we finished

"With you" I flirted as he gave me a wink "Anytime"

Drew left to get a drink of water with a bright smile before we waited back to the ring for a playful bout.

"That could be us you know" Braedon said once he saw the coast was clear

"You wish" I retorted shaking my head

"I do" he commented "I really, really do"

I playfully pushed him away then ran to Drew who was on his way back. By now I was accustomed to Braedon's inappropriate words and learned to just brush it off. There was no way I would give him the satisfaction of letting him get to me.

"Come on lover boy" I said dragging him into the ring

Drew and I have been training together since the very beginning and knew each other so well we could practice with nearly no communication already know the move the other would make before they made it. The intricacy and intimacy of each elaborate move felt awe inspiring he was my perfect partner. Wrestling has been a huge part of our lives for a longtime which was a shared passion we were serious about our careers and did not take it lightly, and we strived to be the best we could possibly be. We consistently supported each other giving advice or being brutally honest if we had to as well as treating our bodies like a tool of our trade taking good care of ourselves and each other.

"I fine-tuned The Peace Out" I told him knowing he would be truthful "I want to see what you think"

"Let me see it" he said eagerly

The Peace Out was my signature finishing move and I wanted it to represent me impeccably. It must have excitement, high energy with, hint of danger, and I believed it finally had everything. But with the good comes the bad and the grim reality was that if something went wrong it could be lights out on my career in a matter of seconds which I found made it even more enticing with the fear getting my adrenaline pumping and keeping me on my toes. Man, I really do love my job!

I jumped up kicking him to the mat putting him in position then I threw up a peace sign to let the audience know what is coming. After which I climbed to the top rope and leaped off doing a spiral in mid-air before landing on Drew for the count of three.

"She has done it ladies and gentlemen" he praised my efforts "Miss Penny Lane has hit The Peace Out and it over"

I smiled with pride now fully confident in my move as I rolled out of the ring.

"That was seriously bad ass" he told me "But you really wreck my nerves"

"Thanks bae" I tried to reassure him but knew as long as there was a risk he would never relax "I am a highflyer remember I live for the top rope"

I looked up to see Steve walking into the training center accompanied by a smiling Sarah who made a B-line for me.

"I am so glad I caught you" Sarah said "I really need another goddess to work with"

I flipped my head over piling my sweat filled hair into a bun securing it with a tie then adjusted my lime green workout gear in preparation for another fight. Even with every muscle in my body burning I was still ready to go a little more besides no pain no gain. Right? Across the room Steve was demonstrating his finisher Gunpowder on Drew who made good competition for the 6'4" 285-pound beast. My attention was immediately diverted back to Sarah with a swift slap in the chest. She then took my arm tossing me into the ropes before charging at me, but I quickly hit the mat and rolled out the way. We stood on opposite sides of the ring contemplating how to one up the other stalking each other's movements and studying every expression like a predator hunting prey. Which one of us is the predator and which one is the prey could change with the tics of the clock. I really enjoyed freestyle wrestling getting to test all your skills and wits. It was good fun plus it gave us a chance to improve.

Although the storylines may get cheesy and the outcomes mostly predetermined, inside that ring it was all real and all of us. We each had our parts to play and the impact this kind of work has on the human body while keeping up appearances could inundate some, but I believed it was totally worth it.

Sarah managed to get me down where she intertwined her legs in mine then arched her back up putting pressure on my limbs to successfully execute her finisher Killer Legs causing me to tap out. Sarah was a fierce competitor and I looked forward to the day we get to battle it out in front of a live audience.

"Good try" Sarah bragged about her win

"Next time" I spit back

"Oh yeah" she giggled "We will just see about that"

Finally done for the day we joined our guys at the water cooler as the sweat glistening off Drews body caught my eyes. Oh, my he was so hot I could ravish him right here and now but that would be unprofessional of me therefore I would have to wait until later. Sensing the same animalistic attraction, he pulled me into him by my waist sending a charge throughout my body.

"We are going places bae" he said confidently before kissing me

It has been a long day at the office, but I made sure to reserve some energy to do some wrestling at home with my impressive lover.

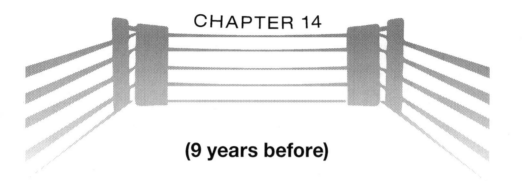

CHAPTER 14

(9 years before)

My eyes fluttered open as I looked around in utter confusion at all the movement around me and the sight of my parents sitting in the rooms corner sent a chill down my spine. Something must be seriously for them to have come here. What is going on? Where is Joey? Where are all my friends? My mind spun on overload completely muddled with unanswered questions.

"You are awake" my dad noticed coming to my side as my mom stayed seated.

"How is Joey" I asked my head full of fog and worry

The silence spoke volumes as they lowered their heads answering my question without words. Oh God please no! This cannot be real I must be stuck in some sort of nightmare. It felt like the room was spinning around as a sinking sensation came over me. Why could no one tell me that he was alright?

"I am sorry Cammie" my dad voiced my worries fears confirming what I was most afraid of.

I shook my head in denial I could not believe what I was hearing. This must be a cruel joke I thought while I stared at the door waiting for him to walk right on in. We were in love, he was my future, where do I go from here? I glanced down at the ring he had given me it was a promise of forever. The ring is still on my finger so where is Joey?

I began to panic as I tried to get up when I asked, "What about Drew?"

"I am not sure Cammie" my dad said sitting me back down "You have to calm down"

As the shock started to wear off, I could feel a soreness in my ribs before I lifted my hand touching my swollen face running my fingers across the gash on my forehead that had been stitched up. Every single part of me hurt as pain throbbed throughout my body but it was nothing compared to the sadness I felt in my heart. The not knowing was the most horrible part. God, if Drew is gone, please take me too do not leave me here completely alone, I would never make it. Finally, the greatest relief came over me when that familiar face burst through the door.

"Oh Andrew" I exclaimed watching him push my dad aside and take my hand "Thank goodness you are alright"

Looking into his bloodshot eyes and tear-stained face I could no longer deny it and finally it began to sink in that it was all real and Joey was gone. I would never see him again. Drew was all scratched and scraped but he was alive and here with me which for that I was endlessly grateful. Together we sat in the solitude of the cold dim hospital room as we cried together with the knowledge that a piece of us was lost. What do we do now?

"Camille Landry?" the doctor said walking in clipboard in hand.

The doctor then glanced up at Drew displeased "Mr. McEnrowe what are you doing?" Dr. Guidry asked "you should be in your room"

"I am right where I need to be" he responded defiantly

"Yes, I am Camille" I said redirecting the doctor's attention.

"Are you aware that your pregnant" he asked bluntly

Pregnant? Did I hear that correctly? My life was turned upside down by the loss of Joey this was all too much. I could feel myself quickly starting to spiral out of control. My parents appeared to be in shock as Drew squeezed my hand warmly in support after hearing the news.

"No…" I answered seeing the doctor lower his head to his clipboard as if it had some magic words "I had no idea"

"Considering the accidents severity" he responded before hastily exiting the room "It is a miracle, but you and the baby will be fine"

I fought back tears while I tried to digest all the information in my head. Drew gave me a reassuring look like it would be alright, and I wanted so very badly to believe that was the truth. I broke down crying with the reality that Joey would never have a chance to hold his own child, be a father, or a husband. He would never get to chase his dreams and never get to grow up he was permanently frozen in time, taken too soon, our innocents so swiftly stolen. If I had known it was going to be our last night together, I would have made sure to leave no words unspoken, held him a little bit closer, and shared one last kiss, one last I love you. I took a slight comfort in knowing I would see him again even if it is only in my dreams standing underneath our tree staring at the sunset with the face of an angel, the beauty of a picture, and a voice sweet as a song. Now only the memories remain. I just do not understand how he could possibly be gone when I never let him go.

"What do you want us to do Camille" my mother said coldly "Your 16 and carrying a fatherless child"

"I would expect you to do what you usually do" I said furious at her callous comment "Nothing at all"

My parents have always been screwed up, but this was an all-time low even for them. I wish they could at least act like real parents for once in their lives and show real concern.

"This baby will have a beautiful life" Drew snapped angrily at them "You two make me sick"

I saw a fury in his eyes unlike any I had seen before and could tell he was serious. I knew I was not alone in this and had an angel watching from above.

"Just get out" I demanded emotionlessly pointing to the door.

I stared blankly at my parent just wanting them gone. They had never been there for me any other time so why I expected today to be any different is beside me. My mom looked at me with disgust before her and my father left without argument. Me and Drew were left alone as his quiet confidence gave me the solace I needed in this moment.

"You and me against the world" he proposed "I will take care of you"

"Plus, one" I added

"Plus, one" he shook his head placing his hand on my belly.

For a longtime it had been just the three of us, now only two of us remained. The despair inside of me was unexplainable, it was like screaming at the top of my lungs, yet no one could hear me, it was the most hopeless feeling in the world. I loved like there was not a tomorrow positive that it would always last, believing we had forever, only to have my dreams cut short by tragedy. Does this kind of pain ever really go away? Will his memory linger sweetly or leave a bitterness on my soul? I would gladly relive every bad day I have ever had for one more good day with Joey. Everything seemed so unreal how long will this haunt me?

"How is everyone?" I asked concerned about my friends

"Laura is beat up but other than that alright, Billy broke his leg and bruised his ribs" he informed me "Ginny hit her heads really hard she is unconscious in ICU"

My friends meant a lot to me, and I cared greatly for them besides they were all the family I had. I was relieved to hear that Billy and Ginny would be fine but prayed Laura would soon wake and make a full recovery. I do not think I could handle another devastating loss.

"I am scared to fall asleep" I voiced my fear "I am afraid I will wake up and you will be gone too"

"I am not going anywhere" he guaranteed as he laid down in the bed beside me "I promise"

Laying in the dark holding Joey's hand he told me *I will never leave you; I promise* so promises do not mean what they use to in my eyes

"Then I will do my very best to keep the two of you safe" he said

"Thank you" I responded

I held his Drews hand securely in mine and rested my aching head against his shoulder physically and emotionally depleted. I closed my eyes feeling safe with Drew. The medicine flowing through my body made my head foggy and I soon drifted off to sleep where Joey awaited me in beautiful dreams.

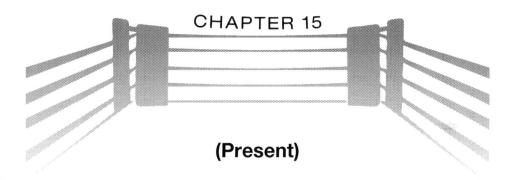

CHAPTER 15

(Present)

Me and Sarah typically wasted time by the hall's backstage during live tapings and tonight was no exception. We were both camera ready decked out in our ring gear with hair and makeup complete. I was trying out a new outfit and I loved how it felt to have my hot red wrestling boots on, I thought they made the outfit pop, and they made me feel powerful, sexy, like a Goddess. We were ready to go in a moment's notice at times having to think on our feet. When Sarah stopped me abruptly near one of the televisions broadcasting the show in the back.

"Hold up were about to be on" she noticed

Last week during Knockdown we filmed a brief montage to set up my latest storyline and it was about to air for the first time. Seeing myself on television was still foreign to me filling my stomach with butterflies and soul with pride.

The screen went black then the camera focused in on me, Sarah, and Drew standing together. Drew had his arm draped around my waist as we smiled and chatted when Braedon and Steve entered the frame.

"Who is that?" he asked Steve as Drew hugged me before leaving

"That is Penny Lane she is Cajun's girl" he warned

"Well," he said patting Steve on the back before approached us "I do love a good challenge"

"King Braedon" he said confidently introducing himself and extending his hand out to me.

"Miss Penny Lane" I smiled innocently as he kissed my hand with an evil smirk.

Sarah and I grinned happily satisfied with our short cameo. The montage got my blood pumping, and I could not wait for tonight's performance.

"Looking good" Titan said with a wink as he passed by us in the hall "The camera loves you girls"

"Damn" Sarah said eyeing him closely "He is hot"

"Yes indeed" I had to agree

Unable to help myself I had to turn for a harmless second look. Titan was The TWE Heavyweight Champion and face of the brand. Half of the fans adored him, and the other half loved to hate on him but regardless everyone knew his name. It also did not hurt that he was extremely easy on the eyes resembling a Samoan Warrior with his long silky black hair, matching dark eyes, golden skin, and tribal tattoos across his arms and chest. What is not to like? Titan turned his head back then gave me a slick smile when he busted me checking him out causing my cheeks to flush red with embarrassment.

"Naughty girl" Drew teased sneaking up behind me after witnessing the exchange.

"I am only human" I defended my actions.

"But he does not have anything on you babe" I giggled looking him up and down please with what I saw in front of me.

I did love the way that his black spandex wrestling pants fit the curves of his body. or my personal favorite his rear, just right and the sight of his beautifully sculpted muscles made my heart beat a little bit faster. He knew darn well that he had nothing to worry about because he was certainly more than man enough for me.

"So, babe" Drew asked as Braedon walked up "You ready for tonight?"

"Of course, she is" Braedon butted in "It is not like tonight is our first kiss"

"You are not kissing me" I reminded him with a scoff before he slithered away "You are kissing Penny Lane"

Drew looked perplexed unsure of what to think he asked, "What does he mean by that Cammie?"

Oh man this was not what I was expecting at all Braedon was a snake in the grass I knew for certain now. I wish I had just told Drew about that stupid kiss my one moment of weakness. I hope he is understanding about this whole situation because this is last thing I needed right before a live performance.

"It was one kiss" I admitted "Before you came back to me"

"Do I need to be worried?" he questioned

Should I be offended that he was questioning my intentions? He already knows the answer to that he was just being smug now.

"I like him, but I love you" I ensured him "You are irreplaceable"

"Good to know" he replied giving me a loving kiss

Drew flashed me his bright white tender smile that always gave me an air of confidence while we headed to wait in the wings with Braedon. It was time to put on our game's faces, set aside any personal issues, and go out there to engage the millions observing from around the globe.

There was always a slight tingling in my body and some faint fear that went along with the building anticipation I felt before walking out onto the stage. Taking on the responsibility of putting on a flawless act was intimidating at times yet also exceedingly glorious once you have pulled it off. Enthusiasm dashed throughout my entire being as the seconds ticked slowly by. Without a word I tapped Drews tattoo with my fingertips and he tapped mine back which was our silent intimate sign to one another. Just then his music hit, he gave me a wink then took off down the ramp as his fireworks reverberate through the arena. Yes, they gave my man some fireworks I could not be prouder

"Your contender standing 6'5" weighing in a 246 pounds from New Orleans, Louisiana, The Crazy Cajun" the announcer belted as he made his way to the ring.

I hopped around shaking my head with an anxious vigor attempting to knockout a few nerves before going out there. Braedon gently squeezed the back of my neck giving me a genuine smile seeing my tension grow.

"We got this" he encouraged

His words were helpful, so I nodded my head in agreement while my ears perked up hearing the crowd cheering for The Crazy Cajun which filled me with pride for my adoring husband. Within seconds Braedon's music gave us our que to walk out to the ramp where the heat of the bright lights shone down on us. Braedon strutted with a cocky confidence as I followed directly behind him carrying his jewels and thumbing nose up at the crowd while me and Drew gazed intensely at each other. I know I deserved to be in that ring and not on the sidelines, but this could be a great step up.

"And your reigning Shining Star Champion, escorted to the ring by Miss Penny Lane, from Pittsburg, Pennsylvania standing 6'7" weighing 255 pounds King Braedon" the announcer introduced then twirled and exited the ring.

Drew stood opposite the ramp swaying back and forth getting amped up for the fight. I stood off to the side while Braedon entered over the top rope then stood in the square hollering trying to intimidate his opponent who walked to where I was standing and looked down upon me outside of the ring. I stared back up until Braedon noticed what was happening and began to fuss causing me to put my head down in shame as the bell rang signaling the start of the match up. As my adrenaline pulsed, I could feel the beating of my heart in my chest while I listened to the commotion coming from the rowdy crowd. The fans sounded divided with some cheering for The Crazy Cajun while others rooted on King Braedon and there were even a few undecided stragglers whistling for Miss Penny Lane. My spirit was charged with vibrancy as I slapped the mat encouraging Braedon to beat up Drew and doing my best to keep the crowd hyped up. This work is a wild ride that gave me the best buzz I have ever had because no other feeling compares to being right in the thick of it with thousands of fans going crazy around you. It certainly fired me up watching the two of them go at it, keeping everyone on the edge of their seats with each back-and-forth blow.

Knowing my spotlight moment was coming up quickly gave me nervous knots and an immense rush that engulfed me. According to plan Braedon threw Drew against the ropes and charged to kick him but Drew was able to counter the move getting the upper hand putting Braedon in The Voodoo Vice insuring his victory and The Shining Star Championship. However, I raced over to the corner where Braedon had a pained expression on his face with his hand in the air ready to tap out when without hesitation, I reached in the ring yanking Drews leg and breaking his grip. Drew looked at me in pure shock as I shrugged my shoulders like I had done nothing wrong.

"Penny" he asked appearing hurt "Why are you doing this?"

My distraction gave Braedon the opening he needed to recover pulling himself up and standing behind Drew. I pointed behind him with a mischievous grin causing Drew to turn around and receive Braedon's signature move The Royal Punch sending him flying to the mat. Braedon immediately capitalized covering Drew for the three count and dashing his chances of become The Shining Star Champion for now.

"1….2…3…" the referee counted then sounded the bell to end the match.

I jumped in the ring joyfully raising Braedon's hand in victory while Drew laid on his stomach with his head raised looking towards me as if he was wondering how this all went so wrong.

"Please Penny" he begged for mercy

I looked down at Drew sympathetically then glanced at Braedon then back to Drew weighing my options before smiling wickedly.

I cruelly shook my head and commented "I do not date losers"

Braedon then grabbed me bringing me close for our prearranged kiss. However, what was not planned was the way he kissed me passionately catching me off guard sending goosebumps across my skin. It took a second to recover which I prayed went unnoticed by Drew who was fighting for my honor. I brought my hand to my lips blowing Drew a tainted kiss before pressing my boot to the back of his head pushing his face into the mat laughing viciously.

After completely humiliating Drew me and Braedon walked out to a mixture of cheers and jeers as my theme song played proudly. I had chills as I reveled in my few delightful moments of fame. Once we hit the wings backstage and were out of sight, we celebrated our success since the audience totally bought what we were selling them tonight. I hugged Braedon who picked me up and spun me around when our eyes momentarily met but I promptly turned my head away. I was relieved when Drew joined us, and I wasted no time jumping in his arms for a commemorative embrace.

"We did it" I beamed

"We sure did" he happily agreed

I followed Drew down the corridor with my body still prickling from the exuberant show when Braedon crept up behind me putting his hands on my hips startling me for a minute.

"I know you felt it" he whispered low into my ear "Even if it was only for a second"

I did not waste my time responding to his nonsense only glaring at him them taking Drews arm as we walked briskly away. There was no way I was going to make the mistake of letting Braedon's head games get to me because it was nothing more than a ridiculous assumption. I love Andrew and only Andrew, so I would not let these absurd accusations come between us.

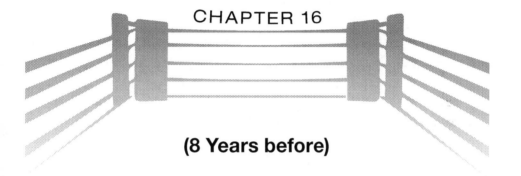

CHAPTER 16

(8 Years before)

I started my day as I did most mornings by waking with the sun after a relatively sleepless night then turned to see the picture of me and Joey at our special spot that I had framed onside my bed. I reached out rubbing my fingers across his face wishing he was here as the feeling of his touch slowly became another fading memory. I felt I had lost my zest for life and the days can be so long and lonely. Not yet has a day gone by that I have not cried and some days the sheer weight of my scattered heart seemed almost unbearable.

How do I even begin to recover from such a traumatic loss? You cannot prepare yourself for that type of devastation, there is no rehab for a broken heart, I am left to my own vices to help me navigate through this uncharted territory. These days I feel like a real life walking dead girl because Joeys death killed me, yet I continue to breath trapped in this harsh frigid place. It is not until times like this that you are reminded how important physical touch is and how chilly it is without it. People keep telling me that everything happens for a reason, but I cannot find one good reason for any of this.

I had no choice but to come to terms with the fact that my parents, if they were even deserving of that title, had completely turned their backs on me in shame however, I cannot say that I am at all surprised by the decision. In the long run their absence in my life is more than likely for the best since I did not want my child to grow up in the same kind of environment I came from. But I suppose I have been lazy enough this morning and it was time to get up and about.

"Hold on" Drew said popping his head up from across the room "I will help you out of bed"

There are no words to express how much I appreciated Drews warm welcome into his home and that his dad agreed to let me stay there. Since Joeys death his father has not raised a hand towards Drew, he just primarily walks around in a somber state as his drinking gets progressively worse. AJ, the twin's father, stays gone a lot then comes in at all hours of the night normally making a loud ruckus before passing out wherever he landed but luckily our paths seldomly cross.

Without a doubt my biggest blessing is having Andrew in my life as my best friend and biggest supporter. I could not tell you how in the world I would have managed without him all these months, he is my rock. Alas, considering the situation I got myself into, there were not only some negative consequences for me but also for Drew who was nothing more than innocent bystander. We had both dropped out of high school to make ends meet becoming little more than another teenage statistic, yet we were left with very few choices when our childhood was cut maliciously short that dark December night. Drew thankfully landed a decent paying job at a shipyard in town, but its hard work outside all day long with the hot Louisiana sun beating down on him. I was also fortunate enough to pick up a few shifts bartending at a local hole in the wall, Whiskey Paradise, thanks to my very convincing fake ID. Although the further along I get the more my muscles seem to ache I was not going to let anything stop me from doing what needs to be done to give my child the best life I possibly could. Having experiences growing up with absent parents who left me craving for a love they were unable to give me prompts me make darn sure that my child gets all the love and attention they deserve.

"Thanks" I said politely as Drew assisted me out of the bed

He let out a soft chuckle watching as I stretched my ever-growing body with a moan. Working nights was not kind to me these days.

"You try being pregnant" I lightheartedly scolded him when I suddenly felt the baby move.

"Ow" I remarked enlivened by feeling the tickle of the baby's kick.

"Can I feel?" he asked with an animated smile.

I nodded then placed his hand on my stomach where the baby had just moved. I could see the astonishment in his widening grin as he felt the kick of the tiny foot. We both lit up as we shared this special moment with our eyes connected and locked on each other. What am I thinking looking at Drew this way, it breaks all the rules? Or does it? Please do not do this to yourself Cammie I begged my conscience as I turned away. I had to admit that it did feel extremely good to make some happy memories once again.

"Are you ready" Drew asked breaking the tension "Time to see if it is a boy or a girl"

"Yeah, I am stoked" I answered eagerly on the short drive to the doctor's office.

My suspense grew the longer I waited in the lobby of Dr. Thibodaux's office for my sonogram appointment. I was enthused to learn the sex of my sweet baby to be able to better prepare for the arrival.

"Camille Landry" the nurse called

Standing up we followed the lady to the back where she put us in a sterile room. Dr. Thibodaux joined us shortly and applied the cool gel to my skin then rubbed the machine across my growing belly. I stared at the monitor in wonderment as a small head came into focus and was in awe by the sight of my precious child and the sound of the tiny heartbeat.

"Mom, dad, it is a girl" the doctor proudly announced

"My sweet little Josephine" I said gaily looking at Drew

The heartwarming expression on his face and light in his eyes beamed lovingly. I could already tell that he was going to be an excellent role model and will love her as he would his own. We stopped correcting people who assumed Drew was the father because it was just a whole lot easier to just go with it than to keep retelling our painful past.

"A girl" he grinned

"A girl" I cheerfully confirmed

Drew was beside me the entire time as he had been since we first got the news. He has never missed an appointment and was my most prominent advocate throughout all of this. Watching his face brighten brought a smile to my face. What would I do without him? Pulling back up at home I noticed Ginny's car in the driveway. Drew opened my door helping me out of the car before walking inside together where we found Ginny in the living room sitting patiently waiting on our return.

"What is the verdict?" she asked curious of the outcome.

"Josephine" I said with a smile

"Congrats" Ginny said bubbly as Drew took a seat beside her and gave her a kiss "A girl that is totally awesome"

Since the accident Drew and Ginny had fallen into a pattern of fighting, breaking up, then making up on an almost weekly basis but as of today they were obviously on again. I had always been genuinely happy seeing those two together however they now struck me as being toxic for each other at this point. Drew was a great caring soul and I hated to see him constantly getting hurt because they could not make up their minds. Could I be secretly jealous because I missed having someone to hold and love? Am I? Man, these pregnancy hormones were the worst!

I excused myself, slipped passed the couple, and headed straight for the bedroom. I sat on the edge of my bed cradling my head in my hands as I cried while a mixture of emotions encircled me. How I wish I could turn the hands of time back to when nothing really mattered, our futures looked bright, and life was easy. Our eyes were shut unaware of how things could change within a matter of seconds. At times I just felt like screaming at the top of my lungs until all my breath was gone.

"You promised you would never leave" I scolded Joey wanting so badly to hear his voice "You lied"

It was not all that long ago when we are making plans to escape together leaving everyone else behind when all we had was love and all we needed was time. There was this gigantic world out there and it was ours for the taking. Closing my eyes, I allowed myself to be temporarily transported back to warm Louisiana nights laying on the dewy grass next to the one I loved underneath the stars wrapped up in one another taking full advantage of being young and free. Those are cherished times that I will never forget.

"You are not alone" Drew said startling me as he entered the room "He left me to look after you"

Drew frowned "I feel like I am failing"

I forced a smile and dried my tears not wanting to make him feel any worse. He was being way too harsh on himself and has in no way failed me. He never failed to have my back, comfort me when I was sad, and was always there to lift me up when I fell.

"That is far from the truth Andrew" I told him "I would be lost without you"

"Please go back to Ginny" I advised him.

I plead in vain for him to not worry about me so much. I hated to watch him put his life on hold for me it made me feel like such a burden. The only people responsible for creating this mess was me and Joey why should he be responsible to help clean it up? My guilt-ridden conscience nagged at me.

"No" he said defiantly "I sent her home"

"Why?" I inquired "I do not want you pausing your life for me"

"First, you are not causing me to pause anything" Drew said "You are my family all I got Cammie, I want to be here"

"And when it comes to Ginny it is just not meant to be" he explained "I know love and that is not love so why keep wasting both our time"

It was mind boggling to me how much the two of us have changed in only a few short months. I was once the incurable optimist and life of the party but now somedays it is hard to even smile. On the other hand, Drew who was usually my meek sweet boy soon learned to speak up to defend himself and the ones he cared for. Although we can never be the same people we were before our world abruptly fell from under our feet, we were determining to be the best versions of ourselves we could be even with a total lack of guidance.

I often catch myself reading back through the pages of my diary trying to get a taste of those times once more. I can still feel the joy in my words and vibrancy in my writing when we were carefree, holding nothing back, giving freely of ourselves, yet life feels much more sober nowadays. I needed to make peace with my circumstances and take comfort in knowing that all was not lost since time does eventually heal all wounds and life carries on right down to the smallest of lives like the one growing inside of me. She does not deserve a depressed mother.

"Being happy does not mean we forgot him" Drew tried reasoning with me "The length of our sorrow does not determine the amount of our love"

Was there an appropriate amount of time to mourn? Perhaps Drew is right that I have punished myself enough and should stop feeling guilty every time I smiled because Joey would never have wanted to see me like this. Although I knew logically what he said was true getting my emotions in line with my brain was a harder task. When Joey left, he took a piece of me with him leaving me to wonder if I would ever be whole again. How can I love with only half of a heart?

"One step at a time Cammie" Drew begged to pull me out of this darkness I found myself in "That is all I am asking"

"I will be here when you are ready" he continued "Even if it takes an eternity"

I have been denying it for some time now but finally realize that I needed to allow myself to heal and was almost ready to admit it out loud. Regardless of how scary or how tough this maybe it was time I learned how to function in my new reality if I can just make it through today then maybe tomorrow will be a little bit easier. Although I might never have a last cry for my lost love, I am hoping that the tears will start falling further apart.

"It just seems unfair for this responsibility to fall on you" I expressed to him

"I am the one still here with you" he responded "I got the better end of the deal"

"Me and my brother would stay up late into the night talking about you" he reminisced with the hurt clear in his eyes "About how you accepted us without question, the way you defended us, and how you were the best part of us"

And for the first time I could see my own pain reflecting at me through Drews eyes. I should have been more sensitive to his emotions besides he had lost his twin brother, his other half and here I was a constant reminder of his loss. I will never, nor do I want to, forget Joey but there must be a way out of this darkness and back into the beautiful rays of light. I was poised to come to terms with the fact that Joey was gone and was never coming back Even if the only way is to take it one step at a time as Drew said.

"I am petrified" I admitted

"You are not alone" he promised "It is ok to be frightened of the unknown"

"I want to be held again someday" I cried for myself

Drew got in the twin size bed with me sweeping me up in his arms while cuddling me with a tight grip. It was pure and innocent. Just two people craving the feeling of having someone who loves you giving you that human touch. Even if it is only a platonic love.

Drew got in the twin size bed with me taking me in his arms while cuddling me in firmly. It was pure and innocent. Just two people craving the feeling of having someone who loves you giving you that human touch. Even if it is only a platonic love.

For the first time in a while, I could picture a light at the end of the tunnel and permitted myself to release a tiny piece of Joey back into the universe.

Then I joked lightheartedly "Man, you two have some messed up DNA"

"Yep, that is true" he grinned at me "Because our DNA was created to love one woman"

"Well then God royally screwed you two if that woman is me" I laughed

It honestly felt fantastic to laugh like that again. I had not laughed in so long I had practically forgotten how. The experience of being inside of Drews arms was an entirely different feeling from Joeys. Looking back now it was a ridiculous theory to have thought that just because they were identical twins, they should also feel identical which could not have been further from the truth. Drew was not his brother he was unique with his own personality, own smile, own touch. And own eyes that allowed me to see him in a whole new light.

"Shut up" he rascally nudged me "Go to sleep or something"

His laughter delighted my ears and I refused to continue apologizing for my happiness. It was time for me to move on not only for my sake but for Drew and Josephine as well. In the end we may just find a way to make the most of thing called life if we do it together.

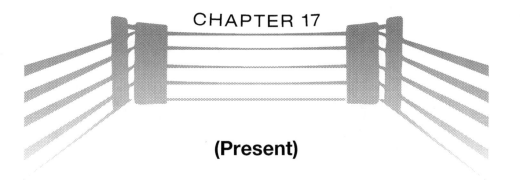

CHAPTER 17

(Present)

I stood in baffled silence wondering what I had done to make Drew this upset when we should be relishing our flawless adrenaline filled live performance. Unfortunately, his mood did not change, and his sourness continued all the way into the hotel room.

"What is wrong?" I asked becoming irritated

"That kiss is what is wrong" he answered with an angry tone "It was a little to convincing"

"You got some nerve!" I immediately lost my cool offended by his off handed comment "Do not believe everything you see on TV Andrew"

What in the hell was he thinking right now? Where does he get the nerve to look me straight in the face and accuse me of such preposterous things? Yea the kiss could have been shorter but was not my decision and that does not compare to the things he has done to me. I could have sworn he knew me better than to assume I could betray him so easily it was like a dagger through the heart. Could he have seriously changed that much in my absence?

"You and only you are the one I love" I tried reasoning with him in his irrational state "I have been with two men my entire life and they have the same DNA, you have won"

"I am a grown woman now if you have not noticed" I said with fire in my voice "You can trust me or you can leave me"

There is no way he can be serious right now. Does he truly believe that I have been with him all these years only because Joey was gone? I did love them both but in separate ways and for completely different reasons. Joey was my first love a crazy, young, wild, and carefree kind of love. While Drew one the other hand was my soulmate, the love of my life, and the man I chose to take as my husband of my own free will until death or adultery do us apart.

"I swear I do not even know who you are right now" I confronted him disappointed by his childish behavior "I feel like I am talking to a stranger not my husband"

"I am out of here" I shouted slamming the door behind me before one of us said something that could not be taken back "See you"

Walking out I regrettably ran into Tweety who I would have rather just ignored but luck was not on my side tonight.

I took a calming breath to stop my natural reaction to punch her right smack in her nose. I jerked away staring at her with an inferno of rage burning within me.

"Stay away from Braedon" she warned which I found laughable "He is mine"

"Give me a break, if I wanted him I could have him" I shot off in anger "But I do not so back the hell off"

Tweety may have inadvertently received some of the wrath intended for Drew, but she was certainly asking for it. She just did not know when to stop and kept on constantly pushing my buttons until I snapped.

Alone in the quiet confidence of the elevator I pondered about the time I kept Drew at arm's length afraid of letting him get to close and now here I was the one being locked out begging to be let in. Have I not already repented for my sins? How long must I stay on my knees before I am forgiven? I headed to the hotel lounge where I ordered a margarita and found a peaceful corner to hide out in. I wanted to disappear while I drowned all my sorrows away.

"Well, who do we have here?" I recognized Braedon's voice "It is my beautiful Cammie"

It appeared that my mission of hiding was a complete and utter failure. I laid my head on the table admitting defeat as he took an uninvited seat next to me.

"Braedon you are the root of all evil" I said before lifting my head

"Ouch!" he responded humorously clutching his chest laughing "Trouble in paradise so soon?"

"First off its none of your business" I retorted "And secondly tell your attack bird to back the hell off me"

"Awe, what is wrong?" he asked amused "Tweety been pecking at you?"

"Yeah, and I am just about ready to peck her back" I remarked "All I wanted was to make a good impression here"

I tend to portray myself as sweet, innocent, and even a little ditsy. Which goes to show that perception can be distorted because those close to me know me as a fireball and when you cross me you may end up getting burnt. As far as I was concerned Tweety could antagonize me as much as she wants because I was not going to let anyone, especially someone like her, intimidate me. I have come to far, worked too hard, and accomplished too much to allow her to get the best of me.

"You made a good first impression on me" he smiled slyly

"Perhaps to good" I countered with a sarcastic grin

"You are a very intriguing Cammie" Braedon commented "And so is Miss Penny Lane"

I had to admit that Braedon did somewhat pique my interest because hard as I may I could never quite figure him out. At times he was a complete and utter ass, other times he could be very charming, and of course he could also be inappropriate. And this man really loved a three piece suit.

"I wanted the best Goddess" he flirted "And I got her"

"Yeah, yeah" I jokingly punched his shoulder "I am sure you tell all the girls that"

"Only the prettiest ones" he said with a half-smile as I rolled my eyes at his back handed comment "But this time I really mean it"

Glancing over my shoulder I notice Tweety sitting at a table intensely eyeballing us. That girl is evidently a weirdo and made me quite uncomfortable If looks could kill, I would be long gone. She surely had a few screws loose.

"Stalker alert" I warned Braedon

"If that crazy chick kills me, I will be back to haunt you" I told him as we both chuckled

Tweety was clearly obsessed with Braedon and made no effort to hide the fact that she despised me. The best thing I can do right now is just ignore her and hope she goes away.

"Be honest with me" I asked seeking answers "What is the deal between you and Drew"

Braedon replied "You should really ask Drew"

I looked at him with an expression that told him I was not going to give up until I got to the bottom of their shared aggression.

"Are you positive you want to know?" he advised but I already had my mind made up "Somethings are better left unknown"

"Yes" I shook my head hoping I would not come to regret this decision.

"The truth is it all started with your friend Tweety" he responded before pausing for a moment.

My arch enemy was at the center of this controversy? Why? How? I was not prepared for that but now my curious mind needed to know what all this chaos had to do with her.

"Me and Tweety had been dating for a while and I was really starting to fall for the girl" he began to explain in a monotone voice "It was her birthday and I wanted to surprise her, but I was the one who got surprised when I found her and Drew in bed together"

Although he tried to hide it, I could see the pain radiating from his eyes as he told his story making my heart ached for him and angered that Drew would be so selfish. The thought of my husband and my arch enemy together literally made me sick to my stomach. Where has my sweet boy gone? I needed badly to find him and pull him out of this deep hole he has gotten himself into before he self-destructs. I was not stupid or naive I knew that Drew had been with other women but hearing about it made it a lot more real. I think Braedon is a good guy deep down inside even if he refuses to admit it however hurt and betrayal does take its toll and can make you bitter. After hearing that story who could blame him for hating Drew. I sure could not.

"So then are you using me for revenge?" I asked a bit hurt

I was going to get to the bottom of this one way or another because I was not going to permit anyone to use me as a pawn in some sick game. I am a living breathing human being with feeling and emotions.

"No Cammie I swear" he said honestly giving me some relief "I love your passion and intensity I have not seen that kind of talent since Dallas still fought"

I touched his arm gently thanking him for his kind words as he looked at me with eyes that shine to hide his sadness. I could easily relate to his heartache and find solace in his presence which scared me some. I quickly moved my hand into my lap thankful for my strong willpower to not give in to lust.

"I just do not want to end up a pawn in someone's chess game" I told him

"Kings do not waste their time fighting over pawns" he said with a slick smile that made me blush "You are the queen Cammie"

I could tell that this war was far from over and nothing I could do would stop it. However, Braedon was getting into a war that he could not win because I already had my irreplaceable king even if he was not acting very royal in this moment.

"Checkmate" Drew said boastfully coming out of nowhere staring down Braedon then kissing my cheek.

Drew was acting much more territorial than normal, and I was not sure what he overheard but I hoped that it was enough to wake him up and get a grip on his jealousy.

Braedon stood to give me a hug before leaving and whispered low in my ear "If he hurts you, I am here anytime and I can kill him just so you know"

I listened then gave him a peck on the cheek and told him goodbye.

Once we were alone Drew apologized "I am sorry my love"

"I know" I said giving him a warm kiss

"You are the most beautiful girl here or anywhere for that matter" he said genuinely "So I know I will always have competition, but I trust you"

"Do you get it Drew?" I responded "When it comes to you there is no competition"

"But do not ever question my intentions again" I warned

"I never will" he replied

"No more second chances" I let him know straight to the point

He pulled me in close for another kiss. There was not another person on this planet anywhere who could ever come close to replacing Drew or stealing me away. I only wanted him.

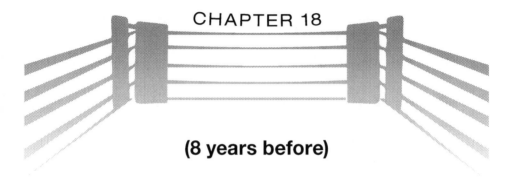

CHAPTER 18

(8 years before)

Looking through the bedroom window gazing out into the backyard full of good memories I could still picture the three of us outside playing in the grass so innocent and clueless, full of life giving no thought to our futures. The last few months has given me plenty of time to contemplate my circumstances and reflect on the recent trials in my life. That reflection gave me the belief that the first time you fall in love is the strongest because you enter the relationship naive, giving openly of yourself, and not yet knowing what heartbreak feels like. When a love is as pure as that the agony of its loss can be crushing. It does not end easily and cuts us deeply leaving a scar to remind us that the past was real. Once we have become accustomed to that type of pain and grief do we admit defeat, or do we fight for survival giving ourselves a chance to taste the sweetness of romance one more time. Being that hindsight is 20/20 and knowing how it all ends would I do it all over again? Yes, I would do it a million times over all the good, the bad, and the ugly. Even if our time together was brief, I was just grateful that for each moment we shared. In my opinion being able to say that you truly loved and have been loved back was an extra special offering since not everyone can say that and those of us whom can were the lucky ones.

The memories I have of me and Joey use to bring me sorrow because I did not have him here with me, but now I realized that I should think back happily letting them bring me pleasure and help to lift this heavy burden from my soul. I learned the hard way that this world could sometimes be cruel but no matter what happened, how deeply anything hurts you, the earth will not cease to spin, and you will continue to breath. The world is not going to stop for a broken heart. Therefore, I have decided to take delight in what time we are given since tomorrow is not promised to any of us so why not make the most of everyday. I also theorized that there is no such thing as goodbye because each hour we spend together, the look in your lovers' eyes, every stolen kiss, and all the whispers of love are not vain since we could live forever in those small intimate moments we shared.

"You really have the most beautiful smile" Drew complimented "It is nice to see it again finally"

"I am just happily reminiscing" I told him

Turning back to look out the window I was hit with a sudden pain so sharp that it caused me to double over before I knew what was happening.

"Are you alright?" Drew said rushing over to me in a panic

I closed my eyes tightly taking a deep breath in as the pain began to slowly subside. For a split second I thought I was going into labor but was relieved to be wrong. This was a first for me and my nerves were on extreme edge thinking of what was to come.

"Yeah, I am good" I nodded "False alarm"

With my due date only days away Drew was on high alert. He was very attentive and the way that he watched out and doted on me was the cutest thing. I have yet to meet anyone as loyal or caring as him and was sure he would grow into a wonderful man. The girl who is fortunate to catch him better hold him tight and never let him go. Before I could finish my thought the pain that had passed a few minutes earlier came back with a vengeance as an unusual warmth trickled down my leg.

"Drew I was wrong" I shouted with the intensifying "It is time!"

"Just breath" he reminded me of my Lamaze techniques "It will be fine"

He put his arm around me helping me to the car as each contraction struck worse than the one before filling me with fear. How much worse could this possibly get? Am I strong enough to do this? Will the baby be, okay? My mind whirled with endless questions on our trip to the hospital where Drew put me in a wheelchair and rushed me in.

"She is in labor" he dashed to tell the man behind the desk who quickly shuffled me into the delivery room.

"Are you family?" the attending asked Drew stopping him at the door.

"No...But" he tried to explain

"I am sorry" the guy interrupted "I cannot let you in"

"Drew please" I called out reaching for him "Do not leave me"

Right now, I needed him more than I ever needed anyone in my life. I could not begin to imagine having to do this all alone without his support and guidance.

"That is my child about to be born" he countered pushing the man aside "I am going in"

"Geez dude" the man seemed stunned at Drews aggression "Sorry"

"You should know me better than that" he assured me after forcing his way in "I would never leave my pretty girl"

Following us in shortly after a small statured grey-haired nurse surfaced then proceeded to check my vitals and progression while attaching me to numerous machines and monitors. My anxiety was beginning to peak when a dark complected man in green scrubs, who introduced himself as the anesthesiologist, walked in the door. He took his time calmly explaining the procedure step-by step to elevate some of the pain which was a more than welcome suggestion.

"Just focus on me" Drew said feeling my hands shake as the nurse prepared my back for the epidural.

"Alright Miss Landry" the anesthesiologist instructed "I need you to lean into your husband, take a deep breath, and be very still"

I did as instructed taking a deep breath, leaning into Drew, and burying my head deep into his chest allowing myself to relax as I focused on listening to his rapidly beating heart and synchronized my breathing with his helping me to keep me calm and focused.

"Now try get some rest" the sweet natured nurse recommended before leaving us alone "You will inevitably need all of your strength"

Once we were alone Drew asked, "Are you mad I said she was my baby?"

"No" I answered "I would be mad if you were not here"

The truth of the matter is that over the last few months me and Drew have grown close and created a nearly unbreakable bond becoming each other's best friends and main confidant. My life without him looked bleak and I could not picture my life without him in it. Staring into Drews loving face I could sense that it was time to let go of the past, stop worry about right and wrong, and follows what feels right to me even if it does not turn out as I expected. But how do I begin to explain all of this, all my feelings.? What if he does not reciprocate my feeling and I end up looking like a total fool? If this goes wrong, I have everything to lose.

"Andrew" I said grabbing his attention

"I never want to be without you" I opened up

"Do not worry" he replied "You never will"

"My sweet boy I do not think you understand" I admitted it all out loud "I am in love with you Andrew"

He was visibly shocked by my confession and his silence filled my heart with dread. Did I just make the hugest mistake of my life? Had love been right in front of me this whole time but I was too deep in my fog of grief and now I may have missed my chance. Am I the world biggest fool? There is no time frame on love is there? When you know you just know?

"I have waited a long time to hear those words" he responded with his light eyes glowing brightly "I love you too Camille, I always have, and I always will"

"The world looks different with you by my side" I told him through joyful tears "You made me want to live again"

Drew tenderly wiped my eyes and kissed the weepiness away letting me feel the love I thought I would never have again. We focused on each other letting our eyes speak a thousand soundless words. Each word we heard and understood. Before we could get a word in Dr. Thibodaux walked in followed by his staff as I held my breath unnerved with the unpredictability ahead.

"It is time to have a baby" he announced as I felt my heart about leap from my chest.

I allowed my mind to go blank while I listened closely to Dr. Thibodaux's instructions. I lost track of time unsure of how long I had been pushing using all the energy I had. At this point I was expended running on fumes with nothing left to give when Drew wiped my face, brushed back my sweat filled hair, and kissed my forehead.

"You got this" he confidently encouraged making me believe what he said was true.

Somehow, he always knew just the right words to say when I needed to hear them. I focused on Drew trusting him completely, letting the rest of the world disappear as I pushed a few more times until I heard the most beautiful sound that has ever graced my ears, it was the sound of my newborn daughters first cry. I flopped back on the bed entirely empty with welcome tears flowing freely when the nurse laid my minutes old baby girl across my chest and seeing her precious face made it real that my life would never be the same again and I could not wait to start my new life with Josephine and Drew.

"Hello Josephine" I spoke to the tiny piece of me "I am your momma"

Drew watched over us like any proud father would. The admiration on his face as he stared at Josephine finally registered in my mind that she was not only a piece of me and Joey but was just as much a piece of Drew she does have half his DNA.

"How does daddy sound to you?" I asked

"Sounds beautiful" he cried tears of joy

"And this is your daddy" I spoke proudly handing her to Drew who beamed brighter than the sun.

I felt complete watching him with our daughter who wrapped her tiny finger around her daddy's as they gazed quietly at each other. The love that naturally illuminated from those two was heartwarming and in that moment, I knew I was exactly where I wanted to be with the two people I belonged with.

"That is right Josie I am lucky enough to be your daddy" he whispered before handing her back to the nurse "And your daddy in heaven will be watching over you and your momma"

For the first time I saw what a real family is supposed to look like. There was no way I was going to mess this up especially not with the most innocent of lives hanging in the balance.

"You did good pretty girl" he smiled at me

"Oh, my sweet boy" I said rubbing his face in my hands as we brought our lips together.

I feared his kiss may have a similar feel but was very pleasantly surprised by its own unique breathtaking quality. It was without a doubt one of a kind better than I could have ever wanted for. His kiss was soft, warm, sweet, loving, and lingered on my lips leaving my body prickling.

"I love you and Josephine" he said from his heart "More than you will ever know"

"And I love you" I reciprocated "Thank you for loving us"

"No, thank you" he kissed me "I now have the family I always wished for"

I wholeheartedly believed that love was not meant for me anymore and out of the question. However, I now know that I could not have been more wrong and was looking forward to starting our new lives together. Worn out from the day's events I closed my eyes saying a prayer thanking God for the blessings he has bestowed upon me then I spoke to Joey thanking him for our adorable daughter and watching over us. I reached out holding Drews hand before giving into exhaustion and drifting peacefully off to sleep.

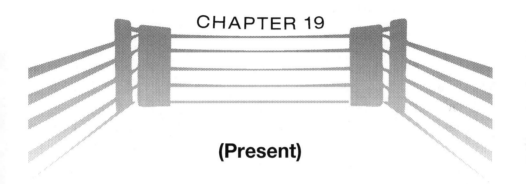

CHAPTER 19

(Present)

Dear Diary,

Life is full of mysteries many for which I have no clear answers. Birth, death, ecstasy, grief, success, failure, rich, poor, good, and evil are all somehow connected in this tangle web of life. I have tasted the bitter as well as the sweet yet still find it hard to tell the difference between the two at times. The only firm belief I have is that in the end we are all judged as equals before we ascend into the great unknown. Maybe I am being a little philosophical, but it seems that the older I get the more I want to analyze and take inventory of my short 24 years one this earth. Somedays I look back and it is as though I have barely lived and others when I feel like I have lived a thousand lifetimes. Whenever I get a sense of overwhelming, I remember the advice Drew gave me years ago "Take it one step at a time" words cannot explain how much I love that man. Well, that is all my thoughts for now. Peace!

I slipped my journal careful not wake to Drew then crept back underneath the covers in the stillness of the morning watching the rise and fall rise and fall of Drews chest with every breath he took. It was in these quiet moments before the start of our hectic day that I treasured the most. The peaceful look on his face reminded me of the boy I feel in love with when we were young. And now the way he smells, how he tastes, and the way he feels is permanently embodied in my mind, body, and soul I rolled over rubbing my finger over the bareness of his chest reflecting on how fortunate I was to be able to wake up next to my soulmate every morning.

I set me eyes on him when we were apart and like a beautiful vision, we found our way back into each other's arms like a moth to a flame. We were at our strongest together having already come directly in the path of various trauma and clasping hands we conquered it. We were never ashamed of where we came from or hid our struggles, we gladly owned them and wore them like battle scars denying them power over us by turning sorrow into success. We were the kids from poverty expected to become nothing yet here we stood two throw away kids chasing our dreams in the TWE. Life is a crazy ride and can change so fast you have to make sure not to get whiplash.

"Good morning pretty girl" Drew said opening his eyes and stretching his limbs.

"Good morning" I smiled at my handsome husband

"Two more days" he said eager from some alone time "Then I get you all to myself"

Since our reconciliation we have spent much of that time on the road therefore I was looking forward to being free of a schedule and getting plenty of time together to do as we pleased. TWE gave us just enough time off to have some sort of personal life but not enough time off to get lazy, it was a perfect balance of work and play for me. Drew rascally clutched my arms throwing me down kissing me with his tongue tasting strongly of lust. His body was warm against mine and his breath hot on my neck causing my body to quiver. Regaining control, I kneeled over him as we kissed vigorously while I wrapped my fingers in his dark silky hair.

"Did you not get enough last night?" I teased

"Nope" he answered rolling onto my back and nibbling my neck "Never enough of you"

"But duty calls" he relented releasing me from his dominance.

I stayed in bed awhile longer allowing myself to cool down from his advances and suppressing my desires.

"You are such a tease" I yelled to Drew who laughed in response

I suppose it is time for me to kick myself into action for tonight's pay-per-view event TWE presents Revenge. This will be my first pay-per-view, so I was pumped and honored to have been chosen to participate in it. Approaching the bathroom, I could hear the shower running as I entered a cloud of steam which had greeted me where I let me clothes fall to the floor then joined Drew. I paused admiring the sight of the water falling on his well-defined body as his eyes connected to mine and he rubbed my wet face in his hands then ran his finger over my lips.

"What is wrong love?" I asked as he stood motionless staring at me

"Sometimes I have to touch you to make sure you are real" he revealed "I am scared I will blink, and you will disappear"

"I am real" I ensured him "And I am not going anywhere"

I would give anything to be able to feel like this forever because love has the highest of highs and the lowest of lows and his love was my elixir. When life handed me a heavy load to carry Drew was my strength. Is this love or obsession? I frankly did not care because whatever it is it is mine.

"You are my love and my savior" he voiced mirroring my feeling as if he was inside my head "You always seem to know when I need rescuing"

"And you save me" I replied kissing him while the water ran down our skin "We were made for each other"

"Cannot trump DNA" he reminded me of his words long ago

I relished the time I spent lost in his gravity both feet planted firmly on the ground while my body floated in his orbit. Time crept by us each minute better than the one before as we surrendered to our carnal cravings. Once our lust infused blur cleared from our vision, we grasped just how long we had spent adrift and swiftly grabbed our bags and headed to the stadium trying to avoid the consequences of arriving late.

Stepping out the vehicle I stuck to my rock roots in my jean shorts, Ozzy mid-drift, and my classic black Doc Martin boots while Drew dressed comfortably in his jeans and representing in his Crazy Cajun apparel with his shirt. Glancing at the barricades I spotted a small gathering of groupies with hopes of catching a peek of their favorite Totalstar or Goddess.

"Cajun, Penny" they shouted jubilantly

The commitment the patrons displayed and delight they exhibited for the characters we personally created carved a special place in my heart for them. Our livelihood depended heavily on the fans and the passion they had for what we did. Without them we would literally be nothing. They made all the bumps and lumps well worth it.

"Come on bae" I begged leading him to the growing group "Please"

"Okay" he conceded "Anything for you love"

The congregation was thrilled when we greeted them, and their cheerful demeanor was contagious firing me up for tonight performance. Meeting everyone was indubitably a confidence booster although I still have a hard time of feeling worthy of such admiration. As I signed a few autographs I noticed a mother making her way through the crowd with a toddler on her hip who inquired about a picture, and I readily agreed. I held the adorable curly brown headed little girl in my arms while posing for a snapshot.

"Miss Penny Lane" the child spoke "I want to be just like you"

"Mommy I want to be just like you" I heard from a memory

"You can be anything you want to be" I told the child squeezing her tightly "You just have to work hard and never give up"

Being a role model had never crossed my mind until now. The image of that sweet innocent face staring up at me brought memories of days passed flooding back and the distant look in Drews eyes told me he was likewise thinking of our own brown headed daughter. A particular silence blanketed the air between us as we left words unspoken because speaking it aloud was just too painful.

We had a troubling tendency to sweep bitter issues under the rug and immerse ourselves in a world of make believe where only the two of us exist engrossed in each other. Both of us knew it was crazy, but everyone deals with grief in their own ways. I was not sure if he was my cure or my poison, but I did know that I would rather die with him than live without him. I promised for better or worse and accepted the hand I was dealt so now it was time for him to be the man I deserve.

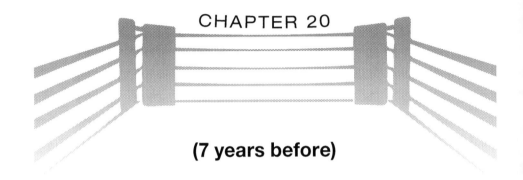

CHAPTER 20

(7 years before)

Sitting on the couch I had to giggle watching Josie running across the floor sippy cup in hand. It is as if as soon as she learned to walk, she started to run. Where has the time gone? I took enormous pleasure in seeing everything she did as she developed and grew. Witnessing her first steps, first words, and first tooth was astounding to experience. I felt honored to be her mother and only wanted to do right by her and would not change her for the world. I heard the creek of the front door opening then saw my hunky working man walk in through the door.

"Dada" Josie shouted running straight into his arms

He swept her up covering her in kisses then blew on her tummy as she let out a contagious laugh that had the three of us all chuckling. The sight of them two together always brightened my day and gave life meaning. Finally, I have the family that I use to dream of as a little girl. I had a cute loveable daughter and her breath-taking sumptuous father who belonged to me. I found it remarkable how drastically our lives have changed in such a short period of time and how properly domesticated we have become.

"Bae in case you did not know" I said "You look super-hot got me burning up"

Drew looked up giving me a satisfied grin and his I will see you tonight wink. I am unfiltered I just say what I feel then things come to fruition.

"And I would never forget my pretty girl" he said giving me a smooch then sitting beside me.

Once seated he said with apprehension "There is something I want to talk to you about"

"Alright, what is it?" I responded curiously

"When we use to talk about our dreams when we were younger what did we always say?" Drew asked me

"TWE" I smiled because it was still my dream

"Do you remember Psycho Dave?" he asked me "From Swamp Boys Wrestling?"

"Yea…" I answered

Swamp Boys Wrestling (SBW) was a small wrestling organization that was popular in these parts and mainly comprised and run by locals. Wrestling was by far our favorite past time therefore we attended nearly every SBW show and never missed TWE on Mondays and Thursdays. I admired the Goddesses because they were not only powerful but beautiful and confident everything a woman should embody.

"Dave works with me he told me they were looking for some new recruits" he explained "He thinks I would be a good fit, but the training is $300"

"Not just that" he continued "he needs a female wrestler he will train you for free"

"300" I said slightly hesitant caught off guard by his proposition.

Drew worked extremely hard pulling long hours and overtime under the punishing Louisiana sun to provide for his family, giving us a nice home and taking wonderful care of me and Josephine. We lived as comfortably as our finances allowed and even had some money saved, so how could I possibly deny him after all the sacrifices he has made for us when he did not have to? Is this too good to be true? Probably but I am a dreamer and that is just what we do.

"Okay" I approved watching his face light up "go for it"

"Thanks bae!" he kissed me with excitement "I am one lucky man"

I smiled then nabbed up Josie and headed to the kitchen to finish up supper while Drew went to clean up. I stood over the stove with my girl on my hip stirring one of Drews favorite meals spaghetti and meatballs which Josie somehow always managed to get more on herself than in her mouth.

"Camille" I heard my dad call from the front door

"In the kitchen" I called back

After the fit my parents threw not wanting Josie, I was pleased that my dad was trying, unlike my mean-spirited mother, to be part of our lives. However, the truth is that some things never change and his continuing battle with drug addiction appeared to be a losing fight no matter how desperately I tried to keep him sober. After several stints in rehab, getting sober for a few months, then relapsing repeatedly I had to face the fact that my hands were tied and only he could save himself.

"Josie" he said taking her and freeing my hands "Paw Paw came to see his little princess"

"Hey dad" I said greeting him with a kiss on the cheek when I caught a disappointing glimpse of his glassy eyes as Drew walked into the kitchen.

"Are you high?" I asked angry yet not surprised

The look of shame on his face spoke volumes as Drew protectively snatched Josie from him. This was just another in a long pattern of disillusions and I do not even know why I keep putting myself through this time and time again. Despite how incredibly screwed up he was I still loved him and held on to hopes that is perhaps one day he could be a real father instead of a dad who breaks my heart then leaves me alone to pick up the pieces.

"I think it is time to be going" Drew advised him

My dad said goodbye to me and Josie before leaving with no resistance fully aware of his faults, false promises, and tense relationship with my other half.

"I do love you Camille" he maintained as he exited my home

"I know dad" I responded "keep trying"

I deeply wanted to believe that was the truth, but I was not sure if he had the capacity to love in his drug fueled daze. Besides if he really did care that much than I do not understand why he could not stay sober for only a short visit. A solitary tear snuck out with that thought letting my emotions for the circumstances get to me then quickly wiped my face but not before Drew noticed.

"He is not worth your tears" he consoled me gently drying my eyes "Me and Josie are your family now"

"You have always been my family" I stated

Drew smiled that boyish smile I loved so much then gave me a sweet wondrous kiss that made everything feel right again. Visits like those made me appreciate the life I have now even more. I never want my child to have to feel the kind of hurt I felt at the hands of her parents. I was fortunate to be able to provide Josie with a stable sober home, a happy healthy childhood, and two very loving parents. Being a mother and partner may not be the easiest job in the world, but it is certainly the most rewarding. Although if I am being perfectly honest at times, I feel closer to 30 than to 17 but these were the choices I had made and was alright with that because I was truly happy and content with where I was and had no complaints.

Finished with supper I strapped Josie into her highchair while Drew kept her attention making a few funny faces before sitting down to all eat together. This whole family thing was foreign to the both of us hence we were learning as we go, and I think we are doing a pretty good job if I do say so myself.

"I love watching her zip around here" Drew expressed "You would never guess she had a heart problem"

"Yep" I responded hating to think about that subject "She is a handful"

Josephine was born with a congenital heart disease and the doctors warn that she would one day need a heart transplant and to be put on a list for heart. However, I did my best to brush it out of my mind, not to be cold but to keep from driving myself crazy. I just wanted to enjoy her growing up instead of constantly worrying that something may go wrong.

"Did you come up with a ring name yet?" I asked as we ate

"Swear not to laugh" he made me agree

"Swear" I agreed

"The Crazy Cajun" he lit up

"I like it" I approved pleasantly surprised

"I was afraid you might say Dashing Drew or something" we chuckled at the thought "Then I may have had a hard time of keeping my word"

"And you?" he asked

"Miss Penny Lane she is a happy hippie" I answered

"Fits you perfectly" he smiled

It was easy to see by his proud grin that he really did want this, and I was going to back him all the way. Plus, it would be amazing to for us to chase our dreams of performing in the ring while us and Josie took turns cheered from the sidelines.

"I can hardly believe it" I smiled at Josies spaghetti filled face "She is really going to be one tomorrow"

"And it is our anniversary" he said as if I would forget "Where does the time go?"

"Oh, by the way" he said as he cleaned Josie off and put her down "I have any early gift for you"

"Andrew…" I said suspiciously

"Go get daddy the present for mommy" he instructed Josie

Sneaky, sneaky those two made the perfect partners in crime. She raced as fast as her little legs would take her to grab the gift then pitter pattered back with a big cheesy grin. Once Drew had the present in his hands, he dropped down to one knee opening the box to reveal the dazzling diamond ring inside causing my heart rate to quicken.

"Camille Jolee Landry" Drew began with his blue eyes shining brighter than ever before "Will you make me the happiest man on earth and marry me?"

Although I was completely unprepared for this it was the most wonderful surprise I have ever received besides Josie. I stood up in shock trying to catch my breath as my eyes teared up in delight. I cannot believe this is really happening right now.

"Yes" I answered still in disbelief "A million times over I would say yes"

"I love you so much" he said slipping the ring on my quaking finger with tears in his eyes

"I love you to sweet boy" I reciprocated touching his angelic face then sharing a full-hearted kiss.

Josie tugged at Drews shirt staring up at him with her big brown puppy dog eyes feeling left out and insisting on being included so Drew picked her up embracing us both. I lived and breathed for my family without them life would be meaningless.

"Go relax in the bath" he suggested "I will put her down"

Accepting his offer, I emerged myself in the nice warm tub where I found more surprises. Drew had put me a glass of wine, rose petals, and candles around the tub he knew I could not resist a hot bath. The ambience from the candles was incredibly soothing as I drank my wine soaking up how marvelous the water felt floating across my skin. Laying back I closed my eyes reflecting on my day still trying to wrap my head around the fact that I was now engaged and one step closer to being complete. It was as if all my wishes were beginning to come true and this is my fairytale in its own strange way.

Stepping out the tub I caught a glimpse of my maturing face in the mirror. Gone was the baby fat that once plumped my cheeks and added was few fine lines which was a far cry from the 12-year-old picking blueberries to the young woman I have become. I slipped on my silk ruby red nighty then pulled my robe tight around me before lightly brushing on a bit of rouge and adding a splash of color to my lips. Afterwards I found Drew still in Josies Hello Kitty room and joined him onside her bed.

"Mama" Josie shouted jumping into my arms

Holding my precious gift in my arms who looked up at me with her daddy's eyes was a feeling that words could just not express.

I laid her back down giving her a goodnight kiss "Night, night sweet girl"

Drew pulled up the covers, tucked her in, and kissed her forehead as we softly sang her favorite lullaby "You are my Sunshine". I saw her blink her eyes as her lids got weaker until she gently floated away to dreamland allowing me and Drew to have some alone time.

I closed our bedroom door behind me nibbling my lower lip while locking in on Drews baby blues that were filled with lust. Standing in front of Drew he delicately ran his hand down the closing of my robe then watched as it hit the floor.

"Beautiful" he remarked pulling me to him

His hot lips against my skin sent chills up and down my spine as we let passion take the wheel. This was the man I intended to marry, the person I would growing old with, and the man I chose to give my forever to. He was the young boy I seen grow into a young man with our continuing odyssey I could not wait to share every piece of my existence with him.

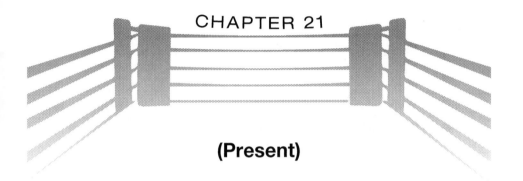

CHAPTER 21

(Present)

Entering the famed Madison Square Gardens, for TWE's biggest pay-per-view of the year there was an energizing vibe in the air. Me and Drew parted company heading to our assigned locker rooms but not before sneaking in a parting smooch. Walking up to join Sarah, she pulled me aside.

"I wanted to give you a heads up" she alerted me "Braedon's been creeping around looking for you"

"Does he ever give up?" I asked shaking my head

As if he heard us talking, right after her warning, I caught a glimpse of Braedon out of the corner of my eyes.

"Can we talk a sec?" he asked with a hint of desperation

At first I was just going to say not I responded when I thought oh what the heck man may

"What is up?" I asked straight to the point

"Are you ready for tonight" he danced around the real topic "I know it can be intimidating"

"Come on Braedon!" I said in a huff "What is this really all about?"

Getting the run around really irritated me and I made sure to let it clearly show. Braedon lowered his head taking a deep breath appearing to build up the courage to say what it was that seemed to be of importance to him. Then he looked up with his eyes fixated on me.

"Cammie, the truth is I find myself with feeling for you" he admitted "Drew is not a good guy he hurts people"

"He is my husband" I defended my relationship "You do not know him like I do"

"I get it, I will not bother you but if you need me, I am here" he stated then sweetly kissed my forehead "Anytime I am only a call away"

I was seriously shocked by his bold confession as well as his unsavory opinion of my husband. How could someone come to that conclusion about Drew? What type of reputation has he created for himself here that warrants such a negative view? Do others see him in this same derogatory light? Tons of questions swirled around the vastness of my mind that threatened to consume me unreservedly. I went back and forth with myself wondering if I would be able to handle the whole truth or was Braedon right and some things were simply better left unknown.

The Drew I knew and fell in love with would never hurt anyone which was in stark contrast to the person I heard characterized since arriving here. He was always there for me, went through the fire with me, held me when I was frightened, and carried me in times of weakness. He had never been anything then genuinely good to me and had only mistreated me with other women. So, this whole situation totally boggled my mind but none of us are perfect, we have all made our share of mistakes, and I refuse to let the past ruin my future. Only the present matters now and it is all that we can control in the present.

"You are up in makeup" Sarah called out snapping back to reality

I hastily changed from my street clothes and into my customized ring gear before racing to hop up in the cosmetologist chair. My anxiety rose as the finishing touches were put on Miss Penny Lane and each minute that ticked by brought me closer to my inaugural appearance on a pay-per-view event. With the image of my alter ego complete I sprinted off to wait near the wings with my cohort.

"Well, it is the best-looking hippie I ever did see" Drew complimented as he put his hand on the small of my back while I relaxed into his touch.

"You are pretty desirable yourself" I remarked checking him out and toying with him "Yummy"

Leaning back against Drews chest my nerves slowly began to fade into his embrace as I luxuriated in the calm before the chaos. If there was anything vicious about him, I was totally oblivious because I could not see it, nor did I want to. Unfortunately, my peace was interrupted by Tweety staring me down looking more unhinged than ever which I honestly thought was impossible.

"Tweety freaks me out" I said glancing at her "She is completely obsessed"

"Do not let her get to you" he told me "That is exactly what she wants"

"You do not understand" I said distressed "It is like she is stalking me"

"She is just jealous bae" he said trying to ease my mind "She wishes she could be a fraction of the woman you are"

I brushed the iciness of the encounter away refusing to let her get one up on me plus there was no sense in worrying about things beyond my control and redirected my focus to the match I had coming up in mere minutes as Braedon joined us flashing a bright smile that I returned as we gathered in place. Tonight's battle was the highly anticipated rematch between King Braedon and The Crazy Cajun in a no disqualifications title match to settle this feud once and for all even the Shining Star Belt was on the line. This meant that anything goes, nothing was off limits, every man for himself, good old-fashioned throwdown. An ecstatic vitality flowed around us as I fed off the roar from the thousands of fans who were awaiting our emergence. I warmed up bouncing around to get my blood pumping when Braedon's music began which was our que to get on out there. I tapped Drews tattoo, and he tapped mine back with a confident wink before following behind Braedon putting on my best servant act.

"Ladies and gentlemen, your reigning Shining Star Champion" the announcer belted "Weighing 255 pounds standing 6'7" from Pittsburg, Pennsylvania, King Braedon"

Braedon entered stepping across the top rope then kindly held the ropes apart for me to step in and stand beside him with a contrast of mixed opinions coming from the audience.

"And escorting him to the ring Miss Penny Lane" she continued

I reveled in hearing my name announced over the loudspeaker which was a small victory in what I hoped was the first of bigger victories to come. Braedon raised my hand in the air twirling me around proudly showing off his newest trophy. After which Drews music blasted like a shockwave through the stadium bringing me and Braedon to a halt the audience to their feet. That reaction was what wrestling dreams are made of and I was one hundred percent proud of everything he has achieved thus far in TWE.

"And your contender standing 6'5" weighing 246 pounds from New Orleans, Louisiana" the announcer finished before twirling then exiting the ring "The Crazy Cajun"

Drew wasted no time with pleasantries instead opting to charge towards the ring and sliding under the bottom rope while I instantaneously jumped out the ring as the bell tolled. The guys immediately locked up as I watched them fight listening to the delectable ohs of the fans that went back and forth with each blow. With the pressure building my heartbeat sped and a surge thrummed through my blood standing beneath the hot production lights with all eyes on us as the cameraman broadcast our picture across the world.

It was practically impossible to put into words how I was feeling right now in the moment because there was nothing more enthralling than witnessing this pure marvelous madness and seeing how the fans faces lit up. If I had to find a way to explain it, I would compare it to scaling the world's tallest mountain and finally reaching the top then looking down at the boundless lands wishing you could stay there forever taking splendor in your achievement lost in a euphoric cloud. This was my idea of bliss.

The captivating match persisted on while I observed Braedon beginning to fade as the fight took its toll on the both of us. Braedon desperately motioned my assistance and without forethought I reached underneath the ring grabbing a steel chair and tossing it over to my master. Catching a second wind he then hit Drew in the back twice sending him rushing to the mat. With Drew unable to move Braedon smiled pleased with himself then gestured for me to join him where he handed me the chair commanding me to hit Drew adding insult to injury.

"Do it!" he hollered

I held the chair above my head standing centerstage feeling everyone looking at me while my heart throbbed. Drew gazed up at me alone on the mat preparing for the blow to come making me take a momentary pause.

"Come on get this done NOW" he screamed again growing fiery

Braedon's forceful demanded combined with the sympathy I felt for Drew caused a change of heart and breaking Braedon's grasp on me. Love always wins I thought with a vengeful look as I turned catching Braedon cold then tossing it aside.

"No one tells Miss Penny Lane what to do" I yelled angrily

Drew swiftly seized the opportunity crawling over and pinning him.

"1...2...3..." the referee counted then rang the bell

"Your new Shining Star Champion, The Crazy Cajun" was declared over the loudspeaker with Drews hand lifted in sweet, sweet victory.

I squatted down hushed in the corner feeling guilty for my betrayal. I shined him a bright smile and nodded a congratulations before standing and pivoting to leave him to celebrate in peace.

"Penny" I heard Drew call bringing me to a halt on the top step "Wait"

Drew jumped out the ring offering me his hand as I gazed at him all starry eyed accepting his hand down the steps. Before my feet could touch the floor, he tilted me backwards making a point to give me along steamy kiss while the audience erupted in applause. The atmosphere was brisk with pleasure as the crowd whistled, clapped, and shouted exuberantly. They finally had a champion they could be proud of, the good guy, and fan favorite was now their new Shining Star Champ. The TWE Planet could once again be complete with Miss Penny Lane and The Crazy Cajun reunited reveling in championship glory.

"My husband The New Shining Star Champ" I said backstage "How does it feel?"

"It feels damn good" he said patting the huge belt across his shoulders

"That's right bae" I picked "should always take the women advice

I was nearly jumping with jubilation for Drews successful achievement. He worked fiercely to attain this, and I felt grateful to have the opportunity to see it happen firsthand and sensed many more wonderful things to come. I did not influence his win because every match is already pre-determined, but I was there every time they maybe need and extra, to take part.

"Great job out there gorgeous" Braedon complimented as he paused to kiss my cheek intentionally ignoring Drew.

"I hate that guy" Drew grimaced

"I know bae" I said softly sweeping away his hair "I am sorry"

"Do not be sorry it is not your fault" he told me "I am just glad you chose me"

"Always choose you" I ensured

"Time to hit the showers" he said

"Yep" I agreed "Time to become us again"

Tonight, Drew took a humongous step in his career with this win moving him closer to the possibility of one day earning The TWE Heavyweight Championship which is the highest prize for any Totalstar to be awarded. Yet as elated as I was for Drew, I felt selfish for wanting to get the chance to show off my in-ring skills and work my way up the ladder of The Goddess Division to clinch a belt of my own. I understand that nothing worth having happens overnight it takes tremendous discipline, hard work, and major determination. At least after tonight's unique co-starring role more people know who I am which was half of the battle. This just made me hungry to press on and take the next stride in my Total Wrestling Entertainment experience.

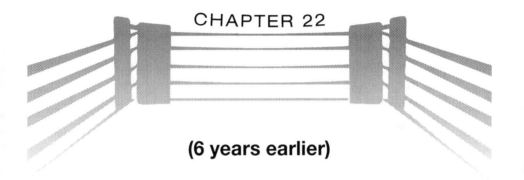

CHAPTER 22

(6 years earlier)

Today is first day of the rest of my life. I am scarcely hours away from becoming a wife and having the privilege of getting to marry my best friend and soulmate. This was no longer just a sweet dream; it will soon be my glorious reality when I become Mrs. McEnrowe. How crazy is that? All this fuss over me was unbelievable I thought glancing at my little Josephine's smiling face racing my way.

"Hello sweet girl" I spoke covering her face with kisses "Momma loves you"

She was enchanting with her brown hair pulled back in a French braid wearing a charming white satin dress with full tulle skirt, an emerald sash secured around her waist with a giant bow in the back, and matching petals lining the bottom of her skirt. She is undoubtedly the loveliest flower girl on the planet. She resembled are real life Disney Princess complete with a tiara atop her head to finish the picture.

"Oh, my goodness Cammie" Laura exclaimed squeezing me tight "I still cannot believe you are actually getting married"

Me and Laura have been through hell and back together creating a sacred bond of sisterhood between us. After the wreck, we grew even closer than before. She was my best girlfriend, Josie's Godmother, and my maid of honor pairing her with Billy who was serving as Drew's best man. Although the two of them ended they are on again off again relationship over a year ago they somehow managed to remain friends. They shared a long history together from first kiss to high school sweethearts and certainly loved each other even if they were no longer in love. It was better for them to move on then try to relight a love that was out of fire.

So, that pretty much summed up our whole wedding party Josephine, Laura, and Billy. It was a small intimate wedding just as I envisioned with close friends and family in attendance. We did not need any lavish event instead we chose something sweet and simple that would mirror our lives and personality.

"So, what do you think?" Laura asked modeling the dress picked for her "Pretty?"

I responded with a smile "You look simply divine"

And she did look exquisite with her strawberry blonde hair pulled up into a bun accentuating the one shouldered emerald satin dress which complimented her lightly freckled face. There was a lavender sash pulled snuggly around her waist with one side of the dress cascading beautifully down sweeping the floor. But I was most eager to see how handsome Drew was going to look in his tuxedo. I can already imagine how dashing he will appear.

Due to our mostly untraditional relationship, we decided it would be nice to toss in a few more traditional customs. For instance, I did not allow Drew to see me in my dress and we spent the night before our wedding apart. It felt odd not having him beside me but at least I had Josie to cuddle up with. The expectations of today's special occasion had me on pins and needles with 5 o'clock not coming fast enough.

"Almost done" the stylist informed me "Just a few last touches"

I felt like queen for the day with so many people fussing over me. I was pampered having my hair and make-up done designing a semi-neutral appearance with a light pink blush, powder, and some shades of brown on my eyes that was flattering against my hair and skin tones then finished it off with my favorite color of classic red across my lips. Afterwards she carefully curled my lengthy brunette hair, piling it atop my head, and leaving a few curls dangling down framing the sides of my face. Then my hair was topped with a veil of Chantilly Lace accented by light silver flowers and ribbon paired with precisely places pearls and crystal for added sparkle. As things began coming together, I started to feel more like a bride and seeing my refection I barely recognized the image staring back at me. For the first time in my life, I could see how I glowed which was astounding.

"Time to finish getting ready" Laura pointed to the ticking clock "Not much longer"

I stepped into my wedding dress made from an ivory shade of satin pulling up the A-line gown with a charming sweetheart neckline, keyhole back, and fitted bodice connected to a princess waistline with vertical seams down the skirt that gently flared wider at the bottom. The dress was accessorized with, and emerald belt of Chantilly Lace incorporated with pearls, crystal, ribbon, and light silver flowers that matched my veil. My look was completed by an elegant 3-foot chapel train trailing behind me. Shuffling over to the full-length mirror I lifted my head slowly and exhaled before turning my head up glancing at myself. The unfamiliar sight staring back at me was not the poverty-stricken teen mom all I saw was a beautiful bride that left me breathless. Could this polished person in the mirror really be me? Tears of delight started to build behind my eyes, but I managed to hold them back refusing to mess up my make-up.

"Aww...Cammie you look whimsical" Laura complimented putting her arm around me "I have never seen a more dazzling bride"

I smiled resting my head on her shoulders then made a goofy face in the mirror as we laughed together lightening the air around us.

"Only you could be silly at a time like this" she giggled "I would be a nervous wreck"

"That is why you love me" I retorted

"Absolutely" she confirmed with a shake of the head

Then I heard Josie's sweet voice behind me "Mommy pretty"

I turned gleaming at the mini version of myself, she was my little princess, and she knew it. I held Josie as we watched the photographer finish setting up when there was a sudden unexpected knock on the door. Laura opened the door to find no one until she peered down noticing an envelope and handed it to me. I passed Josie off to Laura freeing my hands as I saw my name on the envelope and opened it removing the paper inside when I recognized Drews handwriting.

To my soon to be wife,

I know without a doubt that in only a few short hours I will officially become the luckiest man alive. My dream of being your husband and you being my wife is about to come true and we will have succeeded in creating the type of family Josie and we deserve. I am blessed that you have chosen me to give your love to therefore I swear to never take you for granted and will tell you I love you every day. You and Josephine are my reason for living and I cannot wait to spend the rest of my days loving you.

Your soon to be husband

I pressed the freshly pinned note firmly against my heart where there was not one single inkling of reluctance. Beyond a shadow of a doubt, I knew I wanted to marry him and was on cloud nine thinking about becoming Mrs. McEnrowe. I found it humorous how truly he believed that he was the lucky one when I knew it was me who was lucky to have him. Anytime I needed him he was there, he held me when I was afraid, wiped the tears from my eye, always saw me as beautiful despite my flaws, he was a father to Josie even though he was under no obligation, and he breathed life into my body when I was lifeless. He was my better half in every sense of the word and now we would soon be bound together by an unbreakable pact.

"It is time" Laura called out gleefully

My pulse gradually increased while we inched our way to the huge ballroom doors where we took our places. My ears perked up as I listened to the random chitter chatter of the guest while they awaited my arrival which I am sure contributed to my wedding day jitters. The sheer thought of having all those eyes focused on me was terrifying. Oh,

Lord please do not let me trip on my feet and fall on my face because that would without a doubt be beyond humiliating.

I listen to the songs we selected playing while the wedding party made their way down the aisle and snuck a peek at the procession through a faint opening in the door. I watched Laura and Billy walking arm in arm followed closely by Josephine holding her small white basket filled with rose petal that she threw along the walkway. She looked quite fetching in her flower girl gown resembling a little lady who made her way straight to her daddy. After which I softly closed the door taking a step backwards awaiting my big moment. I peered over at my dad beside me feeling serene having him here and sober as he prepared to walk me down the aisle to give me away.

"You look gorgeous Camille" my dad said with teary eyes holding my quailing hands "I am so proud of the woman you have become"

Hearing him vocalize his pride in me for the first time warmed my heart but not only was he proud of me I was proud of him as well. I also appreciated my father's acceptance of my decision to have Josie and to marry Drew even if my mother still refused to, also choosing to not come her only child's wedding. I was never one to make excuses for him or deny that he had been an awful father in the past who has made countless mistakes, yet I never turned my back or give up on him. My situation taught me the power of a daughters love that gave me the fortitude to forgive all the pain he has caused me. However, the forgiveness was not purely for him I had my own selfish reasons like helping me to heal my soul because holding onto that type of awfulness could eat you alive and I have two very important people to live for.

I inhaled deeply trying to calm my nerves as my dad gave me a reassuring pat on my hand. And now my moment has finally arrived as "Here Comes the Bride" played, and the double doors slowly opened for my grand reveal I turned my mood ring Joey had given me twice on my fingers. In memory of him. All the guests stood up turning around to watch me enter the room. There was nowhere for me to hide, the time has come, no turning back now. I stood statuesque taking in the astonishing beauty of the room lit with white lights and candles shimmering from the glycinin white roses amidst a sea of emerald and lavender highlights. I scanned the room across the small group of guests when my eyes were drawn to the alter where Father Courville was holding his bible with my Prince Charming waiting for me.

Standing up there was the man of my dreams appearing more handsome then ever in his tuxedo smiling confidently at me washing away all my anxiety and worries. I could not wait to be up there alongside him where I belonged, I thought as I walked down the aisle securely gripping my dad's arm keeping in step to the music while never taking my eyes off Drew. It felt as if I was visibly beaming even while surrounded by a room full of people, I could only see Andrew. Upon reaching the alter my father lifted my veil giving me a peck on the cheek then handed me away.

"Who gives this woman away?" Father Courville asked

"I do" my dad proudly said

"Hey pretty girl" he whispered with a charming grin

"Hey sweet boy" I greeted him "Fancy meeting you here"

Father Courville started the ceremony, but I could not hear a word he said finding myself distracted by Drew's unwavering gaze getting lost in his shining blue eyes and youthful smile that always melted my heart. I could envision us fifty years from now holding hands on the front porch swings while we watched our grandchildren running around the yard and climbing our great big ole oak tree.

"It is time to reciting your vows" the father informed us.

Andrew,

My sweet boy. There was once a time I felt unworthy of love and certain that I would never fall in love again. However, you managed to show just how wrong I had been by never giving up on me even when I had given up on myself. You have been right there beside me through thick and thin, lifted me when I was weak, provided me with a soft place to land, and accepted me despite any of my short comings. I value how you make me laugh, the way you never forget to kiss me goodnight, and how you love me unconditionally. I want to be by your side when you need a friend, to be your loudest cheerleader, to lift you up when life beats you down, and to celebrate alongside of you in times of joy. I vow to cherish you, support you, and love you until all the breath is gone from my lungs. I look forward to better or worse if I get to do it with you.

Eternally your pretty girl

As hard as I resisted, I could not contain my emotions as the tears streamed halfway through my vows causing Drew to do the same. After concluding my commitment oath Drew softly pulled my chin to him giving me a small kiss then wiping the tears from my face.

"Man, I love you so much" he said with a lump in his throat "More than words can ever express"

"I love you too bae" I responded feeling the love floating in the air

Father Courville paused momentarily to let us gather ourselves and get control of our emotions. Then he nodded at Drew to let him know he could continue to his vows.

Pretty girl,

Camille, when I look into your big brown eyes, I see the most beautiful woman I have ever seen or will see, a magnificent mother, and sometimes I can still glimpse that sassy 12-year-old girl I met when we were young. I loved you then, I love you now, and I cannot wait to spend the rest of my life loving you even more. You tell me all the time that I am your rock, but the truth is I am only strong because you are beside me. You have a special power to calm me with a glance or sooth me with a touch which is both magical and mesmerizing. There is no one like you on this planet, you are certainly one of a kind. You never cease to amaze me finding perfection in my imperfections, making me smile no matter how mad I am, and how you make me feel undeniably loved. I promise to be your defender, to be your best friend, to always kiss you goodnight, to be your rock, and to protect and honor you so that even death cannot tear us apart.

Forever your sweet boy

I cried feeling my spirit being deeply touched by the words Drew had spoken from his heart. Drew never went a day without telling me how he loved me which made it easy to feel his love however hearing him express that in the beauty of his own words was significant to me and I would eternally hold those words in a special place. Billy then handed Father Courville the rings he had kept safely tucked in his pocket. The wedding ceremony continued as we repeated after the father and exchanged wedding bands.

"I now pronounce you husband and wife" he announced the words I was eager to hear "You may kiss the bride"

Our lips touched for the first time as husband and wife with Drew tipping me back in his enchanting playful manner.

"I am proud to introduce Mr. and Mrs. McEnrowe" Father Courville concluded the ceremony

We raised our hand united with tear filled faces rejoicing in our new union. Laura and Billy were the first hug us congratulations before we welcomed the other guest as we radiated with pure exhilaration. I saw Josie making a b-line for us her arms lifted in the air as Drew swiftly swooped her off her feet and tossed her into the air. She let out a loud laugh from her belly and hugged Drews neck whilst she tagged along to finish greeting everyone. I have never seen anyone so proud as Drew to be a dad and she was obviously a daddy's girl. We were indeed two lucky gals.

"Can I have the newlyweds to the dance floor" the DJ requested

After passing Josie to Laura, Drew took me by the hand and lead me onto the dancefloor. He pulled me in tightly wrapping me in his affectionate embrace while I rubbed his heavenly face as we swayed to our song "Groovy Kind of Love" by Phil Collins it is quite an old song but suits us perfectly. The song was not our typical type of tunes but when I landed on a station that was playing that song and it was if it could have been written especially for us.

"I love you Mr. McEnrowe" I expressed

"And I love you Mrs. McEnrowe" he replied before we shared a truly passionate kiss

It felt like I was walking on air, the universe flawlessly aligned, and I was exactly where I should be in the arms of my newly minted husband. All the crazy twist and turns my life has taken lead me here making each mile walked totally worth it. My little family was finally complete, and I looked forward to filling the rest of my days with plenty of love, laughter, and joy. Looking into Drews beautiful blue eyes was thoroughly intoxicating like getting a glimpse into heaven as we danced, I sensed tranquility within his arms. For better or worse was the vows we took so no matter what life throws at us I to love him through it all. Now comes the Grand Finally thing to do is have my husband carry me over the threshold which he did with such ease.

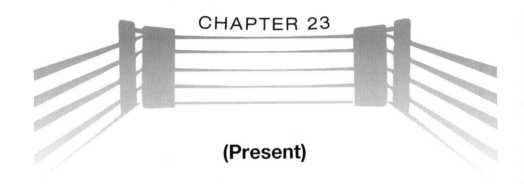

CHAPTER 23

(Present)

Dear Diary,

There is nothing more comforting to me than going to sleep knowing Drew will be there beside me when I wake up. Over the years I learned not to take the little things for granted because life is tricky, and things can change in a moment. Since my character turned on Braedon a few months ago it is as if Miss Penny Lane was given a fresh start as one of the good guys sending my alter-egos popularity soaring and even managed to snag a spot on the main roster. It was a tremendous feeling to be notice for my talent, knowing all my hard work has paid off and was not futile. I am super excited for tonight because me and Sarah are joining forces in a tag team match against Tyree and Egypt on Knockdown, I am delighted to be paired with my best friend. This ought to be fun! Peace out!

Drew reached across me taking the diary from my hand placing it on the nightstand then leaned his head down to my stomach tenderly kissing my skin as I laid there calmly aroused with my breath quickening until he reached the spot just above my belly button. His lips brushing ever so lightly against my skin tickled causing a natural reflex to jerk away and automatic laugh out loud. Afterwards Drew put his head back on his pillow with his hands behind his head and a look of self-satisfaction while he laughed already knowing the reaction he would get.

"Way to kill the moment" he teased

"Sorry" I spit back "I need to conserve my energy for later"

"Good excuse" he grinned before jumping to his feet

I followed him shortly out of the bed to start my daily routine the only change is that we are in a new hotel room, in a new city, with our clothes strewn across another floor. It was a different day, same pattern as we attempted to find some semblance of normalcy in an abnormal situation. Since my professional life could be hectic and unpredictable, I found comfort in the daily grind. Things like staying up late into the night talking and waking up to the sun on my face however it does not lessen the thrill of boisterous nights where you get down and dirty in the ring draining every bit of your energy then become revitalized by the electrical charge of thousands of cheering fans.

Once we were both up and ready, we walked over to The Pancake Palace Restaurant out front of our hotel passing a few co-workers on the way and saying hi. TWE was like a surrogate family considering, we spent more time with each other than we did at home which is most likely the main contributing factor to the multiple divorces and co-worker relationships. However, that was a subject no one approached or wanted to, it was a taboo topic, the industries dirty little secret. After finding a booth in the corner we scanned the menu when an older plump woman grey haired woman came to take our order which we rattled off. As the waitress turned away Drew took my hand entangling his fingers in mine, our matching wedding bands touching while he smiled at me with adoration on his face.

"Now, that is a beautiful sight right" he said affectionately squeezing my hand

"Yes, it is" I agreed

Having the knowledge of what it meant for us to put our wedding rings back on was a decision we made together and one that I did not take it lightly. They were a symbol of the love and commitment we have for each other and a reminder of the vows we took for better or for worse. Right now, we were in the better stage, and I wanted nothing more than to never forget how good it feels because I was not close to being prepared for worse yet. We have been through worse already, buried six feet under, but we tend to beat the odds and find a way to rise above it all. If he just steers, clear of the women it will be alright. I hope my faith in him is not tested.

"I love being your husband" he said warmly

"Well, that is good to hear" I responded with sincerity "Because I love being your wife"

Taking advantage of our alone time we leaned across the table for a single tender kiss. It was these brief periods of time that I thrived on. It is the simple things like sneaking a stolen kiss, a kind touch, or a special look that turns me into putty in his hands. He was my one true weakness.

Crunched for time we ate quickly being that we tended to lose ourselves in each other. Before leaving I made a point to hand the waitress a generous tip for her great service then headed to the coliseum. Pulling up with not a minute to spare as we reluctantly raced passed screaming fans to get inside where Sarah was waiting on me.

"About time" Sarah said leading me to the seamstress "Wardrobe is ready for us"

Since me and Sarah were partnering up in a tag team match, we decided to go with ring gear with shades of green and purple colors and the letter GG sown on the back representing our tag team name The Groovy Gals. Even I had to admit that the name was a bit corny but so were we and that is what made it even more fun. Our spirits were high having the audience's permission to act as silly as we wanted because we were the heroes, and our competitors were villains. I was bursting at the seams waiting for this match.

"Love you" I managed to tell Drew giving him a parting kiss before being drug out

"Love you too" I heard him yell out bringing a smile to my face

Me and Sarah witnessed the seamstress, Mrs. Peggy, working her magic bringing the visions in our heads to life. Trying on the new ring gear got us fired up and we were extremely pleased with the outcome we saw reflecting in the full-length mirror. We now looked like a legitimate team.

"Damn we look fierce" I commented raising my eyebrows

"Yes, we do!" Sarah boasted "The Groovy Gals are in town Whoo!"

While we merrily danced around admiring our cool matching style in the locker room Tweety walked in ruining the mood, staring at me with an icy cold gaze.

"You are aware that I had your beloved husband when you umm shall we say were away" she said wanting to stir up some trouble.

"Key word there is *HAD*" I retorted angrily "But do not be mad at me because he does not want you back, you were nothing but a placeholder for me"

"Well then" she declared trying to piss me off which was beginning to work "We will just see how long that last"

In a blind rage I hopped up wanting to grab her by the throat and ring her neck but thankfully Sarah intervened pulling me back and stepping between us.

"Save it for the ring" Sarah advised calming me down "She is not even worth it"

"She is trying to get to you" Sarah continued "Mess you up"

"She will have to try a hell of a lot harder" I voiced sternly

Never have I ever wanted to tear someone apart so badly I thought seeing Tweety scurry away like the vermin she was. The rage I had built inside towards her was ready to overflow and she knew it. In hindsight I felt quite ignorant for taking the bait and playing right into her hands. I should have been more professional since I had no reason to doubt Drew's love or commitment for me, yet I still let that witch get under my skin. Why would I do that to myself? I honestly had no clue.

"Time to go" Sarah reminded me with our match soon approaching

"Come on and do this thing" I asserted putting on a smile tapping into Miss Penny Lane

We stood in the wings doing our preshow rituals and wished Tyree and Egypt good luck before they were summoned to the ring.

"The defending Goddess Tag Team Champions from Bristol, England Tyree and from Cairo, Egypt, Egypt making The Worldwide Killers" they announced

My heart was beating a million miles a minute and we were ready and raring to go when we heard our que, and it was game time. We danced our way down to the ring acting like two silly gooses then took a bow from the ropes.

"Together here for the first time from Tupelo, Mississippi, Sensational Sarah joined with Miss Penny Lane from New Orleans, Louisiana, "The Groovy Gals" They announces as the bell rang.

Sarah and Egypt were the first to face-off in the squared circle as they studied each other with a snarl and dirty looks. Egypt was a chestnut toned exotic beauty with dark hair and eyes to match her fiery temper. The two fought exchanging blows while me and Tyree yelled horrible unpleasantries back and forth. Sarah walked to our corner with a steel grip on Egypt's arm. I jumped from the top rope hitting Egypt's arm with mine causing her to scream in pain and hold her arm while me and Sarah did our sassy handshake snap before turning our attention back to our opponents when we heard the slap of Egypt tagging Tyree in.

Tyree was the most powerful Goddess in the division and was built like a brick house with ebony skin, raven hair, and mysterious eyes. I have been waiting for the chance to meet her on this turf because she was a beast inside that ring, and I did love a good challenge. I somehow managed to hold my own against her for a while until she got the best of me tossing me aggressively to the mat knocking the wind out of my body. I slowly crawled to Sarah with my arm outstretched and my back still feeling the sting of the impact. I immediately slapped Sarah's hand then rolled under the bottom rope dropping to the floor where I stayed a minute to regain my air. Once recover enough I pulled myself up just in the nick of time to watch as Sarah applied "Killer Legs" on Tyree when Egypt tried to intervene and double team Sarah, but I hurried to jump in the ring and clotheslining Egypt just as Tyree tapped out.

"And your new Goddess Tag Team Champs, The Groovy Gals" was announced as I ran to Sarah for a gleeful hug before energetically dancing our way out in victory.

Finally, I was a champion me and Sarah were officially The Goddess Tag Team Champions. Having that belt around my waist felt fabulous and heavier than I thought. I am working my way up bit by bit and do not plan on stopping until I touch the top. After the match I came out expecting celebratory praise from Drew who I could not find which was very unusual. Yet then again you never know what to expect here so I was not alarmed by it.

"I must go meet Steve by Kraft Services" Sarah informed me

"Alright, I am going to find Drew" I told her before parting company

I roamed the halls backstage cluttered with roadies, staging equipment, crates, and numerous random items still full of vigor and pride. Passing one of the side halls I halted in my tracks when I heard Drew's voice and turned to head that way. I only got a few feet when I came to another hallway and peered down it and what I saw was a sight that shook me to my core. I could not trust what I was seeing where my eyes deceiving me. I hid behind the wall to stay out of sight hoping this was some weird misunderstanding.

Drew and Tweety were alone standing closely, laughing, talking, and touching each other. How could he have ditched me after my big match to be with her? Why is he flirting with my arch enemy does he just want to hurt me? I closed my eyes tightly wishing this was nothing more than a mirage or my mind playing an evil trick on me. And when I thought it could not get any worse, I opened my eyes and saw the two locked in a kiss that Drew did not seem to resist. I had honestly believed that Drew was made for me but maybe he was made to hurt me.

I placed my back firmly against the wall fearing I might fall because my legs felt as if they were made of Jell-O while I pressed my hand over my heart as it shattered. What did I do to deserve this? Did I not show how much I loved him? Why was this happening? I thought staring blankly ahead as I slid slowly down the wall looking at my wedding band feeling a heaviness in the air as silent tears rained from my eyes. Titan saw me on the floor and came to my aid kneeling beside me with genuine concern in his face. He glanced down the hall hearing laughter then helped me to my feet in a nearly vegetative state.

"Good job asshole" Titan yelled at Drew as he walked me away

"Do you ever get tired of trying to fill that void you must have inside" I shook my head "Never make me cry again yeah right"

Drew looked at us in utter shock and sprinted towards me as Tweety stood there with a smile of self-satisfaction.

"Cammie, please" he pleaded frantically "It did not mean nothing"

I was reeling unable to even form a response after that. I thought it was different with us, ignored red flags, and pushed aside warning so I could relinquish myself to him completely and now feeling like the world's biggest fool. How could my world have been ripped apart by something so trivial and dumb yet life altering at the same time? I ignored Drew putting my head down in shame as shock and sadness enveloped me.

"Camille, I love you" he begged me to understand "You are my best friend, my everything"

"Well then I guess you just proved that friends could break your heart too" I responded in deep sadness

"Come on baby girl" Titan said guiding me out of the situation "Let us get out of here"

"Damnit!" Drew hollered punching the cement wall with his fist

Titan aka Jonathan leads me out the backdoor and onto his tour bus. I sat down feeling beyond low Tweety had won she had stolen the man I loved and what hurts the most is that she did it with such ease.

"I am sorry for all the trouble" I apologized

"Do not be baby girl" he said with a kind smile handing me a glass of whiskey on the rocks

"Thank you" I expressed warmly

"Looked like you could use it" he responded

"Yeah" I commented revealing a slight smile as my tears began to dry "That is for sure"

"I just want you to understand that I did not bring you here to take advantage of you in your moment of weakness" John explained "I have been in your shoes and thought you might need a place away from prying eyes awhile"

"You are like a real-life Superman" I said thanking him in my own style

"Not quite" he responded when I caught a glimpse of that distant look, I knew all too well

"I get it" I told him "I am broken too just packaged skillfully"

"Well put" he said with his dark eyes glistening in the light "I can relate to that"

It felt as if I had found a kindred spirit bonded by heartache. I did not know his story and he did not know mine but there was a familiar vibe we both clearly recognized in each other. I was grateful for the distraction because the last thing I wanted to think about was Drew and my failed affair of the heart.

"You are the main event tonight right" I reminded him noticing the time

"Yes, but your welcome to stay" he offered "I have some clothes you can borrow if you want to jump in the shower, make yourself comfy I will be back"

The kindness that Jonathan showed me restored my faith that not all men were bad. After showing me where everything was, he turned to leave for tonight's performance.

"Hey Superman" I called out stopping him in the doorway amused that he responded to his new nickname

"Warning do not go falling in love with me" I joked lightening the mood making him laugh

"I should be the one telling you that" he replied as I rolled my eyes playfully shrugging his comment away as he left with a smile

I grabbed a t-shirt and boxers to put on after I showered when I heard my phone ringing nonstop, so I grabbed the phone off the couch and was surprised to see Braedon's name pop-up.

"What the hell is going on?" He asked heavy with worry "Drew is acting like a crazy man, he even tried to start a fight with Titan accusing him of hiding you"

"You were right Braedon" I admitted out loud "He hurts people"

"I promise you that jerk will get what is coming to him" he said sounding sincere "But right now I am just concerned about you"

"I am safe, I promise to call you later" I told him before ending the call "Right now I need a shower"

I hung up without any goodbyes refusing to let my life become consumed by this. I took a hot shower letting the streaming water hit my back and neck helping to relax my stressed muscles. Stepping out the shower I wiped the steam away from the mirror looking into my own eyes.

"I guess it is just you and me" I commented talking to my reflection

I went to the front of the bus and laid back on the couch drained of everything I had and emotionally exhausted. If I could find a way to free myself of Drew things would be much easier, but I knew we were not quite through yet since we were partners and a TWE power couple therefore I had to act normal or risk my entire career which was all I had now. The silence surrounding me allowed my mind to roam rapidly. I truly believed I had my marriage firmly back together, but it appears I had left some pieces behind. Will I ever get the chance to be whole again? Right now, it was too soon to answer that question since I first had to get past the stunning developments which left me gasping for air today. At least I knew I would come out on the other side of this because I was still here and still alive, so I knew I would survive this too.

I though Drew was the medicine I needed but instead, I ended up overdosed by love. I closed my eyes desperate for sleep that would give me a break from feeling the horrid ache. Laying there I felt my dreams drifting away and the life I had so neatly constructed come crashing in on me.

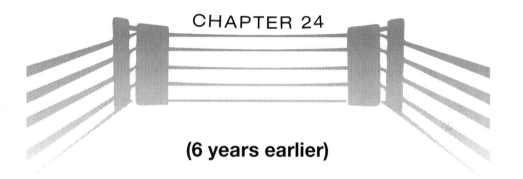

CHAPTER 24

(6 years earlier)

Dear Diary,

Last night me and Drew decided to finally go through with getting the matching tattoos we've been talking about more often. We created an image we consider our family insignia a permanent symbol of the love we shared. We had the letter M representing our last name entangled in an infinity sign of thorns to remind us that no matter how prickly the path may get together we can overcome it all. Drew had his placed above his heart while I had mine put on my right side near ribs. The sound of the tattoo gun was quite intimidating, and I was terrified but once the artist started it was not as bad as I imagined besides what is a little pain for love. Sorry to cut it short but I hear Josie waking. Got to go! Peace!

I hurried to shove my diary beneath my pillow then closed my eyes pretending to be asleep as Josie climbed onto our bed and happily bounced on top of us.

"Wake up daddy" she smiled sweetly getting a kick out of her morning ritual "Wake up mommy"

"Who is this strange child jumping on me?" Drew asked grabbing and tickling her

"It is me, daddy" she said through laughter

"Oh, it is my little princess" he acted surprised before covering her in kisses

I loved seeing the heartwarming interaction between Josie and Drew. It was made even more special with the knowledge that he was the father he did not have to be but instead chose to be. He wanted to be her daddy and they were as close as any father and child could be. I could easily watch them all day long, but I knew my dynamic duo would soon be getting hungry.

Drew took Josies hand following me to the kitchen where he gave Josephine her morning medication as I started breakfast. I cracked some eggs into the pan scrambling them while I added my secret selection of Cajun seasonings which was my super-secret recipe for Cajun Eggs. Drew placed Josie in her highchair putting her bib on her then made his way up behind me grabbing my waist and tenderly kissing my neck.

"Morning pretty girl" he said in his sexy tone

"Morning sweet boy" I responded turning my head towards him to taste his honeyed lips

I plated our meals then took a seat at the table smiling at my darling daughter with her face full of eggs in her pink Hello Kitty nightgown. Her lovable presence always brightened my day.

"What are todays plans?" I asked as we ate

"I figure we would leave around noon" he suggested as we continued to eat "So we can help set up and hopefully squeeze in a little practice"

Tonight, we have a Swamp Boys Wrestling (SBW) event. Things were just starting to get interesting now that Miss Penny Lane and Drews Crazy Cajun character is gaining popularity. The Crazy Cajun was a hot, tall, with flowing dark hair, finely built, and well-liked wrestler who wore tight leather pants and matching alligator skin boots and vest. I am also having a blast and glad that Drew brought SBW to our lived. I designed an eccentric persona Miss Penny Lane for myself who is a free spirited, fun, sexy, hippie, Swamp Chick.

Joining the company and getting involved by jumping in headfirst into the entertainment business has been a life altering experience for me. Although there was only one other woman with SBW I was happy to at least have a competitor and enjoyed acting as Drews Manager. I have learned so much and had so much fun in the last few months that I cannot wait to see what was around the corner. It has opened my eyes to a new passion that adds a unique spark to my existence.

After breakfast we fit in some family time playing on the floor with the building blocks when Josie walked over to me falling into my arms and giving me a long hug.

"She is tired today" I told Drew as I rocked her in my arms humming a soft tune

"She will be fine" he comforted me "It is just one of those days"

"I know" I admitted "I just worry"

"I get it my love" Drew responded coming sit beside me kissing my forehead and embracing us "It is hard not to"

There was a light knock on the door then Laura walked right in as she normally did.

"Where is my baby at?" she said loudly causing Josie to pop her head up always buoyant to see her nanny who continually spoiled her.

"Nanny!" Josie hollered grinning from ear to ear as Laura swept her up

"She is tuckered out today" I informed Laura and she shook her head understanding the circumstances.

"I will take good care of her" she assured me "Try not to worry too much Cammie"

"Thanks for everything I know she is in good hands" I said gracious for her help and how she loved Josie "Our careers would not be possible without you"

"No need to thank me" she responded hugging me "We are family"

"Want to come read a book" Laura asked Josie to distract her giving us time to sneak out

"Yea!" she agreed delighted following Laura to the bedroom to pick out a book

Drew stood up extending his hand out helping me up from the floor then I grabbed our luggage with all our gear I had packed earlier then quietly snuck out the door. Once we arrived at the auditorium, we barely got a few steps in the door when Dave called out for Drews assistance.

"Come grab the corner of the ring" he commanded "Before these fools drop it"

"Alright coming" he replied dropping his bag and running to help

While the guys were busy setting up the ring, entryway, barriers, and chairs I joined Debbie aka Darlin' Debra Doll, who was the other Swamp Chick, as we began to assemble some of the merchandise booths. Although no one ever said anything negative towards us or treated us badly we felt like we were primarily considered arm candy and something pretty to look at rather than as professional wrestlers. But we all must start somewhere, and this was my beginning even though I certainly was not planning on being here forever. Therefore, in the meantime I was going to take full advantage of the tools I had at my disposal and spent much of my down time learning, practicing, and shining up my wrestling skills. I turned the radio to the only rock station we could catch before getting to business setting up the booths.

"How are my girls?" Dave asked as he walked around checking on the progress

"Good" Debbie answered "Thanks for asking"

Dave, who was better known by his stage name Psycho Dave, was the founder of Swamp Boys Wrestling and somewhat of a hometown hero. SBW was a homegrown company comprised mainly of local wrestlers and the usual group of fans and clingers on. I quickly learned the names of the typical faces in the audience at each show which I found made for a more intimate feeling.

From the first time I walked through the curtains as Miss Penny Lane I was completely captivated and instantly knew that this was what I was made for. Early on I ascertained that you either must be passionate about the industry or have a humongous ego fed by small town fame to really commit yourself. The money was scarce, training was tough, and the toll it took on your body was even tougher. Plus, theses were not the most comfortable or new rings out there, but we did not let it stop us. Call me crazy if you will but I was absolutely hooked, and it had nothing to do with my ego. For me and Drew to pursue our wrestling ambitions we supplemented our income by selling merchandise we made ourselves such as t-shirts, hats, and wristbands along with photos and autographs. Since we depended heavily on the fans, we did our best to keep them happy and interact with them, so they would feel more like a part of the show than just onlookers. As me and Debbie finished folding shirts and laying out photos organizing everything neatly her husband Steven, aka Steven Starr, and one of the other Swamp Boys Shawn, aka Cosmo Kid, joined us at the table.

"Need a hand?" Shawn asked putting his hand on my hip like he was slick or something

"Nah, I am good" I responded kindly moving his hand

I could see the dirty look Drew was giving him even from the opposite side of the room, there was no love lost between them. Shawn did not care to hide his long-standing crush on me which I found flattering and harmless. However, Drew did not agree with me and tended to let his jealous streak show which Shawn found very amusing.

Noticing the line growing outside, me and Debbie went to collect tickets at the door after which we rounded up the crowd and helped everyone find their seats. From there I checked on the concession stand and all the merchandise booths making sure they had everything they needed before heading to the back to get changed. I recently accepted an offer from Dave to be his right-hand man and help him manage the company. Without hesitation I took him up on the spot eager to learn all the ins and outs of the business since I planned on turning into a long career. As the SBW manager I was responsible for advertising, inventory, paychecks, orders, and daily operations, in addition to also being a ring girl, announcer, wrestler, and most importantly a wife and mother you could say I was pretty much going non-stop but that is just the way I like it.

In the back me and Debbie reluctantly changed into our ring girl outfits, if they could even be considered clothing at all, consisting of not much more than some tight black elastic mini shorts, a bikini top with the SBW logo on it, and some black high heels. To say the least I found no dignity in how scantily I was clothed and felt like I belonged more on a pole than in a ring. I constantly reminded myself in these moments that this was merely a steppingstone on my journey to the top. Walking out the entrance and down the walkway I could feel all the leering eyes on me as I listened to whistling and cheering while I strolled around the ring announcing the match between Wayne "Wildcard" Leblanc and Fast Freddie to get the audience warmed up. With the first match underway I went about my supervising duties and tending to the guests needs. I took immense pride in being an integral part of the operations around here despite the nearly X-rated attire.

"My turn" Debbie said passing me by to make her round in the ring "Yippie"

"Woot, woot" I grinned at her making fun of our so-called "sexpot" status

She announced the next bout between Bayou Bill Boudreaux and Kid Cosmo before meeting me behind the entranceway. As we made our way to the back to prepare for our upcoming performance, we bumped into Shawn on his way out to his match.

"This one is for you sha" he said giving me a wink

I rolled my eyes playfully paying him little attention as we entered the locker room where we switched into our slightly more conservative wrestling gear which made me feel more like myself and certainly more comfortable. Tonight, Drew and Steven were going head-to-head and us girls would be their beautiful ring escorts aka arm candy. Luckily for us our awesome men devised a plan to share a bit of their spotlight with us even if it is only for a short while it would still be a chance to see us shine.

"Ready love?" Drew asked

"Hell yeah" I replied dancing around doing my preshow ritual to loosen me up and get my blood pumping "You know I am"

"Good luck" I said wishing our opponents luck but not victory

"We do not need your luck" Steven spoke with a cocky tone then bust out in laughter at our playful banter "But thanks anyways"

The four of us had grown close over the last couple months from training together, hanging out, barbequing, playing cards, and double dating always having a blast no matter what it was we were doing. They also had a daughter Chloe that was only a year older than Josie, so we had a lot in common plus it was nice to have someone to talk to and exchange advice with. Josie and Chloe loved each other lighting up each time they saw one other, and we practically had to pry them apart whenever we left.

With the last match finally over it was now time for us to meet at the ring. We made our way out to start this battle proudly escorting our other halves. As the bell rang me and Debbie took our respective spots to cheer on our brawling beaus. With our spat coming closer to play my part I became increasingly keyed up while I watched on intensely as the time ticked slowly by. Towards the end of the match Steven gained the upper hand using his finisher The Superstar Twist knocking him out then covering him for the win while I stood by looking shocked and disappointed. After being defeated he started to stir while he came back around when Debbie hopped in the ring walking to where Drew laid and gave him a malicious kick in the side before laughing and puckering her lips simulating blowing him a kiss. Witnessing this unfold caused my rage to secretly boil over. Enraged by the treatment of my husband I slid under the ring with lightning speed grabbing Debbie by her red curls dragging her to the corner of the ring where I viciously beat her head into the top turnbuckle. By now Drew had gotten back on his feet and when Steven Starr saw Drew standing sternly staring him down, he made a mad dash away leaving Darlin' Debra Doll to fend for herself. Unconcerned with the guys I continued my assault on Debbie flinging her to the mat then stomping on her ribs.

"How you like that, huh?" I screamed as Debbie lay curled in a ball defenseless "Huh, do you?"

"Enough baby" Drew grabbed me from behind pulling me away and forcing me to the back "She gets it"

"Damn bae, good job" he complimented once we were behind the curtain "You are quite the actress"

"That was fun" Debbie said joining us grinning "Can we do it again?"

I held Debbie's hands as we danced a jig overjoyed with the act we had just put on. But there was little time to celebrate as the main event featuring Psycho Dave and our special guest of the week The Wizard, who was a TWE Totalstar of yesteryears, got underway. Now it was time to man our merchandise booth where I could see the appealing view of a line of folks already beginning to form. It gave me a huge thrill getting to meet the fans that were fond of Miss Penny Lane who has become a part of me. I also enjoyed having the opportunity to interact with the fans during my performances letting them have a ball right alongside of me. We spent the next hour signing autographs, taking pictures, and selling merchandise while having fun meeting our admirers.

At last, with the show over, people gone, and everything packed up it was time to head home and chill out for a while. It was after midnight by time we arrived home and Josie was long asleep in dreamland. We quietly tip-toed passed Laura asleep on the couch then slipped into Josie's room to steal a goodnight kiss. Finally, I was ready to climb into my warm comfy bed and straight in the arms of my husband which in my opinion was the opportune way to end to an incredible day.

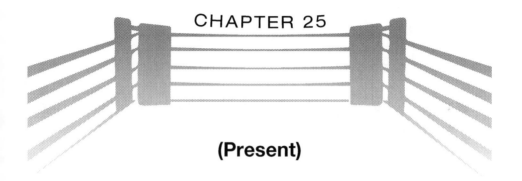

CHAPTER 25

(Present)

I woke from my slumber to the sound of the bus doors opening and footsteps walking inside. I sluggishly rubbed my sleepy eyes trying to get my wits about me as I turned over onto my back looking straight into Jon's face.

"Sorry" he apologized while I yawned still a bit drowsy "I did not mean to wake you"

"I will forgive you this time" I grinned as he flippantly rolled his dark eyes "I am sure it is hard for the man of steel to make a quiet entrance"

"Well, well little miss Cammie" John chuckled hitting me with his shirt "You are certainly in a class all your own"

"I am an acquired taste that is for sure" I returned his laughter with a deviant smile

Unable to help myself I covertly tried to eye John's perfect physic, but I knew my mission had been exposed when he lightheartedly shook his head and flashed me a sparkling smile before walking into the bathroom.

"Hey, got to find a reason to smile" I told him

How is it that I incessantly find myself in these insane predicaments? Well, at least I can never complain about my life being dull because whether good or bad it is ceaselessly full of colorful events. No matter what the situation I am in my life and will always find a way carry on even when I do not want to.

Alone I pulled my knees up to my chest sitting comfortably surrounded by the silence and solitude getting lost in my thoughts. I foolishly trusted Drew, so the sting of betrayal caused a kind of pain I have never felt before and the terror of what is to come scares the hell out of me. But never mind how awful the incident I just do not know how to stop my heart from missing him. He has been a huge part of me for a very long time. How do I leave all that history behind me when he is in every memory I have ever made? And now I have the brutal task of exploring my capacity for breaking down and reconstructing my life from the rubble that is left behind. I truly appreciated Jon's diversion in such a trying time. He helped occupy my mind and took the edge off the pain steering me away from the road to madness which I could have easily gone down. Maybe I should make the future count for a lot more than the past. Stop walking backwards and start running forwards. That may be my solution.

"How about some dinner?" John asked stepping out the bathroom

"Umm…" I hesitated unsure if I was ready to show my face "I do not know"

"You cannot hide forever" he proposed "you got to eat"

"Fine" I relented deciding not to hide and let them win "Just food"

I changed into some clothes Sarah was kind enough to drop off along with my coveted diary then I did what I could with my face and hair, so I would not look like a hot mess. Afterwards we walked to the hotel restaurant where we were quickly seated away from many of the guest. The place was packed with familiar faces most of whom looked at us in confusion wondering what we were doing there together. I sighed a breath of relief and was able to relax after looking around to find that Drew was nowhere to be seen. However, news travels fast off the tongues here and I knew there would soon be a confrontation, but I was not yet ready for that and just wanted to enjoy my time out for dinner.

"You clean up well" Jon told me

"Thanks" I smiled shyly "You do not look too bad yourself"

"Do not mind the stares" he informed me "Nobody has ever seen me out with any Goddess before"

"Whys that?" I inquired

"None of them have ever piqued my interest before" he smiled at me

I looked at him quizzically like why me, but it was complementing either way. We made idle chatter as we ate while Jon politely avoids any topic of gossip. It was nice to be able to close that away in the back of my mind for a while and get to take delight in our pleasurable conversation before we were interrupted.

"Hey beautiful" Braedon cut in pulling up a chair "Glad to see you out and about"

"Do you mind" he asked Jon who gave him an unfavorable glance after the sudden intrusion

"That is up to Cam" He answered avoiding a confrontation

I shrugged my shoulders aware of his persistence and not wanting to be rude. Plus, I understood that he meant well even if he tended to go about it the wrong way.

"Can we talk after you eat?" Braedon asked

"Not tonight" I answered wanting to forget about it all for the night "I am not up for it"

"I just want you to know you are not alone, I was in love with Tweety" he said with sadness reflecting in his eyes "I know how you feel"

I reached across the table taking Braedon's hand in mine trying to bring him some comfort in our shared agony.

"I am sorry Braedon" I apologized "Thank you for being such a good friend"

I stared down at the table feeling guilty for everything that went down. If I had never shown up here maybe none of this would have happened. Jon gently tapped my chinned to get my attention causing me to raise my head and look at him.

"Hey, it is not your fault" he said peering into my eyes "You cannot blame yourself for any of this"

"Maybe its karma" I said softly

"That is not Karma Cams" he assured me

I was relieved when the waitress arrived with the check. The three of us stood to leave as I gave Braedon a long hug feeling the connection from the horrible heartache that bonded us together.

"How about lunch tomorrow?" I proposed "I am exhausted"

"You got it beautiful" Braedon responded kissing my forehead before walking off "Remember I am only a call away"

"You have quite the number of suitors?" Jon noticed

"I was told it was my aura or vibes that pull people in or that I am just a witch" I said

After saying our goodbyes, me and Jon walked back towards the bus. As we rounded the corner, I stopped dead in my tracks at the sight of Drew leaning casually against Jon's bus waiting on me.

"You good" Jon asked out of concern

"Yeah" I assured him "I will be fine"

"I will give you two a minute" he warned then left us to talk "I will be right inside"

I had lied I was not alright at all, I did not want to do this now, but it did not seem I had much of a choice. There were a million things I wanted to say yet nothing was coming out as I stood there in silence.

"So, you and Titan huh?" he said in an ugly tone as if to insinuate I had done something inappropriate

"Seriously Andrew I waited 2 years for you I only slept with you and Joey, and what did I tell you last time you questioned my intentions I thought you knew me better than that" I spit back instantly silencing him "But honestly its none of your business after what you did to me"

"You said no more second chances" he replied

"And I meant it" I said "I deserve someone to love only me"

Staring at him standing there I could still feel a power he held over me which somehow made my heart race even though I felt as empty as a ghost in the night. I was submerged in his beautiful pain fighting to keep my head above water.

"I love you so much Camille" he said with tears building in his eyes "Always will"

Without thinking I wrapped my arms around him wanting to savor what I knew could be our final embrace. I realized my actions were wrong, but I did not know how to simply shut off my feelings. I breathed him in one last time before forcing my body to pull away. Allowing myself to be that close to Drew was like being in a danger zone and all I wanted from him now was some real honest answers.

"I meant it when I said for better or worse" I said honestly "But this is past worst it is infidelity I need time"

"I understand" He replied "I am just scared you will not come back"

"And I may not" I admitted "You claim to be in love with me when right now it feels like you are killing me?"

"I never meant to hurt you, I was stupid" he tried to explain without success "I was set up and it is not hard to figure by who, it will never happen again"

"You kissed her back! Was I not enough?" I asked in sorrow "With those few fleeting moments you broke my trust and pushed my love away. I really hope she was worth it"

"What about all the dreams we worked so hard to make come true do they count?" he argued "We can get past this; we have overcome worse"

"All the sorrows we have seen and the memories we have made, I remember them all" I said my mind at war with my heart "They make the pain of my broken heart that much worse and harder to repair I am only listening to you because of our history"

"Why was I never enough?" I cried "I just wanted to be enough for you"

"You are enough" he cried "I have only loved one woman"

"This is a pattern of behavior Drew" I fussed "You need to be alone for a few weeks no placeholders"

"We are not done yet I felt it in our embrace" he told me "You did to"

Deep down I knew he was right because I could not say with confidence that I was done, we had to much unfinished business. I did love him and perhaps always would, but it did not make it right. There had to be a light at the end of this tunnel. I wanted him so badly to be my person for eternity however I was not sure anymore if he should be or even want him to be.

"What you felt was me missing who you use to be. Where did my sweet boy go?" I responded mournfully "You once were a better man who would never hurt me like this"

"He is still here it is not too late" he said in vain incensing me "I wish there was some way for you to understand how I feel"

"How you feel...is that a joke?" I said overcome by emotion "I get too standby and watch my entire life slip away like a bad dream I cannot wake up from"

As I stood motionless studying the face of the husband, I have loved so long I caught a short glimpse of my sweet boy with those shining blue eyes now turned sad as tears ran down his angelic face. Cammie why do you torture yourself like this? Do you find pleasure in the flames of this ever-enticing pain? How do you stop loving someone you cannot picture your life without?

I knelt coming eye to eye with Drew where he had fallen to his knees.

"Why do you cry?" I asked seeking the truth

"What is wrong with me?" he questioned himself "How could I hurt the only woman I ever loved and who loved me so completely"

"Only you have those answers" I replied "you should get help"

"One stupid kiss, I cannot believe I am about to lose everything over one kiss" Drew apologized "I am sorry Camille, it was not worth it"

"That one stupid kiss made me feel like the world's biggest fool" I tried putting my feelings in words "Here I was chasing a fairytale thinking I found my prince charming blissfully unaware that I was about to walk into a horror show"

"I do not want to lose you Camille" he begged as he tried to regain his composure "You taught me how to love, you are irreplaceable, please forgive me"

For the first time since the recent events, I let my face turn soft as a calm washed over me allowing my body to finally relax. All the hate a rage I had inside of me was released. I had to let go of the anger to begin the healing process. Carrying a burden as heavy as that could darken one's soul and I felt much lighter free from all that extra baggage.

"Andrew, you showed me how to love again, you were the man I chose to marry" I told him honestly "But you are also the man who shattered my heart"

"I do forgive you, but you must fix yourself" I explained "Before you can love me the way I deserve"

There were no more words left as I turned to enter the bus leaving him alone in the night as a solitary tear escaped my eye which I instantly wiped away. I took a deep soothing breath looking back at Drew one last time before turning and disappearing onto the bus. Walking away from him was the hardest thing I have ever done but it had to be this way. The damage he inflicted cut deep and would leave a nasty scar that would take a long time to mend.

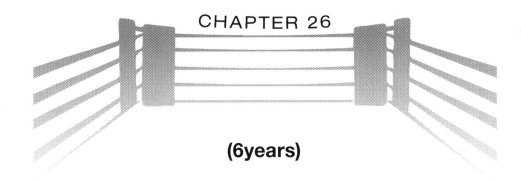

CHAPTER 26

(6years)

I absolutely love Halloween it is so much fun getting all dressed up, flying around on a sugar high, and watching Josie's joy while she is trick or treating it is a total blast. I dressed my sweet girl in some black tights and pink leotard topped with cat ears and tail.

"Meow" Josie said making me smile as I picked her up to sit on the counter

"Sit still" I told her while she wiggled around

I completed her look by drawing a cat nose and some whiskers on her face with my eyeliner. Then I slipped on her patent leather shoes with a bow on top and let her down to run free. Afterwards I headed to my room to change into my sexy pirate costume with a low-cut red top, short black and red stripped skirt, black thigh high stockings, and black high heeled boots. Walking out the room I found Drew in the living room all decked out in his pirate costume that matched mine. As I gently got a feel of his pants from behind,

"You are one hot pirate" he commented

"Your pretty hot yourself" I said in return

Taking a step forward I put my arms his neck as we shared a loving kiss until we were interrupted by Josie running towards us with her arms raised. Drew snatched her up kissing her sweet face.

"What a cute kitty you are" he told her

"Meow" she responded with a huge smile as me and Drew shared a laugh

"We better hurry the party is about to start" he warned looking at the clock

As I turned to grab my hat Drew slapped me on the butt which in our world was a term of endearment. I could feel the winds of change coming our way opening the real possibility of making our dreams come true. We had recently been offered a spot on The International Wrestling Association (IWA) roster. I was in shock at first it felt utterly unreal to me, and I could hardly believe that out of the hundreds that auditioned they chose us. It was surely one of the best days of my life. Our great friends wanted to throw us a Halloween costume party in celebration of the new adventures we would soon undertake. We decided on a backyard barbeque where we could enjoy delicious food, good fun, and the company of our awesome friends.

Accepting a position with IWA was going to be a life changing decision in every aspect. We would once again be starting at the bottom, but we would have the chance to be seen by more people since this was a larger company with a greater following. However, getting here was on half the battle now it was up to us to keep the crowd entertained and make them want to watch our characters in the ring. If they do not like us, we would be done with no questioned asked. Best case scenario is they love us worst case is they hate us but regardless we were going to give it our all and see what happens from there. We prepared ourselves for spending a lot of time on the road traveling and performing all over the US, yet we were not abandoning The Swamp Boys we planned on coming back as often as we could.

Walking in front of the full-length mirror I stopped to checkout my tight-fitting pirate costume and adjust my hat with a big feather on top. Looking at my reflection I could see that the Cammie of yesterday was gone emerged was Camille of today more mature and self-aware.

"You look beautiful my love" Drew complimented "But our guests are waiting"

He put his arm around my waist leading me outside where we were greeted by all our friends. Out of the corner of my eyes I saw my little kitty running around playing with the other kids making my heart happy. After which Dave walked up to personally welcome us.

"Congrats guys" he said shaking Drew's hand and hugging me "I am proud of you both but I hate to see you to go"

This was obviously a bittersweet victory for me. I was enthusiastic about the opportunity presented to me, yet I was going to miss the people who took a chance on us, taught us, and backed us as we steadily transformed ourselves from fans to professional wrestlers becoming family along the way. Today we have a new lease on life that would have otherwise been impossible without the encouragement of the friends and family here celebrating with us today. I was aware of how truly blessed I was to have that many outstanding people in my life. Friends, family, and food what more could anyone ask for?

"Thanks Dave we are going to miss you to" I assured him "Promise we will not be strangers"

Scanning the crowd, I notice Laura all alone leaning against the old oak tree across the yard in her zombie get up. She smiled waving at me pretending she was fine even the make-up could not hide the red rims and puffiness around her eyes which unmasked that she had been crying. I walked to my best friends' side, who I knew needed me right now, to give her a comforting hug.

"You, okay?" I asked her

"Yes, I am really happy for you two" she confessed holding her tears in "Sometimes I am just scared to lose the only family I have"

"You are never go losing to us" I told her "Besides family sticks together"

I met Laura when I thirteen years old in seventh grade English class. We bonded almost instantly over our so–called misfit status and dysfunctional home life and have considered each other as family ever since. The thought of leaving her behind and separating her and Josie pained me greatly.

"I am going to miss that baby" she said dismally deeply loving the godchild, who loved her back, having built a special connection between them.

"Come with us" I proposed excited at the prospect of Laura coming along "No one loves Josie or knows her condition better than you"

"Are you sure?" she asked enlivened as a huge smile covered her face

"Yes" I repeated "Come with us"

"Okay then" she said letting happy tears fall from her eyes "I will"

The hardest part of this is leaving the only place and people I have ever known behind but having Laura on the road with us will give me a piece of mind. Joining IWA was an epic step in my goal of making it to the top but making it to the top and staying there are two totally different things. I just had to grab the audience's attention and get them invested in my character hoping they will want to see more of Miss Penny Lane.

"Cammie" Debbie called out holding up a beer "Over here"

Before heading her way, Laura grabbed me giving me a long hug.

"Can you believe were actually getting out of this town together" I smiled excited to have Laura going on this new odyssey with me "Exactly like we always said we would"

Then I took her hand as we walked over to Debbie.

"Bottoms up" she said handing me and Laura a beer

The three of us cheered clinked our bottles together then all took a swig.

"I do not know what I am going to do without my other Swamp Chick to help me battle the boys club" she told me "Not going to be the same without you"

"I know that is right, but I will be back" I assured her "Going to serve them some act right"

"I am going to hold you to that" she replied

"She will be back" Shawn chimed in "We all know how obsessed she is with me"

"Damn, I thought I hid it so well" I responded giving me and Shawn had a laugh

"You know what?" I admitted to Shawn "Believe it or not I am actually going to miss you"

"Who am I going to harass now?" he jokingly asked

"I am sure you will find a replacement" I smiled

"No one can replace you" he said and although I was not sure if he serious or being a clown, but I found it an honor either way.

After talking with them a while I walked around conversating with all my friends making sure to included everyone when Dave tapped his glass to get the groups attention.

"Quiet, quiet" Dave commanded bring a hush over the guest

"It was not all that long ago when these two were nothing more than teenage fans. I would see them in the audience every weekend without fails cheering me on and having a great time. Then one day Drew approached me wanting to join the company and it did not take me long to realize these two were a package deal. I was skeptical at first, but they took me by surprise seeing how fast they learned. I thought that they would not even last a month, yet they fooled me with their God given talent and unrelenting drive. Not only did they love entertaining, but they also had a special love for each other. Their a once in a lifetime couple and I have no doubt they will take IWA by storm. I am going to miss the hell out of you both. Congratulations go get um! To Drew and Cammie"

He made his touching speech as the guest raised their cups to us.

"To Drew and Cammie" they repeated

The beautiful speech made me misty eyed as Drew put his arm around me. I felt like a Starlet for the day having so many people behind us.

"We love you two and will miss all of you" Drew told everyone "We could not ask for better friends"

"I love and will miss of you" I managed to say with a lump in my throat

I took a deep breath and composed myself before grabbing two beers out the ice chest and walking over to the barbeque pit where Drew was flipping some burgers on the grill. I handed him the cold beer as he kissed me thank you.

"Yum… looks good" I compliment smelling the sweet aroma of the barbeque

"Not as good as you look though" he said being his usual cornball self

We spent the next few hours hanging out with our friends talking, eating, drinking, and having a total blast on this awesome autumn evening. With trick or treat fast approaching and the sun beginning to set, most of our company had left and we were finishing up the with the cleaning. Picking up the last few cups a sadness washed over me thinking that this could possibly be the last time for a long time that I get to spend time with all my friends together like this again.

I can remember I always wanted to be free of this little town but now that I am about to leave, I can finally appreciate the charm of small-town living. However, I was nonetheless exhilarated to be venturing to the IWA at the same time I was scared to death. I was on the cusp of uprooting my whole family on a wing and a prayer, but you must take big risk to get big rewards. It eased my mind seeing all the love we were shown to today which indicated that we always had a place here at home. So, I was ready to throw caution to the wind, face my fears head on, and take the wrestling world by the horns. It was my time to truly shine.

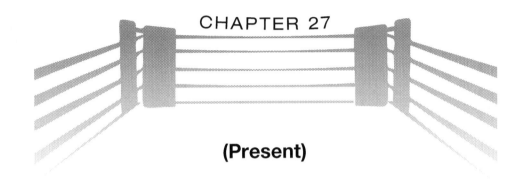

CHAPTER 27

(Present)

I hastily wiped the trail of tears from my face and tried to put on a brave façade which did nothing to conceal my bloodshot eyes. I was mainly hoping that he did not here us fussing outside because I was embarrassed by the entire situation and could not stand the thought of being a burden to anyone. Walking back onto the bus I found Jon sitting upfront like a defender waiting on me to come in safe and sound. I did what I could to act normal even flashing him a half-hearted smile but the look on his face told me that he saw straight through my masquerade.

"How did it go?" Jon asked although I was pretty sure he already knew the answer

"I do not mean to pry" he interjected before I could reply ever the gentleman "You do not have to answer that"

"It is ok, it went fine I suppose" I shrugged my shoulders pretending all was alright "As good as possible considering the circumstances"

"You know you do not have to act tough in front of me" he said seeing past my charade

I rubbed my face stressfully in my hands as I took a deep breath in and exhaled trying to calm my being. I felt as if I was being crushed by the turmoil of the day crashing down on me like a ton of bricks. Am I a beacon for torture? I wondered. Sometimes I feel cursed and anyone who gets too close to me ends up burnt. I was well versed in tragedies, but betrayal was a whole new ballgame with a terrible sting and a different type of hurt. Welcome to the real-world Cammie this is not your fable world anymore I scolded myself.

"I should go" I said racked with guilt as I turned to leave "I hate being a bother"

Jon reached out delicately taking my arm gently spinning me to face him.

"You should not isolate yourself right now" He told me sounding genuine "I should have never made you go out, stay"

"I am cursed Jon" I said feeling confused, hurt, and exhausted "I do not want you to get hurt"

"Do not worry, I can handle it" he said bringing a smile to my face "I have big shoulders"

"You sure do" I smiled

I relented sitting down on the couch feeling downright defeated. Now it was time for me to pick up the pieces to rebuild my life or at least something resembling one and I had no clue where to start. But at this moment I just wanted to forget for a while, I believed I owed myself that much. Jon had a seat next to me sitting silently putting his arm innocently around me literally lending me a shoulder to cry on. Feeling comfortable with Jon allowed me to calm down and relax inside his peaceful presence.

"See, I told you that you did not have to act tough in front of me" he assured me that I did not let my guard down in vain

"I do not get comfortable with many people" I explained "But you have such good vibes it put me at ease"

Growing weary of constantly staying strong made Jon's offer even more enticing but I was not one to appear feeble because I was a strong prideful woman. However, one can only take so much before they cannot bend anymore, and they break. I could feel that I was on the verge of breaking, so I decided to take a leap of faith and place my trust in a man I barely knew. I loosened my grip and let go free falling while expelling the demons that held my head beneath the water allowing me to taste the splendor of air filling my lungs again.

"If that idiot could not see what he had right in front of him" he spoke candidly "Then he does not deserve you"

He benevolently swiped the hair from my face and lightly rubbed my throbbing head putting me at complete peace. You would never guess by looking at this huge statuesque man that he was merely a gentle giant who found a practical stranger in need and came to her rescue. It really is like having my own personal superhero. How cool is that?

"What if I am not any better than that?" I asked "I should have never come to TWE"

"I have been with Drew since childhood" I expressed "the only person I ever trusted made me feel foolish"

Jon turned towards me softly taking my chin between his fingers looking right into my face. His dark eyes seemed to transform as his demeanor shifted letting me know he meant what it is he was about to say, and I should give him my undivided attention.

"I have seen tons of women come through here, but you are different" he began to explain "There is a spark in your eyes an aura that surrounds you"

"You have a zeal that makes you unique and you are not afraid to be who you are, one day you are going to be the face of the Goddess Division and even make Dallas shake in her boots" he spoke with words that felt authentic to me "But no one can believe in you until you believe in yourself, do not let anyone put out your fire, let it burn bright and blind all that look upon it because you are a leading lady"

"Wow are you serious or just being inspirational?" I questioned

"100% serious and I never understood what a woman of your caliber was doing with a playboy" Jon commented "I think you should put your childhood in the rearview and look at the beautiful open roads ahead of you"

"He was a good man once then he got here and changed I cannot except cheating will not except it" I explained "Its time to start a new life for me"

"Fame can change people" he said

"Yes it can" I agreed

What is it that other people see that give them such faith in me that I lack to see in myself? Maybe it is time for me to stop searching for acceptance from other and find it within myself. Regardless of the past I do not deserve deceit, I deserve love. Yet even this realization was terrifying uncertain of what the future holds in store. How do you not think of someone who is in every memory you have ever made? Forgiving is easy it is forgetting that is hard.

"Thank you for your beautiful words" I thanked him as I tucked his long hair behind his ears to see his face "You did not have to do any of this"

"No need to thank me baby girl" he said with a sweet smile "I wanted to"

Jon seemed to have a serene effect on me when he stared at me with his kind transfixing eyes. There were no words to explain the gratitude I had for his hallway intervention. And I will never forget him allowing me to borrow his strength when I had none of my own.

"Do you call the chicks you meet baby girl?" I asked curiously

"No, I call them baby doll" he said confidently "I must have saved baby girl for you because never used it before"

Whether that was the truth or solely a line did not really matter to me. Either way it made me feel good considering it looked as though I had become irrelevant to my own husband. Me and Jon sat in quietude the attraction flowing between us was undeniably strong magnetically pulling me to him. I could feel a hunger deep inside me wanting to grab him, kiss him, and feel his touch. I pressed my forehead to his as we shared the same air, and the warmth of his breath brushed the side of my cheek. He rubbed the backside of his hand against my face then traced the tips of his fingers down my neck to the smoothness of my collarbone sending chills down my spine. I put my hand over his holding it as our lips found each other's for a tender kiss before parting while we hovered in one anthers atmosphere neither eager to move.

"Just so you know I want to take advantage of you" he warned

"How do you that was not my plans all along" I retorted

"Well then it is working" he said as we both smiled at the demented sense of humor, we shared

"I do not want you to think I am using you" I said

"I know" he insured me

Jon stood up offering me his hand and though there was not a whisper between us I certainly did understand the implications of his not so innocent gesture. And just like that I found myself at an impasse. Do I stay on the straight and narrow sticking to what is familiar and routine or do I veer off taking the path less traveled and explore what life has for me? Throwing caution away I accepted the sinful offer as he pulled me swiftly off the couch pressing my body close to his causing me to slightly tremble in his arms.

"Do I scare you?" he asked feeling me tremble against him

"I have never felt the touch of another man" I confessed "And no, you do not scare me you terrify me"

He smiled rather charmingly at me sliding his hand under my shirt and up my side. He then breezily ran his lips across my skin delicately kissing my neck making my pulse quicken

"Now you know how I feel" he said in a breathy tone

"Fire" was all I could say as my mind filled with naughty thoughts that preoccupied me

I let him lead me to the back giving no resistance as I followed behind him. When we reached the bedroom door, he turned to me placing his hand on the wall pinning me between it and him kissing me again with the taste of lust strongly on our lips.

"I am not one of those girls" I cautioned "This is foreign to me"

"I already know that which makes you all the sexier and more desirable" he admitted "but just so you know I am not one of those types of guys"

I stared intently my mouth slightly agape watching him slowly remove his shirt. I felt my body pulse while he laid back on the bed pulling me down beside him.

"You do not have to do this" he said offering me an out

"I never do anything I do not want to do" I responded wanting to keep going

I ran my hand across the silkiness of his ripped chest then brought my mouth to his skin making a trail to his neck my lips intense with a sexual craving as my breath fastened. He rubbed his hand up my thigh bringing me closer for a sensual kiss. Jon gradually lifted my shirt exploring my stomach warmly moving his fingers across my belly button prompting my blood to run hot. I instinctually brought my leg up tight against his thigh tangling my body with his.

"I want you so badly" he said pressing his steamy body to mine "But I know you will never be mine"

"I am a free single woman who cannot tell the future" I said "but it looks bright"

Is wanting this wrong of me? Should I restrain my passions? I was tired of having so much self-control I was ready to give in. Watching Jon's face light up with each touch made me weaker and want him even more. He hedonistically pulled my shirt off kissing my skin and moving his tongue around my breast leaving me with a hunger only he could appease. I let out a moan of pleasure that raised his libido as I felt his exhilaration against my skin with his body fully hot and ready. We kissed once more completely consumed and intertwined in each other.

We abruptly halted ourselves breathing heavily while we glared into one another's faces. I buried my head deep into his chest suppressing my salacious inclinations. I wanted so badly for him to just take me but rushing into this and ending up in remorse would not benefit either of us. He kissed me one last time leaving our appetite lingering around us as we laid together skin against skin yearning to feel each other as he clutched me tightly to him. There was an unspoken agreement to honor our affection and potent unsullied intimacy of this affair as we laid their content to just be.

"Sweet dreams of me baby girl" John said kissing my forehead

"Good night superman" I smirked "And remember do not go falling in love with me"

"Are you into witchcraft?" he grinned

"I'll never tell" I responded with a faint giggle

I was placated feeling his heartbeat against me. Jaded by the day I was ready to get some sleep. And as hard as it is to believe for the first time ever since Drew, I fell asleep next to the body of different man.

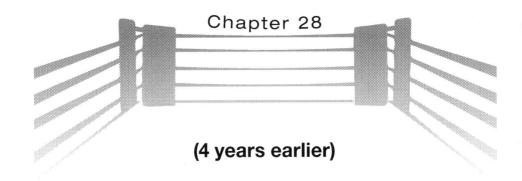

Chapter 28

(4 years earlier)

Dear Diary,

Things are going great at IWA. Drew and his partner Tim Collins aka T-Rex who go by the team's name Extinction are the current tag team champions which I do think is cool. We have made tremendous strides since arriving here and have both been making breakthroughs. Like for an example Miss Penny Lane is the reigning Gladiatrix Champion and I have only been here a year. Just goes to show that you can do anything if you put your mind to it. Josie is getting so big she is 3 going on 30 quite a handful but a wonderful handful and I would not trade for the world. But I am so thankful for Laura's help she is my saving grace I love her like a sister. Well, got to go. Talk soon. Peace Out!!!

"**M**omma, momma" I heard Josie calling

"What is up little love" I asked

"Can we go to the park" she plead with her big brown eyes "Pleaseeeeeee"

Today me and Drew had the day off which Josie knew was her day and took full advantage of our family time together. I loved my career and being the Women's Champion but being with my family is far more important to me. Josie, Drew, and Laura are my family, and I would do anything for them.

"How can I say no to that" I agreed "Go tell daddy and nanny"

She quickly took off with a wide grin while I headed to find her something warm to wear. Then I went back to the living room to wrangle everyone up and get Josie dressed.

"Let us go bug-a-boo" I said so she would have a seat next to me on the couch.

I replaced her nightgown with a pair of jeans, a pink princess sweatshirt, with matching pink Hello Kitty shoes and beanie. After bundling her up we walked over a few blocks to Josies favorite park where she quickly ran to jump on the swing. The wind blew around me giving me a chill from the crisp cool breeze. It was a beautiful day the sun was shining, and everyone was smiling.

"Daddy push" she commanded dangling her little legs back and forth.

Drew happily obliged her but made her count each time he pushed her. She laughed her way all the way to ten enjoying the tickle in her belly before starting back at one. After repeating that a half dozen times as I looked on Laura took over and Drew joined me on the bench. I was loving life right now.

"Is this not the best?" I asked "I hope we can give her a sibling"

"Yea it is" he agreed "and we will give her a sibling in time"

I delighted in wrestling and basked in being the Gladiatrix Champion but above all else I adored being a mom. I realized having another child would put my career on hold just as I am making head way and may never reach that spot again yet to me it is worth it. And even if I lose my career I would be gaining so much more.

"I am sorry Andrew "I apologized my eyes misty with a memory

"Do not be sorry bae" he squeezed my hand "You did nothing wrong"

Although I know he is right because it is my body, I feel I cannot help but carry a bit of guilt anyhow. Me and Drew had been trying over a year to conceive when six months ago it finally happened. When that stick read pregnant his face lit up and he spun me around as we celebrated our growing family. But just five weeks later I ended up miscarrying it felt as if the universe was playing a cruel joke on me. I knew right away when I saw the blood what had happened, but my heart still stung at the doctor's confirmation. Shortly after came the pain and I let my sorrow consume me. Only Drew and Laura knew what had happened and suffered alongside me. Every day I would plaster on a fake smile and pretend to be a happy, normal, sane person fooling the world. Our home became dim and there were no laughs a gaiety as it had been, and I did not know how to shake this loose from me. Then one day it came to my attention that Josie realized something was wrong and I knew that was unfair to her. That is the same day I quit feeling sorry for myself and started to appreciate what I did have instead of dwelling over what I did not have.

"Josie" I called to her "want to slide with momma?"

"Yeah, yeah" she answered excitedly

I walked up the steps behind her guarding my precious cargo from taking a tumble and adding to the scars she was accumulating with her fearless action just like her daddy. We flew down the slide with the wind whipping our hair into a mess, but it was a fun mess. We slide a few more times when I noticed the wind beginning to pick up and you could hear it whistling by as I heard the rustling of the trees all around us. I watched a few leaves scurrying by dancing a waltz with the wind. It was such a pretty day to be outside, but the increasing winds are going to bring a nasty chill, so it was time to head back indoors.

"Time to go little love" I informed her

"No" she protested with a shake of the head

"Yes Josie" I said sternly "time to go home"

"No!" she pouted stomping her feet

Drew grabbed her up as she sulked in his arms like a typical three-year-old who is spoiled rotten. Everyone knew that Josie was spoilt but to us she is perfect, and we did not plan to stop spoiling her anytime soon or maybe ever. Who knows? I like her just the way she is.

"Josie listen to daddy" Drew said to stop her tantrum "do you want to picnic in the living room?"

"Picnic Yah" she replied happily

I smiled at her in amazement of how quickly children could go from one extreme to the other. Tiny humans are interesting you never know what they are going to do next, and they never give you a chance to get bored. Once we got home the phone rang.

"Hello" I answered

"Hey Cammie" I recognized the voice of fellow IWA wrestler Lance "Loverboy" Langston

"Hi, Lance, how are you?" I asked

"I am good" he responded "Just calling to see what you are up to"

"We all just got back from the park" I told him "Now were having a picnic in the living room"

"How is Laura?"

And there it was the real reason for calling. For the past few weeks, I could see sparks flying between Laura and Lance. They thought that no one saw but I have known her since we were kids, so I pretended to be blind to it so that they could enjoy their budding romance. Ever since Billy broke her heart, she never showed interest in anyone until Lance came along and stole her attention. Laura deserves a little romance and happiness it is about time for her to get a personal life of her own.

"She is good" I played along "Why do you ask?"

"Umm no reason" he responds as I lowly chuckle

"Lance, you did not call for me" I told him "But would you like to speak to Laura?"

"Yes please" he said with glee

"Laura, you have a call" I shouted "Its Lance"

She raced into the kitchen with a big bright smile on her face and her green eyes glowing. I passed her the phone then joined Drew and Josie at the picnic to give her some privacy while she talks.

"Is it okay if Lance stops by?" she asked twirling her red hair

"Sure" I agreed

Laura returned to the picnic with a big bright grin as she took a seat next to me and we began our little family lunch party. I gave Laura the I know what you are doing look and she just shrugged her head as if to say oh well. It made me proud that she is finally finding herself she has been lost far too long.

"Were just friends" she stated unconvincingly "That is all"

"It is your life Laura have fun with it" I try to motivate her "and screw what people think"

"But best friends forever so I believe you" I assured her

"Thanks Cammie" she said giving me a friendly hug

Out of the corner of my eyes I could see Josie with an unpleasant look on her face. She hates being ignore always one to the center of attention. So, I shifted my awareness to our little princess who was doing her duty of passing out the food and drinks to everyone. There was knock on the door causing Joey to look up with her face scrunched up to expression says how dare you interrupt my picnic. The impression she cast was priceless and gave us all a good giggle. Laura quickly jumped up and hurried to answer the door smiling like a beautiful blooming May flower.

"Hi" Lance said bright eyed

"Hi" she greeted him back then paused "I am sorry, come in, come in"

Laura stepped aside as she invited him inside with a bashful grin. The twinkle in her green eyes shined bright as a star in the dead of night her cheeks were rosy around her freckles which played off well with her dangling re curls. She was a stunning woman who Lance certainly noticed, and I saw her eyeing him as well. Lance was a striking man he was tall and muscular with rugged golden hair and enigmatic grey eyes. They would make an exquisite couple, but I do not want to get ahead of myself. Laura had a seat back with us and patted the floor beside her inviting Lance to sit.

"No" Josie scowled not taking kindly to the intrusion.

She curled her lips up looking at him disparagingly. But Lance seemed to be a tender soul in a big man's body he gave her a broad smile attempting to ingratiating himself to her by pulling out a lollipop.

"If I give you this" he offered "can I join you then"

She kept her face sneered while thinking over the inciting offer before giving a big smile grabbing the lollipop sprightly.

"Yes" She gave him an endearing hug "sit"

Lance appeared to like Josie's impromptu hug as his face lit up with a heartfelt expression before having a seat. My child was indeed a unique gift to this world. She can make anyone fall in love with her and its looks like she just added another name to the list. Josie continued passing the food and drinks around as the adults blathered on about work, gossip, and life in general. Once we finished Drew took Josie for a bath while the three of us picked up the remnants of the picnic.

"I got this" I told them "You two go on and have a good time"

"You sure" Laura asked

"Of course, I am" I reiterated

"Thanks for the picnic" Lance chimed in "It was fun"

I smiled at him pleased with his gracious manners and cordial demeanor. I could see his charm working on Laura and it is about time that someone finally caught her eye.

"Do you like dancing" Lance asked Laura

"Sounds like fun" she answered readily "but I need to change first"

"Cammie, can you help me find something" She requested, and I agreed with a nod

"I will get the rest of this" Lance said "Go get dolled up although I think your hot just as you are"

Then he gave Laura a flirty smile that she returned with kittenish grin before heading to her room.

"What do you think" she asked "do you like him"

"I do" I answered "He seems like a gentleman"

"He really is" she beamed at my approval "I hope it is not an act"

"I think he is genuine" I assured her hoping I was right.

"Ugh" Laura complained "I have nothing to wear"

"I will be right back" I told her

I went to my room grabbing one of my dresses that would look great on her. I headed back to her room and gave her the outfit. The dress was a curve hugging blue mini dress adorned by a deep V neck, a scoop to display her back with two straps across decorated with silver rhinestones. I also grabbed my most cherished black Louboutin pumps with spiked studs around the heel. I lusted after those shoes for a long time until Drew surprised me with them last Christmas. He knows me so well.

"No way" she said "Not your Louboutin's"

"Yes, you can, and you will" I told her "Best friends always share clothes"

Laura looked downright sexy in the dress and heels. She was ready to set that dancefloor on fire. I cannot wait to see Lances face when he sees her looking so dazzling.

"Do I look alright?" she asked

"You look amazing" I remarked "you will knock his socks off"

She smiled at my compliment which seemed to raise her confidence. Laura was always on the shy side and was one of those people who are drop dead gorgeous but really does not know it. As much as Laura has helped us, I think she deserves the royal treatment and if anyone deserved a prince charming it was her.

"Presenting Miss Laura Lee Melancon" I announced putting her hand in the air and giving her a twirl" Tada"

When she walked in Lances eyes got wide with attraction as he shifted his body standing taller while smoothing his hair back. His lips were slightly opened in awe of her feminine wiles.

"Ready my lady" he bowed "your chariot awaits"

They left with smiles on their faces and excitement in their eyes. I could not wait to hear all about it tomorrow but right now I had to resume mommy duty as me and Drew head to her room with a book. When we walked in the room, we found her already asleep curled up on her bed. Drew picked her up and tucked our sweet girl in. I placed her favorite stuffed animal, a white tiger she named Lady Lulu, tucking it in with her.

"This is a first" I commented "we usually have to force her to bed"

"She did a lot today" he responded "That is all"

His words did little to convince me because I could see the concern written on his face. The doctors warned that with Josie's congenital heart disease she probably would not survive past five years old. But we refused to let her disease run her life and would give her the best life possible. But that did not mean that we were not worried because we were accept, we just did not dwell on it. We wanted our daughter to enjoy her life as we enjoyed having her in ours.

"I am going to stay with her" I informed Drew "You go to bed love"

"You know better than that Bae" Drew replied "Where you two are that is where I belong"

He pulled the covers back to let me in placing the covers snuggly over us. Then he pulled a chair up beside the bed as we settled in. His commitment to family was unwavering and while Laura was searching for her prince charming, I had already found mine.

"Goodnight Andrew" I said softly "I love you"

"I have always loved you Camille" He replied honestly "I have loved you then, I have loved you in past lives, I love you now, and I will love you in another life. Eternally Soulmates"

"I love that it is beautiful" I felt so special

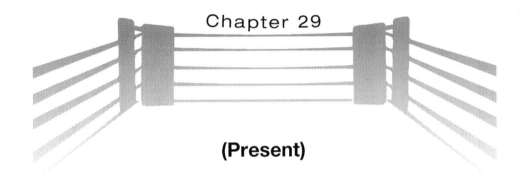

Chapter 29

(Present)

Waking up after one of the worst days and best nights of my life it was oddly comforting to have Jon beside me. Right now, I would ordinarily be starting my daily routine but today was certainly unlike any other day. I looked at Jon still asleep as I laid my head near his arm wanting to center myself and relax in this sweet escape. Jon began to stir around as he opened his eyes looking right into mine and flashed me a beautiful smile. His smile said to me that he was glad to see me.

"Your still here?" he asked rhetorically

"Would you prefer I was not?" I retorted

"Oh, hell no" he exclaimed

Jon sat up putting his strong arm over me hoovering a minute before going in for the kiss. What a marvelous way to wake up. Last night we became more than friends but not quite lovers as we restrained our desires neither of us wanting to feel guilt. If this is sinful, I better start praying now because he felt oh so right last night. He was an Adonis who I know was totally out of my league, and can only end one way, but I may as well relish the ride while I am on if. I have already spent enough time worried about what other people think and trying to do what the world claims is right. But now I say to hell with them all it is my turn to live for me and have some fun in the meantime.

"Before we go past the point of no return" Jon cautioned "I need to tell you something"

"That is never a good sign" I responded

"Remember when I told you I was in your shoes before?" he asked

"Yeah" I answered

"The person I was referring to is Dallas" he told me "She is very jealous, spiteful, and downright evil"

"Oh man" I said surprised "Did not see that coming"

"After four years I caught her cheating" he explained "Then she tried to end my career and will certainly try to do the same to you so if you want to run, I get it"

This information was like a punch in the gut knocking the wind out of me momentarily. I worked hard to be here and to possibly lose it because of someone's crazy ex-girlfriend is insanity to me. Now I am at a crossroads deciding which path to take. I can stay far away from Jon as Dallas wants or I can put my career on the line and hope for the best. What it comes down to is my freedom. I was a free woman and could do what I wanted with who I want to. Why should I give up my freedom and set aside my happiness for someone else's? After thinking it over I have made up my mind and I do not agree I should give away my joy. Although our relationship was not a relationship, it was nothing serious, this was a pure unrelenting lust, yet it still put my freedom at stake, and I plan on keeping it.

"Some of these people have hit their heads so much their crazy" I summarized "either that or I am completely certifiable"

"Maybe a little of both" Jon laughed so sweetly

"I am not afraid of her" I said convincingly "I refuse to live my life on someone else's terms"

"Most Goddesses' would sprint away I knew you were one of a kind" He said "I just do not want to see you get hurt because of me"

"I adore wrestling it is my ultimate passion" I explained "And whether it is TWE or some no name company I am happy either way because money is meaningless"

"I feel the same way" he said "But the money is a bonus"

"Very true" I agreed "But money cannot buy love, happiness, or any of those essentials so what is it really worth"

"You are an amazing woman" Jon commented before kissing me again.

I am acutely aware of the repercussions that my actions my result in my termination, but I was no stranger to starting over. This was about principle no one should hold so much control over you that they believe they can dictate who you can or cannot associate with. And this should also break the burden that Jon has been living under as well. But I refuse to go down without a fight. I do not care how superb Dallas was in the ring and what kind of power she wields she is only human made of flesh and blood same as me. Life is unpredictable one minute your down and next you are on top of the world. You never know what is going to happen so I think everyone should take risks, roll the dice, and gamble a little because it could all be gone in the blink of an eye. I want to experience as much as I can, taste the fruits of my labor, and take time to live before I die.

"Now that everything is out in the open" I looked at Jon "Are you ready to take advantage of me yet?"

"Full advantage" he grinned lighting up his dark eyes

I just nodded my head in agreement no more words now it was time to talk with our bodies. I could feel the heat from his body warming me all the way to my core. Lost in a fog of desire we allowed out inhibitions to float away when we were suddenly interrupted by a knock on the bus door. This is what I call terrible timing.

"Who is it?" Jon called out

"It is Sarah" I heard her respond

Well, she right on time since she did have a habit of having the worst timing ever. But now I must leave the arms who held me and went to answer the door with my body still quivering inside. Jon was good natured and broke my fall went I was falling into a dark abyss. I let him be a Band-Aid putting off the pain becoming lost in his embrace however the vibes flowing between us does not feel like a Band-Aid anymore it feels more like a healing. I felt like a new person and a bit frightened by the way he shook my world I am not sure if he noticed but I am enjoying him way too much. I threw on some clothes on to answer the door when Jon grabbed me by the hips pulling me into his lap, kissing me, and sending my body into overdrive.

"I will be back" I told him as he kept a tight grip on my hand letting it slowly slip away.

"Hi" I greeted Sarah "come on in. What is up?"

Just then Jon entered the front in his jeans that snugly fit his hips as he pulled one of his t-shirts over his head. I grinned at the way Sarah yes widened when she saw him, and I cannot be mad at that he makes it extremely hard not to stare.

"Good morning, Sarah" Jon greeted her

"M…Morning" Sarah replied smiling shyly

Once she got her wits back her eyes became serious as she turned to talk to me.

"Something odd happened today" she informed me with a worried look

"What?" I asked fearing the answer

"It is Dallas, she literally tracked me down and you could tell she was on the war path" She explained "She was asking questions about you demanding to know where you were"

"What did you tell her" I questioned

Well, of course I covered for you" She told me "I said you were back at our apartment"

I watched Jon's eyes glaze over in anger while he quickly tied his shoes and hopped up.

"I have to take care of something" Jon said

He calmed himself a moment looking at me then moved his hand sliding my hair tenderly back then leaned in and whispered low in my ear his breath warm on my cheek.

"I hope this does not change anything" he said in a husky tone "I am going handle this do not worry"

Then he kissed my cheek before walking off the bus and you could tell that he meant business. I knew things were about to get ugly and here I was smack in the middle of the storm. I could see the complete confusion on Sarah's face as she tried to figure out what was going on.

"You are freaking kidding me, right?" she exclaimed "I do not know whether to give you a high five or a lecture"

"It is not what you think" I said

Ok, so I told a little white lie some lies are harmless told to protect you, but other lies can be dangerous. Never any downtime for me I seem to find myself in the most awkward situations. For a split second I thought about running away and not looking back but I refuse to be bullied. I am a grown independent woman who has worked her butt off to be here and would not be put out by a little intimidation.

"I know you are lying to me Cammie" Sarah burst my bubble "But I understand, for now time for go practice and get rid of all that extra energy"

We walked together across the parking lot heading to the coliseum when we noticed Dallas leaving the building. I took a deep breath unsure of what to expect judging by Sarah's interaction with her.

"Hey, remember a friend of yours is a friend of mine "Sarah grabbed my hand "And an enemy of yours is an enemy of mine"

"Thank you, Sarah," I said "But she is not worth losing your career over"

I could see her narrow her eyes into an icy stare that would have shot daggers through me if she could have. Tweety has nothing on Dallas' death stare. She stood there a moment then put her head down and turned around walking back inside. I just let her menacing roll right off my back.

"Well, that was anti climatic" Sarah commented

"Thank God for small miracles" I said relieved

But honestly, her silence scared me more than her words ever could. So, if scaring me was the plan then she succeeded. I had no idea what she was thinking but I guarantee its nothing nice. I am just pleased that I avoided a confrontation for now at least. If I said I was not scared I would be lying because making an enemy of the boss is never a good thing. To think that someone who does not even know me wants to destroy me over jealousy is childish. What she does not know is it is hard to keep me down, I am ready for her, and I believe in Karma it all comes back to you three folds. As we turned the corner, I saw Jon walking towards us, and I lost my train of thought at the site of him and the sun glistening off his tan skinned and his wavy long black hair blowing with the wind.

"Dallas is gunning for you" Jon informed me "I am sorry that I put you in this position Cammie"

"Do not apologize" I pleaded "I accepted the situation"

"You really are exceptional" he grinned "But I have a secret proposition for you"

"Go ahead" I waived

"You never have to worry about Dallas" He suggests "Just listen a minute. My manager Dwayne Jones is interest in having you as a client typically he would not accept new clients, but he will make an acceptation for you because he thinks you have a creative intellect and your versatile and will one day rival Dallas"

"Why me?" I questioned

"He sees good things for you". He stated" But it is your call baby girl"

Dwayne was the most respected manager at TWE and a legend Dwayne "The Dog" Jones knew how to make things happen. I was honored, excited, and even felt like I was cheating undertaking his offer would be career changing he is the best of the best. If I say no Dallas would ruin me so it is an easy choice.

"Okay" I stated "I would love to take that on"

"Great, I'll let him know" he declared kissing my cheek

As he left Sarah gave me that all knowing look, I was terrible at hiding things from her. I know Sarah is full of questions, but I was not sure if I had any answers to give because I was unsure of how to label what me and Jon are. I knew I liked him and enjoyed being in his company, but I also know me, and Drew have unfinished business to tend to.

"Cammie come on with it" Sarah asserted "What is going on?"

"We have not crossed any lines and I do like him more than I should" I admitted "But my feelings for Drew is still right there"

"I do not envy you" she said, "What are you going to do?"

"I do not know yet" I said honestly

"Well, whatever you decide I will back you up" she told me sincerely "I just want you to know that"

"Thanks Sarah" I said giving her a hug "Now let us go get some practice" Sarah is support meant a lot to me. Things are changing so fast right now that it feels like a roller coaster ride. I do not know what is coming next therefore I plan on welcoming the future with open arms. I just hope that my destiny is full of great prospects.

Me and Sarah practiced for a little over an hour preparing for tomorrows show before returning to our neighboring hotel rooms. Alone with my thoughts can be a dangerous place I just have to keep it together. And like it or not me and Drew were a power couple at TWE making it necessary for us to put on a smile and pretend all is well, thank goodness I can act. I laid down on the bed as my mind whirled and I closed my eyes trying to silence the noise and began to doze off before I was woken by a knock on the door. I got up in a sleepy daze opening the door to come face to face with Andrew.

"Can I come in, please" he asked "Only want to talk"

"Alright" I agree taking a deep breath "come in"

He pulled the chair out and took a seat while I sat on the corner of the bed waiting to see what words he has for me although they could be useless.

"First I have to say I am truly sorry that I hurt you the way I did" he said with emotion in his voice

"You should be because seeing that broke me" I told him "You and her are burned in my mind"

"I love you Camille and cannot live without you" he plead "Let me be the man you deserve"

"If you loved me, I would have been enough" I cried out "Why was I never enough for you?"

"Your more than enough I am just a selfish idiot" he told me "But…."

"But what?" I asked

"I do not want to make any excuses" he shook his head "I am just about sure I was set up but that does not change anything, I messed up and it is my fault no one else's"

Could it have been a set up? I wondered. I must get Sarah to convince Steve into telling her the truth. I almost hope it is a farce because then Drew would not be judged so harshly by me.

"Give me the chance to be the man you deserve before you move on" He begged "I am still in here"

"I need time this memory haunts me" I explained "my life revolved around us, now that has changed"

"If you can look me in the eyes and tell me you do not love me" he proposed "I will never bother you again"

"Before that you have to be able to look me in my eyes and you cannot" I rebuffed "You must love yourself before loving me, live completely on your own"

I was tired done, emotionally, drained, with nerves exposed and raw. This was one of the hardest things I have had to do saying goodbye to the only man I ever trusted with my life. I cannot dwell on what might have been because it only brings pain. I lost my balance for a while now it is time to steady myself and move forward

"You know I never wanted to come here without you" He stated "I seriously lost my way and myself"

"I know and I live with the regret of it everyday" I said honestly "But I need time to find myself too"

"I really do love you Camille" he told me

"I know you do but I do not want to know you love me because you tell me, I want your love to be in the things you do like tapping my tattoo, flowers, a poem, a wink, a gesture, it is the little things love put in actions" I explained "not words"

"I love you to Andrew and that will never change" I replied "But then again maybe loves just an urban legend"

The room fell silent as the weight of my last words hit us both. Did I really believe that? I am not sure anymore.

"I spent my life living on love even when it brought me pain, I just do not understand what love is anymore." I cried "Did I ever actually know?"

"You knew it was there Camille" he responded "with Joey, me, and Josephine"

Our silence was interrupted by a welcomed knock on the door. I composed my self-taking a deep breath then opened the door to find Jon standing there like a gentleman holding a red rose in his hand making me smile. He looked in the room giving Drew an ugly stare before looking back at me.

"I saw this and thought of you" he said handing me the rose "Thought we could go on a walk"

"Awe, thank you" I replied "I would like that actually"

"We were in the middle of a conversation" Drew complained

"Nothing left to say tonight" I told him "I want you to go find my sweet boy"

"Man to man she still loves me" Drew said out of spite

I rolled my eyes irritated by his childish behavior. I told him I need some time to sort thing out in my head, but he made me feel very disrespectful putting our relationship out there like that. All he is going to do like that is push me away.

"I know I listen when she speaks but I trust that she can make her own decisions" Jon informed Drew "But I think you really need to feel just as bad as she did that day.

After that comment Jon pulled me towards him by my waist giving me a long hot kiss that sent a bolt electricity through my being. Opening my eyes, I saw Drew his face was red, and his fist were bawled up as he went to charge at Jon. I quickly jumped in between them not wanting to see them in trouble or fighting over something like me.

"Dang it, Andrew restrain yourself" I raised my voice "I am not worth your career"

Drew dropped his head the tone of my voice calmed him down. Seeing the hurt in his eyes pained me but he has scarred me deeply. For a chance of any reconciliation, he had to work on himself, be ready for commitment, give me the time I needed, and had to be a good man. He had a way to go but it was not impossible because regardless of his actions I still loved him even when I did not want to.

I looked Drew in the face putting my hands on the sides of his face then kissed him on the cheek.

"Get your life together" I told him "Find out who Drew is"

I walked away with Jon and was glad to leave that situation alive once we got outside the brisk air in my lungs cleared my mind. He put his arm around me rubbing my shoulder to warm me up on this chilly October night since in all the chaos I forgot to get my leather jacket. Then like the gentleman he was he took off his jacket putting it around my shoulders.

"You good baby girl" He inquired

"I am now" I smiled "Because I am with you"

He grinned from ear to ear he stepped towards me caressing my face with his left hand while staring at me with an unbroken gaze. Then he brought my body closer to his making my heart throb before heating up my lips with a steamy frenzied kiss. Once separated he held my hand as we walked along the boardwalk taking the beauty of our surrounding the sound and sight of crashing waves on the shore, the beautiful sand, and the beautiful sky that lit up the night for us.

There was no arguing, no stress, just a delightful peace that washed over me with the serenity I felt with Jon. Standing at the edge of the boardwalk I looked down at the metal rails as Jon stood behind me with his hand covering mine with his body pressed close to mine This is what love should be like just being is enough. We looked out at the ocean turning my attention to the stars illuminating in the translucent night sky.

"Where you serious?" Jon asked "When you said you were better with me"

"Of course, I was" I answered "I am sorry if that made you uncomfortable maybe I should not have said that"

"Do not be sorry baby girl" he said warmly "You make me feel like I am walking on air"

His comment stopped me in my tracks. Did he just admit that he felt something with me? Or was I reading too much into it" I think I slipped into some feelings somewhere along the line. He was supposed to be just for fun, a possible one-night stand, no strings attached but here I am having broken my own rules. I still am a married woman.

"I spent a lot of time telling Drew what my love language was we do not share the same love language we once did" I confessed "but then 15 minutes with you and were already speaking it with no words at all"

"I hope I did not confuse you" I said shyly

"Nope I understand baby girl" he said

John kissed me tenderly on my neck making my temperature rise. His kisses warmed my soul, and his touch gave me sensation that I in no circumstance have ever had before. He just felt so right.

"I do not want to make you uncomfortable or feel pressured" Jon confessed "I have no expectations, I just want to enjoy the time I have with you when I do have you, and let the chips fall where they may"

"Are you preparing to get rid of me?" I asked

"No but maybe scare you off because I may be breaking your rule" He admitted

"And I may break yours, but I am not scared easily" I teased turning in his arms "I am not uncomfortable, I am intrigued, and I am provoked"

What was it about Jon the piqued my attraction the way he did? He seemed warm, compassionate, caring, and his looks did hurt either. In the back of my mind, I thought I should not be doing this because one of us was going to end up hurt but the rest of my mind was delighted in him and did not care.

"What are your plans for tonight?" Jon inquired

"You tell me" I hinted

A devilish smile crossed his face as he took my hand and lead me away. I was not sure what the night has instore for us but the balls in his court. I am sure whatever it is he has in mind I am going to gratified by. Carpe Diem Seize the Day! Or in this case the night.

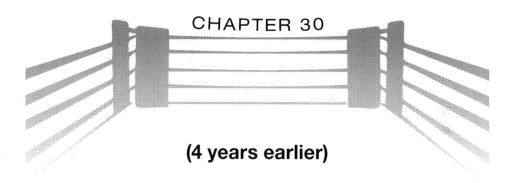

CHAPTER 30

(4 years earlier)

Dear Diary,

This is one of the most difficult entries to make. I am not sure how I am even writing today but there is no one else I can talk to because it is just too difficult to speak about so I will just tell the universe. I need to steal a few moments to collect myself and clear my mind of all the thoughts rumbling around in there. We've spent the last week in the hospital with Josie who has been weak but in good spirits which keeps us positive as we put on a brave mask never showing our own weakness in front of the little girl we love and adore. But yesterday the doctors told us that there was not much more they can do but keep her comfortable so we decided to bring her home where she could be in the comfort of her own room and own bed. I find myself constantly praying for a miracle to a God I hope is listening, but it is in his hands now. My heart weighs heavy in my chest as if it were made of steel. I feel that my love is lethal I've been given so much love only to have it stolen away. The love comes easy, but the loss is earth shattering and certainly life changing. Every loss takes a piece of me with them. I must believe in heaven a place of peace and free from pain where you can spend eternity with those you love and who chose to love you. Heavens all I have got to hold on to and it is what keeps me pushing on through whatever life hands me. Someone's at the door I must go.

I opened my door to see Father Courville who has consoled me in tough times, and he celebrated with me in times of joy.

"My Child" he said with open arms

I fell into his embrace unleashing a flood of tears and emotion. I had kept composed until now having to let go in the comfort of his presence where I was truly safe like a child in their fathers' arms.

"Forgive me Father" I apologized "I have been holding that in for a long time"

"You do not have to apologize to me Camille" he insured me "I have known you since you were a child and watched you grow into this incredibly strong woman you have become"

"Thank you" I said grateful for his confidence in me

"Josie's in her room" I said

I showed him down the hall to her room where he stopped me just short of the door.

"Remember my child" He conveyed "God never gives us more than we can handle"

"I hope that is the truth" I uttered "I really do"

We entered the room where Drew, Laura, and Lance were standing vigils as Josie slept peacefully under her Hello Kitty comforter. A calm appeared to wash over the atmosphere when Father Courville stepped into the room accompanied by a deep sorrow in knowing he was coming to perform The Last Rites.

"Father Courville" Drew welcomed him with a handshake "Thank you for coming"

"Andrew my son" Father asked, "How are you holding up?"

"As well as possible" he answered

Father Courville kissed Laura's cheek and shook hands with Lance. Then he knelt beside Josie who he had recently baptized he softly pushing her hair back and kissing her forehead before pouring the holy water. This time he is softly brushing her hair back and kissing her forehead putting a cross of ashes on forehead. As he finished The Last Rites, we held hands and cries our tears overflowing.

"Thank you, Father Courville," I showed my gratitude

"You do not have to thank me but your welcome" he responded "If you need anything call me anytime"

Father Courville gave me a hug then turned to head for the door. His leaving caused emotions to double because we had no reason to keep our composure anymore. I fell into Drews comforting embrace that was a connection I really needed right now.

We did not sleep that night and at 2:14 AM my sweet little Josephine passed peacefully in her sleep. She fought to stay with us long as she could never wanting to miss a thing she brightened and gave our lives meaning but her tiny heart could go on no longer now she dances with the angels in a perfect body. What are we going to do now? I stared down at Josie's darling face before leaning over and picking my daughter up into my arms for one last time and rocked her in our chair while humming a lullaby. She was still warm, looked as if she was just napping, but I knew this time she was not going to wake up and I would never hear her sweet voice saying "momma" ever again. After some uninterrupted time, Drew came to lift her from my arms as the funeral home arrived. I turned away unable to watch them cover her face and take away my precious child.

Like a ghost in the night, I walked quietly and softly coasting my way almost robotically into my cold lonely room where I climbed in my bed pulling the covers snuggly around me. Words fail me now. I felt empty as another piece of me is taken away. I am glad that we were the ones lucky enough to have had her in our lives for the time we did even if it was short. And unlike with Joey we had a chance to prepare ourselves and to say goodbye. Although I do not believe there is any real way to prepare for the loss of anyone especially of a child.

Following shortly after me Drew walked into the room and laid beside me warming me up in the bed. I suppose words failed us both as we held on to one another speechless. What is the world going to look like tomorrow? Who will we be? I know losing a child can break bonds, but I am hoping this will bring us closer and make us stronger. I have so many questions in my conscience and very few answers. All I can do now is try to get some sleep and wake up to my new reality.

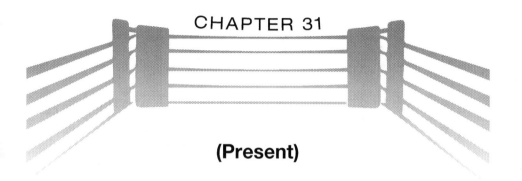

CHAPTER 31

(Present)

Dear Diary,

I cannot quite put my finger on what it was pulling me towards Jon, but it was magnetic. Walking away from Drew was one of the toughest things I have ever done but I just could not trust him anymore and without trust you have nothing. It made my decision no easier, but it had to be done at that moment before we let it all go down the drain. Could Drew who proclaimed to love me be in denial and stopped loving me a long time ago yet still trying to ignite the spark. While Jon has been kind, a friend when I needed one, I know right now were in lust with each other, but I feel more than just that. I realize I am not being fair to anyone with my emotions hanging in limbo. I do suppose there are worst places to be in this world than torn between two lovers. If I said I had no feeling at all for Jon that would be a lie I am just trying to figure out where there going. And if I said I did not have love for Drew anymore that would also be a lie so no matter what I say I end up in a conundrum.

The real question I need to answer is do I love Drew or am I in love with him. This is my cross to bear. I need to get this figured out soon for all our sakes. Got to Go! Peace Out!

I watched Jon walk out the steam filled bathroom from his morning shower with a few drops falling from his hair glistening on his perfectly toned chest, oh man does he look delicious.

"Any plans for the day?" I inquired

"Had thoughts of heading to a state park walk around see the beauty of nature" he proposed "If that is good with you?"

"Ow an invitation" My eyes sparkled "I love communing with nature and you"

We decided to make a day of it where we could be alone, go undetected, and just have a little fun together. We filled a backpack with some granola bars, other healthy snacks, bottled waters, and a first aid kit just in case.

Once we got to the park, we found the trail and started walking onward. I could not help my eyes from getting distracted because he looked hot dressed down in his Nikes, black athletic short, and a snug tank top as beads of sweat developed on his skin. I was comfortable in my tie dye yoga pants, matching crop top tank, and my pea green Sketchers since I do not mind sticking out a bit. It was either extra hot outside or it was just me feeling the flame beside me.

"Hold up their sexy" I called to Jon "Shoe came untied"

"Sure, thing hot stuff" he paused taking my hand "Do not want to lose my Wonder Woman"

"I never pictured those two together" I smiled making him giggle "would be a great looking couple though"

In awe of our surroundings, we walked along holding hands getting a kiss or two in as we listened to the sounds of nature. It was quite enchanting. Birds chirping, whistling of the wind, rustling the leaves, and animals off in the distance. This was exactly what I needed to clear my mind and hit the rest button. It is just so perfect, peaceful, and beautiful out here away from everywhere and everyone.

"Can I ask you a personal question?" Jon asked hesitantly "You do not have to answer"

"I have nothing to hide" I responded

"You never talk about your parents" he observed "Did something happen"

I was not expecting that question but was happy about it because it showed he paid attention to me when I talked and that his interest in me goes more than skin deep. Now that is sexy.

"Well, it is an ear full" I warned

"Got nothing but time today" he responded, "and you?"

I sat down on the plush green grass around the trail and patted for him to sit.

"My parents were hardcore drug addicts almost my entire life" I started from the beginning.

"My mom and I never saw eye to eye" I explained "She blamed for anything that went wrong. I have not talked to her since I was 16 years old, and she has not tried to reach me. My dad tried to be a part of life, but he had a lot of demons to contend with, but he at least does love me"

I then explained what happened with Joey, Josephine, Drew, and all the event that led me to where I am now. May as well see if he is going to run or stay sooner than later. And I could tell he was absorbing everything I was telling him, and he really cared. I think I needed to tell my story and let the past stay in the past. After history it felt good as if it had cleansed my spirit to get it all out.

"It felt so good to confide in someone like that it has been a long time" I told him

"Anytime baby girl" he remarked "I got you"

"I so am sorry you had to go through that" he said sincerely "most would not have made it out"

"You know there is still time to run" I lightened the mood "But thank you"

"Why would I run? I am not going anywhere unless you want me to" He inquired "Now I just think your more amazing than I did before"

"You would run because my love is lethal, it kills" I replied "It is like I am cursed"

He reached out rubbing my hand and looking me in the eyes to comfort me which it did. His presence was always giving me solace.

"Let me worry about that" he retorted "Superheroes have no fear"

I smiled then laughed at his comment. Before gazing off a moment at a few baby birds chirping in the tree to center myself.

"What does not kill you makes you stronger" he commented

"Damn right baby" I retorted "Damn right"

Then he swiped the hair from my face and looked me in the eyes putting my hand upon my chin where I could see and feel the genuine tender affection which warmed my core. I leaned in kissing him fervently wanting to feel a compassion that complied with mine. He then held me close to his chest where I could breathe him into my lungs. His natural scent was tantalizing with a hint of his Giorgio Armani cologne on top. I now know how he smells, and I will not forget his aroma.

"Whatever happened with your dad" he asked

"I am shamed but have no idea he relapsed" I admitted "but I do not even know if he is alive or dead, but I hold hope in my heart"

"You do not have anything to be ashamed of anything with me" he said "You are a remarkable woman, Cammie"

"Now you" I insisted "What is your family like?"

"I come from the Samoan culture, so my family is very close. I have older twin sister Kalani and Lalani and a younger brother Mano" He began "This year my parents will be celebrating their 36th anniversary"

"That is beautiful Jon" I smiled "As a child I use to dream of having a family like that one day"

I examined my peaceful surroundings lost in thought. Here was the beautiful, accomplished, and good-natured man from a great family with the world at his feet, what interest did he have in me?

"Penny for your thoughts" Jon snapped me out of it

"Why me?" I asked "You have everything going for you and I am... just broken"

"Because I enjoy your warrior nature, bravery, talent, personality, there are so many things" He told me "But mainly because I do not want anyone else Cammie"

"Plus, you are not broken maybe just a little cracked" He continued "And I do not have everything"

"I already know I am cracked up" I smiled "Completely bonkers"

He chuckled under his breath while rolling his eyes and shaking his head at me.

"See your spirit is not broken" He said "And you made it here, you are an elite wrestler, you do not give yourself enough credit"

And I hate to say it, but Jon was right I always found a way to blame myself when things happen outside of my control. I would tell myself if I had been a better daughter, girlfriend, wife, mother then things would improve. I have forever been my own worst critic. But throughout the years I have learned to take it easier on myself especially when it comes to things that I cannot change. I sense my affection for Jon is growing and for Drew is dissipating. Looking back with hindsight I missed so many red flags after Josie passed. But it is to late now my heart has moved on.

I took my small battery powdered stereo out my backpack and turned it on a slow song then set it beside the tree. Jon looked at me a little puzzled wondering what I was doing. I smiled as I stood up taking him by the hand.

"Dance with me" I insisted

"I cannot dance" he hesitated

"Take a chance just hold me close" I replied "It is just us"

He stood up pulling me into him with his arms around my waste as I put my arms around his neck as he stared at me with hunger burning in those brown eyes. We danced in the wilderness in sync with threes swaying in the wind. I could feel his heart beating against mine and it felt so right to be here in his arms that felt like a cape of protection around me.

"This is nice" he admitted "But I do not want to let you go"

"I would not complain if you did not" I said meaning my words

As we became comfortable in our embrace the song switched to much more upbeat rhythm. I took him by both hands and started to swing around as we both smiled and laughed.

"I have not had this much fun in a while" he stated

"Good" I retorted "because you never know what you are going to get with me"

I always had a fantastic time with Jon, he made me feel good about myself, making me feel young, yet like a woman all at the same time.

I know we said in the beginning do not go falling in love, but I am already falling and cannot stop it now with a trajectory headed right to Jon's heart. With him the past was not holding me down not that it did not matter but it was not burdening me anymore. You will never get away if you are stuck running away from your past.

As we twirled, I slipped on some dirt beneath my feet sending me tumbling down onto the leaves and taking Jon down with me. We both had a hearty laugh that made my stomach muscles hurt. Jon reached into my hair pulling out a leaf then holding it up as we watched it whirl away with the wind. I listened to the love songs of the birds that were tweeting a sweet tune in the silence of this magnificent forest. I laid with my back upon the ground while he hovered above me as I yearned to kiss him, so I just went for it kissing him lustfully as he returned the gesture without any hesitation.

"That is what I love" he mentioned as our lips parted

"What exactly is that" I inquired

"Feeling that you see me and want me for who I am" he responded "not for my fame, my looks, money, status, or any of that superficial junk"

"You are 100% correct" I admitted "But your looks do not hurt"

Jon was correct I was magnetically attracted to him, and it had nothing to do with anything superficial I loved his kind heart, courageous spirit, and calming aura just to name a few. I wanted him more than I wanted air.

"You are breathtaking" he complimented putting his fingers on my chin lifting my head to face his "Like a true Goddess"

Then he kissed me with a hunger have heightened the senses of his ravenous appetite and I wanted to indulge him in the flavor of me. He moved his mouth down to my neck kissing my skin with a feathery softness causing my blood to become feverish. In my sweltering temperature I took his face in my hands running my finger through his satiny hair.

"I think you are a supreme entity" I stared in his eyes "And I do want you"

Jon kissed me again and we had a hard time keeping our hands off each other as he slid his hand up my thigh, I playfully bit his ear. I never knew that another man could make me feel this way as my body tingled provoked by a lurid pining for his every touch. Just then my ear perked up hearing the crunching of leaves beneath the feet of two hikers coming up the tail bringing us to a halt as we adjusted ourselves.

"Well baby" John said "looks like we almost got busted"

He smiled while wiping the debris off our clothes. Jon reached out giving my butt an extra dusting for his entertainment, but I do not mind one bit.

"That what makes it all the more fun" I smirked

Jon gave me a slick smile back then pulled me in kissing me on the forehead endearingly.

"There is a great place to watch the sunset" he told me

"Lead the way" I responded tucking his hair behind his ears

We hiked a little way up into the woods as I took in the serenity of the breeze rustling the trees while the birds sang a lyric meant just for us, Scanning the scenery I saw a grassy hill that we walked to the top of.

"It is magnificent" I remarked "Wonderous"

"I thought you would like it" he told me

John walked up embracing me from behind as we looked off into the distance. What I adored about Jon is how he makes me feel about myself and I did not know it, but I had been letting some people walk all over me and he has suggested keeping toxic people away helps you stay more grounded and know your own self-worth. Now I know I am worthy. He gives me self-help advice and I give him universe advise we help each other mind, body, and spirit.

"This is so peaceful" I observed

"Let us settle in for the sunset" Jon suggested

He sat in the grass inviting me to have a seat in front of him I laid back into his chest resting my arms on his knees. I let out a long sigh feeling relaxed. I am glad I am right where I am and even happier to be with him.

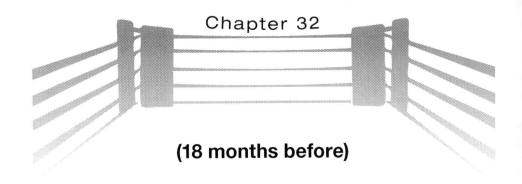

Chapter 32

(18 months before)

Dear Diary,

After all the sorrow over the last year I finally have some long-awaited good news. I am hoping this news gives us that push we need to get over the hump and start ourselves a whole new life. Not this this will diminish the memories of Joey and Josie because I think of them every day and always will, but we been sad too long and it is time to be happy and hopeful again. Last week me and Drew went to tryouts and auditions for Total Wrestling Entertainment and Drew earned a call back which is no small fit and at the callback he was offered a contract and a place on the roster. He is now officially a Totalstar, and I am stoked for him. It does not get more mainstream than TWE. Unfortunately for me I was not as lucky which I went in expecting this outcome because it is considered a man's sport and there is not as many spots available for women, and we must also work three times as hard to get noticed or taken seriously. Drew says he would rather me wait to be signed and we go

*together but I know that is unrealistic and could happen never
so I must talk some sense into my overprotective hubby. There
is not anything I would not do to helps his dreams come true.
Got to Go!! Peace Out!*

"Morning pretty girl" Drew kissed my check straight out of bed
"Morning sweet boy" I said as we sat to eat

"So, my love" I opened up a discussion "How are we going forward
with this opportunity?"

"I do not want to go without you" he replied "I refuse"

"You can and you will Drew" I squinted my eyes in disapproval

*He was just so darn stubborn sometimes. He constantly refuses to
leave me behind, but I would do anything to see him go. It has nothing
to do with not wanting him around because I love having him with me,
but this is a once in a lifetime opportunity being offered to him and I do
not want to carry the guilt for him missing his chance.*

"Then come on the road with me" he retorted

"I will come with you every break I have; I must keep moving
forward" I told him "I will get there soon enough have some faith"

*Although Drew has made it I had not, and I needed the time to chase
my own wrestling dreams. I know I can make it if Drew would be a bit
more patient. Both of us have depended probably way too much on each
other since we were kids and things are great between us yet maybe the
distance can help us become more independent and self-aware. We can
use this distance to work on ourselves.*

"We will hardly see each other" Drew pouted "I just cannot"

"Distance makes the heart grow fonder" I responded

"Will you stop loving me if I am not by your side?" I inquired
wanting to understand his resistance

"No!" Drew said sharply "never"

*I am hoping what I just said was true and the distance makes us love
each other more and does not end up tearing our relationship apart. But
there is no way to know until it happens. I feel that me and Drew have
been seen as a package deal for so long that I was not sure who we were
standing on our own.*

"We can take this time to work on ourselves" I continued *"and our trade"*

"I love you Camille" He responded *"I cannot see life without you"*

"I love you too Andrew" I told him *"That is why I want you to reach for the stars"*

"And it is not forever I will follow soon" I hoped *"It is just for a small blip in time then we will be back as one"*

This was the hardest conversation trying to convince him that I was okay being alone. Perhaps it has something to with him being a twin and having never been alone not even in the womb. I honestly do not even know what I am going to do with myself without Drew. I am shaking inside having this talk but holding a strong front because if I get weak, he will get weaker. But I was looking forward to reuniting and seeing the strong self-supporting man I know he can become.

"So, you want me to leave you" He inquired

"Yes, I do" This was the hardest words I ever had to lie

"Alright then" he said in a sour tone *"I give in"*

"Do not be like that bae please" I begged

"I am sorry I did not mean to sound that way" he said with sad eyes

I remember that morning and that conversation as if it were yesterday. I was trying to avoid regret yet here I am at a TWE event regretting that day and how coldly I went about it. Three months ago, I was positive I had done the right thing but what if I had not and my whole marriage could be on the line. Now here I am sneaking in the back with a VIP badge I had to flirt with a roadie to get. The secret is to act like I belong there. A girls got to do what a girls got to do. I waited outside the men's locker room and Drew spotted me as soon as he walked out and threw a smile my way. He quickly grabbed me up into his arms and I practically jumped into his embrace as we shared a deeply emotional kiss.

"Man, I have missed you sweet boy" I said

"I missed you too pretty girl" he smiled

We walked outside to have some privacy to talk, and Drew knew me well enough to know I would have questions I want answered.

"Why have you been ignoring me?" I got straight to the point

"When I first arrived here the minutes seemed like hours I was so alone" he responded "I looked at your picture every night getting more and more depressed"

"I am so sorry you felt like that Bae" I said

"So, I decided out of sight, out of mind" he said bluntly

Out of sight, out of mind Those words hit me like a missile to my heart. I should have come months ago I was just giving him time to grow but it seems that distance does not make the heart grow fonder it smashes it into pieces.

"Your right, I should have come sooner, I am sorry" I apologized

As we talked a short petite woman with blue shoulder length hair and dark eyes approached us. I knew exactly who she was from watching TWE and she was currently The Crazy Cajuns Ring escort Wendy Wonderful. Most females must start out their careers as ring escorts for the men and only a lucky few got introduced through a one-on-one match up.

"Cajun, what are you doing talking to this roadie?" she looked puzzled

"Umm…" Drew had perfect timing to forget his words

"Oh, I am no roadie" I told her looking at Drews red face "You tell her"

"Who are you?" Wendy asked me

"I am Andrews Wife" I said coldly

I saw her look at Drew her eyes full of questions. I did feel bad for her because no woman wants to find out news in this way.

"I am or was his girlfriend" she said staring daggers into Drew

Although at this point, I was completely expecting to hear those words it does not make them any easier to digest. Her words hurt my stomach making me want to purge. I suppose I had more faith in Drew than he had in himself, and he has never learned to be independent. I know this was my fault I pushed him away, but I really had high hopes for him. What a fool I have been. A fool for love. I never though Drew would be one to break our sacred bond of marriage yet here I am caught in this situation. And it took less than three months to blow up my world. I thought my heart would stop beating.

"You can keep him" I said cheeky "I do not want him anymore"

I turned to hurry and get the hell away from them because at this point, I wanted to punch something, scream, cry, pull my hair out, I do not know where I go from here.

"Camille, wait please" He said "I could not stand the loneliness"

"I love you please" he called out

"I love you too" I said stopped a moment "that is what makes this so hard"

"These girls are not for love but friendship" he admitted

I stopped in my track just friends huh. He must think I am not just looking like a fool but that I am dumb as well.

"Have you slept with anyone?" I asked calling him out

He stood silent which told me the answer it is as if I could feel my world falling apart at the seams. Reality can be cruel.

"I had no one but myself yet I still breath" I said then left

And just like that now once again I am the one who is alone. I have been dependent on Drew for such a long time that I did not know what the meaning of my life is or what it looks like with him completely gone. The chains have been broken but they spared me. I am now more determined to find my way and find my person someday.

Maybe this for the best because I do not have anything to dedicate myself to besides my career, so I am going to become the crème de la crème of elite female wrestler the world has ever seen and get a contract with TWE. I am going to make some waves in the industry. There is no one and nothing left to stop me.

CHAPTER 33

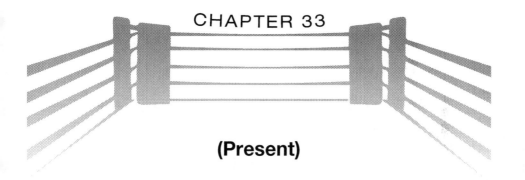

(Present)

Dear Diary,

I feel as if one chapter of my life is closing but a bright new chapter is just beginning. The manager that Jon referred me to Dwayne "The Dog" Jones has taken me under his wing welcoming me to The Dog Pound. The Dog Pound is a few hand-picked royal elite wrestlers who have been champions or is a champion. I too am a former Champion from when me and Sarah "The Groovy Gals" won the tag team championship. I am enthusiastic about my chance in two weeks when I will be taking on Jolene "The Man Stealer" for The Goddess Championship title at the Hell Bound pay-per-view event. Just being one of the female headliners was an honor. Enough about work let us talk about me for a minute. Me and Jon have been enjoying each other's company. The more time I spend with him the more I realize what I want in a man and my feelings for Drew that once shone bright is barely a flicker now. My hope for me and Drew had been banished since my first trip to see him here, but I still loved him, forgave him, and left the past behind for a fresh start then he made me look like a fool once again. Fool me once shame on you, fool me twice shame on me, and I hate being shamed. I am nobody's fool and refuse to be played again. Well time for me to go train. Peace Out!!

I walked to the front of the bus where Jon was sitting sipping on some coffee.

"Here is your coffee baby" Jon said handing me a mug

"Thanks, Sexy" I planted a quick peck on the lips

Jon was kind-hearted he met me at one of my lowest points and offered me his hand when he did not have to. Neither of us knew then that it would become such a life changing meeting of souls. Drew was also kind and caring but he did not know how to support himself and stand on his own instead he found the first person that placates him to lean on. Even though what he was really doing was pushing me to the edge of the cliff. The huge difference in the two is that with Jon I was discovering many new feelings and with Drew my feelings were getting lost. I spent two years on myself working on me. I was owned by no city, no man, nothing but the promoter I worked for. I am grateful for that time because it helped me become the strong self-sufficient woman I am today.

But when me and Drew reunited it was as if I reverted to the old me and looking back, I can tell me, and Drew were self-consuming of each other with certainty it was toxic. When I am with Jon, I feel that we can both have relationships outside of each other. Have our own lives apart and our life together all at the same time. Is he, my person? It sure feels like it, but I am not sure I never put anything past life.

"Time to go baby girl" he said patting my hand

"Yep, Sarah is here" I said "Time to practice"

Jon stood up lifting me into his arms holding me captive in his kiss the electricity his lips gave me cause an extra buzz to sustain me. But we had to hurry out to practice no time to fool around so the three of us walked over to the training center and the heat today in Miami was no joke.

"Feels nice inside" I commented "It is one hot day"

"You are not lying" Sarah responded "Thank goodness for a/c"

"Meeting in 10 minutes" Jon reminded me

"I will be right back" I informed Sarah "It should nott last long"

"Sounds good" Sarah said as me and Jon headed to Dwayne's office

As we walked down the hall Jon stopped me for quick talk. What could this be about?

"You know I have a whole empty closet on the bus if you want to bring some things over" he offered "Not so much back and forth for you"

"Yea, I would really like that" I accepted "Thanks baby"

He then kissed me after the roundabout way of asking me to move in and we entered the meeting.

The Dog Pound was the A-list of elite wrestlers to have ever graced the ring. I felt almost unworthy because I was still new to the company but for the last couple of years, I would spend anywhere from 8-12 hours a day training on my own, with others, and with other trainers so I was fully committed to this dream. But I will not lie I was kind of nervous and exuberant hoping that everyone will except me. Very few people were chosen to join and that is why there is only four members of The Dog Pound including myself and Jon. We also had Neil "Kid Cosmo" who was clean cut, 5'6", high flying, high energy, performer with a finishing move called The Cosmic Kick and his ring gear matched his image perfectly. Then there was Mysterious Mike he was a powerhouse wrestler a big dude preferring to do his fighting on the mat he was 5'9" with a big black mohawk and ring gear that was all black besides the metal spike around his wrist and on his shoulders plus he wore a spiked collar around his neck and his finishing move was The Illusion. The announcers even played up his character by never saying where he was from nowhere, and it worked well pulling everyone in.

"Alright guys and gals" Dwayne said as he walked in

"This is Camille, you may know her a Miss Penny Lane" he introduced me "She is my new recruit"

Then he turned back looking at me and putting his hands on top of my shoulders

"We are the VIP of the elite" He said excitedly "You have made it Doll; how does it feel?"

"It feels damn great!" I said with a cheesy grin

This Thursday night during Knockdown we will be shooting a montage to get the audience hyped to see The Dog Pound and what antics we will be up to for the Hell Bound pay-per-view" Dwayne informed us "You all get together and come up with some fun ideas"

"Alright" all four of us agree

"See you later kiddos" Dwayne said as he walked out the door

"Great to have you with us" Neil said "been waiting to get a Goddess"

"Thanks Neil" I responded

"Yeah, it is about time you are captivating in the ring" Mike told me "And every little girl out there has your shirt on you are a good role model and will work perfectly with us"

"Oh, my goodness thanks I was so worried you all would not like the girl turn" I said

"Your one of us now" Neil told me

"All for one, one for all" Jon put in his two cents

Sounds like soon I will be having an awesome brain storming session with The Dog Pound. I am sure it will be an interesting learning moment. I sure felt magnificent having these well-respected warriors of this industry saying I was the VIP of the elite and being the only woman, he has taken under his wing. We all said our goodbyes and me and Jon walked out.

"So, what do you think?" Jon asked, "Was it all you thought it would be?"

"I thought it was stupendous" I responded "Thank you for all your help, Jon"

"No need to thank me" Jon explained "Dwayne does not get pressured into anything you did this all on your own"

"But you were the catalyst" I smiled "so how bout I thank you later"

"I would never turn you down" he smiled back "he does not typically take women, so he sees in you, what I see in you"

We walked onto the training floor with our hands clasped together. We were no longer going to hide what is blossoming between us. Jon was keeping it hushed because he did not want to see me attacked by the rumor mill. They are going to say I am untalented, fame chaser, or that I slept my way to the top. However, I figure go ahead and let them talk because if I know the truth and the people important to me know the truth then screw what anyone else says.

Me and Jon went our separate ways as he headed to spare with Steve, and I walked to my #1 girl Sarah.

"Hey chic-a-de" I said "How is everything with you and Steve"

"Absolutely amazing" she smiled happily "He is so sweet, kind, loving, and let us not forget hot"

"I am tickled pink to hear it" I said "No one deserves it more than you"

We talked a while as we put our hair up and got ready to start practice. And could converse as we trained because it made the time go by faster.

"Thanks Cammie" she said, "How about you and Jon?"

"He is kind-hearted, caring, fun, and does not care what anyone thinks" I bragged on my man "What else could I ask for with all my drama"

"Drew is drama, you know I have never been a fan" she responded "But with Jon oh girl you got lucky"

"Thank you, thank you" I bowed as we both chuckled

I was on cloud nine with my career and how it headed out into the stratosphere. I spent the last two years perfecting my talent, learning how to draw people in, and keep the crowd's attention. Whether they love you or hate you if they know your name, you are doing something right. I am just pleased that all my hard work is beginning to pay off. And getting to debut in a singles match one-on-one was huge opening for me because that did not happen to often for the women.

Me and Sarah fought a while practicing our moves because there is always room for improvement. However, our tag team reign was over for now because they wanted us for singles action which mean we may be going face-to-face one day soon.

"Hey Cammie" I turned to see Braedon trying to get my attention

"Can we talk a minute?" he asked "I will be quick"

"Sure, why not" I conceded leaning on the ropes "What is up?

"Look I do not want to tell you this" he admitted "but the guilt is eating away at me"

What in the heck could this be about? More drama I sure hope, not now that I am finally content for more than a few moments. Is he going to come and blow my world up again? Please let it be nothing to bad.

"Guilt" I repeated confused "or you trying to breakup me and Jon now"

"Extreme guilt" he continued "Remember when you caught Drew and Tweety?"

"How could I forget" I said sassy "It ruined my marriage"

"Me and Tweety set Drew up" he confessed "And I made sure you would see it"

"I thought you would fall into my arms" Braedon continued "I am really sorry"

Boy he could not have been more wrong. All I could was look at him because I have heard this information already. At one time this would have broken me but now it is only a bruise. What kind of person does it take to do such a disgusting thing? I said I am no body's fool but so far, I have been Drew's, Braedon's, and Tweety's. I feel like a fool right now, but I am not going to let it taint me and what is developing with Jon, all you can do is go in with blind trust and do not worry about it until there is a reason to. Spending time wondering only heavies the soul.

"I thought we were friends" I responded "But your just another asshole"

"I am ashamed and truly sorry" he pleaded "Forgive me"

"I forgive you, thank you for showing me the real Drew" I told him "This conversation is over"

I turned away feeling a bit more confident. So what if it was a setup he still fell for it and kissed the girl. It is too late now to change everything that has happened between now and then I do not regret what happened because it truly opened my eyes. And I surely cannot reverse my feeling for Jon. Having seen Drew clearly I wanted to watch him become his own man, yet he always had a pretty girl beside him making him a little less incomplete. And I want is someone who can walk beside with confidence and not lean on me as if I were their crutch. However, it is only fair to talk to Drew about this and Jon as well although I do not see this changing my mind.

CHAPTER 34

(1 year before)

Dear Diary,

I am busting at the seams to tell someone about this so here I go. Last week they had auditions for TWE and at the last minute I decided what the hell and went tried out. This was my second try, so I was not expecting much of anything besides another experience under my belt. But this morning out of the blue a Total Wrestling Entertainment (TWE) representative called to say they were interested in signing me to the Goddess roster. At first, I thought maybe they dialed the wrong number but once I realized this was for real, I was super excited. I will be flying out to Miami, Florida in a week where their head office and training center is. I do have to admit though that I am a bit nervous about seeing Drew again since finding out he had a girlfriend. I unlike him have not moved on with my love life quite yet because I was extremely focused on my career. It is going to be hard to say goodbye to my IWA family and will miss

*all the relationships I have made but it is time to take another
step up that ladder of success. It is all happening!!! Peace Out!!*

My life will soon be changing but in ways still staying the same.
Another motel room, another city, crowds going wild, living
life in the fast lane. May not sound like one's typical dream but this
was my rockstar dreams coming to fruition. The life of a rockstar and
life of a wrestler are very similar its hard work, travel, groupies, crazy
outfits, roadies, entertaining, and giving a piece of yourself with every
performance. So, if you want a nice quiet life professional wrestling is
not for you but it is absolutely for me.

Once upon a time I wanted the quiet calm life and got it when it
was me, Drew, and my sweet little Josephine. I felt like the luckiest
girl in the world, but it was not meant to last forever only a short time
because every fairytale has an ending. Yet, I would not change one
single second of it for anything in the world. I was rolling through those
happy memories in my mind when there was a knock on the door.

"Hey Frank" I said opening the door "I am glad you are here"

I hugged him hello he has been my main confidant since I came to
the International Wrestling Association (IWA). Frank is better known as
Captain Thunder who is a goofy, comical, and talented wrestler when
he is in the ring, you are sure going to get a laugh.

"Hello Cutie" he greeted me "What is the good news?"

"TWE just called" I said exuberantly "They want to sign me!"

"Congratulations! I knew you could do it" he responded "and to
think you did not want to go at first"

"Thanks for the congrats" I told him "And thanks for talking me
into it"

There were a couple of us from IWA that all traveled together to the
auditions in Miami. It was a long trip but well worth it and I am glad
that I did not quit trying even if it took some coercion because it paid
off big time. It was a group of five of us that went down there. It was
me, Frank, Johnny "Pretty Johnny", and "The Baker Boys" Adam and
Joel Baker. So far, I am the only on to get a call back, but I am keeping
my fingers crossed that someone else makes it too.

"So, when are you leaving?" he asked

"They want me there soon" I responded "Like next Thursday soon"

"Wow that is quick" he said "Good thing you do not have to pack"

"Yeah, the one-time owning nothing comes in handy" I laughed

This was the only time that living out of my luggage is a positive thing. Since starting with IWA, I did not have a chance to spend a lot of time at home in Louisiana and after visiting Drew at TWE I have not wanted to return because home did not feel like my home anymore. And why should it when every memory made in there included Drew who had stepped on my heart and made me feel worthless. It was not a place I wanted to be anymore. So, I stayed living out of motels here and there outrunning the memories of him leaving them behind me in the rearview mirror.

"What are you going to do about Drew?" Frank inquired

"Honestly, I have no idea" I admitted "I am trying not to think about it I want to stay positive"

And that was the truth I had no clue what to do or how things are going to go. Perhaps we will be like ships passing in the night and I will not have to face it anytime soon. I just hope my transition to TWE goes smoothly and the drama stays far away. I do not want him tainting this journey for me.

"I do not blame you" Frank said "Touchy subject"

"No problem" I responded "Do not worry about it"

I may be telling Frank not to worry about it but that does not mean I am not. Because the truth is I am fraught with worry. I am concerned with several things like how I will feel the first time I see Drew it has been such a long time. How will I act to seeing him possibly lovingly with someone who is not me? Will he acknowledge me or ignore me? What will I say if we bump into each other? I remember his icy words "out of sight out of mind" that was like ice water running through my veins giving me a cold chill just thinking of it. Once I am in his face and in plain sight constantly how will he react?

"You should let me throw you a goodbye party" Frank suggested

"No, no, no" I shook my finger" no party for me"

"Oh, come on Cammie" he insisted "Why not?"

"Because I am already sad that I am leaving you all" I answered "You all are like my family"

That was no lie I was going to miss the hell out of everyone because they really were like family, and I feel like I am abandoning them. But for me to be a dream chaser it is just what I must do and there is no way around it.

"You are our family whether you are with IWA or TWE" he said sincerely "You always have a home with us"

His sweet words that were so beautiful brought tears to my eyes. Home is one of those things you miss the most after being on the road for such a long time. It has been some time since I had a place to call my own. I believe people can take it for granted and underestimate the glory of having a permanent residence. Once I get settled in at TWE it is going to be a priority of mine to find a place in Miami to make into my temporary home. Somewhere I can lay my head each night, where I can put my unique touch, and have a closet for all my outfits and shoes. No more living out of luggage for me except for when I am on the road which is a lot but at least I will have a place I look forward to coming back to.

"Thanks Floyd" I said "You are a wonderful friend"

"I have only one request for you before you leave" he asserted "Let me take you out on a date"

I turned to face him with my do not go their glare. He knows I have not been on a date in years so why break my streak now?

"Just as friends I swear" Floyd continued "You definitely need the practice"

"Okay it is a deal" I relented "Just friends and you have to buy me flowers it is only proper"

"Yes mam" he laughed "Have to get you in shipshape for all those hunks you are about to meet"

I rolled my eyes and giggled this ought to be an interesting fake date. Maybe he is right about me needing to get a bit more experience under my belt before I go. And who better to share this experience with than a friend I am positive though that my dating skills are very rusty after gracing the singles scene for so long. I certainly do not plan on keeping that status because I crave a lover's touch and warmth of someone's skin upon mine. My streak may be ended by Drew or by a stranger only time shall tell but I am eager for it.

"Well cutie" Floyd said "it is time for me to head out"

"Okay" I replied "Bye, see you soon"

My life has changed many times and here I go about to modify it once more. I have gone through many transitions from child, teen, girlfriend, mom, fiancé, wife, professional wrestler and now this new revision will make me an elite wrestler. Everyone has different variations we must go through in life and all we can do is roll with the changes and get the most you can out of each revolution by learning and experiencing as much as possible. I am due a modern life and I am elated about this transformation that is coming. Time to turn the page and let this caterpillar morph into a butterfly.

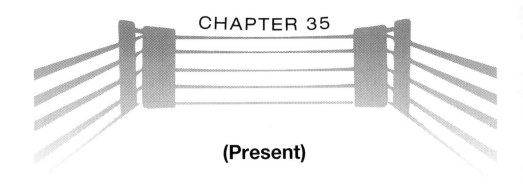

CHAPTER 35

(Present)

Dear Diary,

I cannot believe that Braedon came clean and admitted to me that him and Tweety set Drew up with the whole kiss scandal. But his confession is a day late and a dollar short because what is been done cannot be undone. Plus, I have been judging Drew on what he has been doing and he constantly has a girl on his arm which he swears is platonic (I do not really care either way), but it is not for the show its backstage to, and he will not play me this time. I grew up believing that hell was in a place below us, but hell fell upon my head with Drews cheating scandal. Yet, I rose from the flames like a phoenix and became a superior version of myself. However, I do think that is only right to tell Drew about this and see what he has to say. I am going in with no expectations and seriously doubt this will change anything but that is easy to say when were not face-to-face. Today's mission is to find and speak with Drew. And I absolutely believe the connection that me and Jon have made will be very hard to disconnect. Time to go see. Peace Out!

I hesitated as I pulled up near Drews apartment thinking that there is still time to turn and run away but I am no coward. If I am being honest with myself, I always get nervous when it comes to Drew because he knows me better than anyone else. Yet, I could be wrong because at one time I thought that I knew him better than anyone, but it turned out I did not know who he had become at all.

I walked up the stairs to apartment 12 and gave it a knock holding my breath almost hoping for him to not be home. But as luck would have it, he opened the door.

"Camille" Drew seemed a bit confused "What are you here for?"

"I need to talk to you" I informed him "I do not care if you have a girl here"

"Oh sorry" he apologized "Please come in"

I went in and had a seat on the couch where Drew sit next to me. There was still something invigorating between us that I felt in his presence. If I were to say I felt nothing I would be deemed a liar.

"What do you want to talk about?" he inquired

"I would like to talk in private" I said "If you know what I mean"

Drew dropped his head and let out a defeated sigh maybe I do know him better than anyone else because I am right on the money this time. Drew walked to his room then came back walking a scantily dressed Lucy Lawless to the door. I know her because she is a brand-new Goddess, so I do not hold her to blame in this situation, but I do him.

"Sorry Penny" the kind faced girl said to me

"Do not be, I am sorry for you" I gave her a smile

"We are alone" Drew said

"Me and Braedon had a conversation" I informed him "and he made a confession"

"A confession" he sounded perplexed

"He said that him and Tweety set you up" I repeated the story "and they made sure I would see"

"Those sickos I told you" He said angrily "Why? What for?"

"Braedon thought I would fall into his arms" I explained "and Tweety thought she could fall into yours"

"I was good with you by my side" he admitted "I just do not do lonely well"

"Yes, your right but that is a terrible excuse for cheating on me" I said sternly

I could see the fire burning in his blue eyes that have now glazed over in red. This could be bad for Braedon if he catches him while he is in this frame of mind.

"Please try to calm down sweet boy" I plead "They are not worth losing your career over"

"I blame them for losing you" he teared up

"You not getting comfortable with yourself with being alone is why you lost me" I said truthfully

"Your right Cammie" He relented "I except blame"

Shew, that was a close one because Drew has a temper and just explodes so it is nice to see he has grown enough to get his anger under control. This is one step closer into him turning into a man.

"Do you forgive me" he asked

"I forgave you a while ago" I replied "holding on to anger can make you bitter"

I forgave Drew a few days after being stuck in an exasperated haze. This was not what I wanted for my newfangled life in TWE so I forgave him in my heart where it would not weigh me down or darken my soul.

"I love you Camille I am going crazy without you" he said "these other girls are place holders for you"

"I do love you too Andrew, but I want a loyal life partner" I confessed "The sliver of hope you have is if you can stop depending on others and become the powerful, self-sustaining man that I know you can be with no placeholders just you"

I gently patted his chest atop his tattoo. Drew is kind and loving although I cannot say he is loyal. I am positive if he leaves all these women alone and works on himself, he can become the type of man I know he can be, even if he is not for me, he will be better for the next woman. I did love Drew, but I am not in love with him the feeling that should be there are evaporated been stepped on one-to-many times.

"I am going to show that I can be the man you need and want" he said confidently

"Even then you may not get me back "I admitted "I cannot wait to meet the new and improved you"

I smiled at him and patted his knee. Why did I do that? Force of habit perhaps keep your boundaries Cammie because you know for a fact that Drew is your weakness, I reminded myself.

"Just a parting kiss" he begged

"Do not give me those eyes" I begged "I cannot do it"

"I know where not together" Drew told me "Can we take things slow"

"You have to understand "I explained to Drew "I am seeing Jon"

"I understand" He replied "I just want a fighting chance"

"I gave you chance after, chance after, chance" I said irritated "and you still had Lucy here on one of your chances do you not know how it hurts me"

I hope that none of this drama messes up anything between me and Jon because my feelings for him are growing and he has been the perfect gentleman through it all. But take it from me no one is perfect we all have our faults and scars that make us who we are.

"I always adored you still do" I asserted

I stood to leave as Drew followed me to the door. He hugged me and went in for another kiss I turned my head. I knew his kiss was nice, familiar, and comfortable but far from electric. They are such different people Drew is conventional while Jon is an inferno. I buried my head in Drew chest to take in his scent as I use to which has remained unchanged. I felt I need to do that since this is likely the last time.

"I got to go" I said

"Bye pretty girl" hey smiles

"Bye sweet boy" I smiled back

I pulled out of the parking lot then made my way to Jon's bus in silence giving myself a chance to clear my mind. Jon already knew what I was doing, and I was going to be honest with him about everything. I do not like to keep secrets because they will chip away at your foundation, and I prefer to keep my feet planted firmly on the ground. I walked on the bus and immediately heard Jon.

"How did it go" he pried as I walked in

"As we thought" I reported "He has it in his head he can get me back"

"Being that he was set up do you ever consider giving him another try" Jon asked

"No, that was never the real problem" I said "It is his dependency on women that did it and I am not sharing my man"

"Perfect example" I told Jon "When I got there, he had a half-naked Lucy Lawless in his bed"

Drew has been up and down the women's roster more than once when I was not around and while I am around, so he has no one to blame but himself. When we got back together, we said the past is the past, but little did I know the past was surrounding us so yes something as petty as a kiss set up or not, it takes two, can put me over the edge.

"He always had a woman" Jon commented "whether Goddess, roadie, or groupies even"

"I told him he needed a break from dating and work on himself" I explained "to become self-reliant his excuse I do not do lonely well"

"I hope he heeds your advice" Jon said "because he is burning a lot of bridges"

"I have an admission" I confessed "He wanted to be kissed"

"Cannot say I like it, but you are not tied down yet" he told me "How did it feel?"

"I have no idea I obviously said no" I told him "I mean look what I have waiting at home for me"

"I figured that just giving you a hard time" He smirked

"Speaking of home if you were buying your dream home" he asked "What would be on the list"

"Large kitchen, jacuzzi tub, outdoor kitchen, and definitely a pool "I remarked" But in all honesty I would be happy with a small house, picket fence, and large yard. If it is a place to call my own, I would be happy."

"Honestly Jon any place I could call home is a dream to me" I made sure he knew that

"I have something for you" Jon told me

He pulled a large box out of his pocket and open it. Inside was a beautiful white gold necklace with a heart adorned with diamonds and the matching earrings. On the back of the heart was engraved Jonathan and Camille with today's date. I was so special to me that it struck me speechless and teared me up making me emotional.

"Camille, will you be my girlfriend" he smiled wide

"Yes" I shook my head as he put the necklace on me

"Only my kissing now"

This feels like a fantasy with Jon the past six months have been full of bliss. I love the way Jon can look past everyone and everything and see just me nothing else. And even knowing what happened with Drew today he still wanted me as I wanted him. With Jon I have trust we can go out and do things separately then comeback together as one. There is a freedom in this relationship I have never experienced before. No one has ever made me feel the way he does. I am now an officially taken woman.

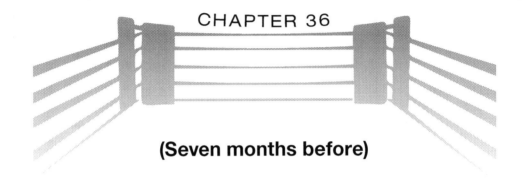

CHAPTER 36

(Seven months before)

I decided I would drive the two-day trip to Miami because I would need my car to get around town and do not want to be stuck taking the bus. I was exhausted but as soon as I saw the Welcome to Miami sign, I was reinvigorated. I felt as if I were on top of the world and I am eager to see what TWE is going to be like. I set my GPS and followed the directions right to the TWE Training Canter. The one thing I am going to have to get used to is the Miami traffic man is it something.

As I walked into the training center, I saw the handful of new recruits and we all looked bright eyed a bushy tailed for now. As I stood there taking in the sights looking around a beautiful tall blonde woman walked up to me.

"Come join us" She invited me "Were all new too"

"Thanks" I said "by the way I am Cammie"

"Sarah, nice to meet you" She introduced herself

I joined the group and we all exchanged pleasantries while waiting on our unknown coach. I am holding my breath waiting to see who we will be learning from. Then a familiar face from the television walked in. It was Timothy "Turbo" Johnson, and he was a legend in the business. He has been here over 30 years, won every belt, and was super talented. Once a year TWE has their main pay-per-view event Wrestle Madness and Turbo has a winning streak because he has never lost at the Wrestle Madness in what will be 28 years this year if he wins.

"Welcome to Total Wrestling Entertainment everyone" he greeted us "call me Tim"

"There are two things you need to begin" Tim said "a memorable name and a stunning finisher"

Thank goodness I have those two things down or at least I think I do guess I will find out soon.

"Everyone partners up" he commanded "Practice your finishers"

Me and Sarah quickly teamed up considering we were the only girls. At least she seems cool to work with.

"Sarah" Tim called "What is you stage name?"

"Sensational Sarah" she responded

"And your finisher?" he asked

"Killer Legs" She answered

"Camille what is your stage name" he asked

"Miss Penny Lane" I answered

"Interesting" he responded "Finisher?'

"The Peace Out" I told him

"Now you girls show me what you got" he said

Tim observed us in the ring and had us do our finishing moves which he approved of thank goodness. He then gave us some advice on how to bring our wrestling up to the next level.

"You ladies keep that up" he said proudly "and you will be introduced one-on-on"

That was what every Goddess hopes for. I hope he really saw something in us, and it was not just a rouse to get us to try harder. We shall see.

"You guys are letting these ladies outshine you" he laughed

We fought for the next few hours getting tip, practicing climbing the ropes, walking into the ring, kicks, hits, and a little bit of everything.

"Congrats everyone" Tim announced "Welcome to TWE see you tomorrow"

"You want to join me for a bite to eat" Sarah asked me "I am starving"

"Me too" I responded "Let us go"

We went to the locker room to change out of our workout clothes and into something comfy like our jeans and crop tops. The difference between us was our footwear I had on my Doc Martin boots and Sarah slid on her black high heels that complimented those long legs. She is much classier than me, but we get along great, and it feels like I have known her forever.

We decided to go to Calvin's Cabana that one of the guys suggested. Walking in there was a Caribbean vibe to the place with matching the decorations and music. I glanced around and saw lots of wrestlers that I knew from watching them on tv which does them no justice. Their even better looking in person. We had a seat and looked over the menu.

"How did you like today" I asked Sarah

"It was splendid I auditioned six times before I made it" she explained "So, I am not taking any of it for granted"

"I hear that" I replied "I got lucky made it on my second try"

One thing I know for sure about Sarah now is that she is not one to give up easily. Having auditioned 6 times and keeping the faith going back time after time says a lot about her character.

"I left my boyfriend behind" she said "I wanted to come here with a clean slate"

"I am perpetually single by choice, so I just grabbed my two bags and hit the road" I said "I bet you do not stay single long"

"Where are you staying?" Sarah asked

"Hotel" I answered "until I can find my own spot"

"Well, I found a two-bedroom apartment near the training center" she explained "Would you consider a roommate?"

"I think that would be awesome" I said "and that is another thing to mark off my list"

First day and I have met all the newbies, got tips from Turbo, made a friend, and found a place to stay. What a massive day it has been for me. I am thrilled that Sarah suggested being roomies because now I can create a transitory home and I will never have to wonder where I am going to lay my head when I am in Miami. I think me and Sarah are going to make great friends.

"Can I take your order" the waitress asked

"I'll have a chicken Caesar salad and water with lemon" I ordered

"Make that two" Sarah requested "Got to keep our figures"

We laughed but we both knew that was the honest to God truth. Although the company will not come right out and say it there are other things they can do. If they think you are getting chunky, they will start messing with you by writing you up for frivolous things. Giving you bad storylines and make your life miserable until you slowly fade away. They like their Goddesses fit and firm, but I believe every woman regardless of her size was beautiful. However, we go into it with our eyes wide open to the situation.

"Wow, Miami is beautiful" Sarah said as our food came

"Yes incredibly" I said

The longer I am in the Miami air the more comfortable and laid back I become. The spirit of a new life is a delightful thought, but I still feel apprehensive about seeing Drew again. From what I hear from mutual friends is Drew lives in an apartment and has a fill-in girlfriend every weekend and they change like the days. I just do not get how you can go from a faithful married man to a cheating man hoe. However, I do not want my day ruined by him because I am over the moon in high spirits today.

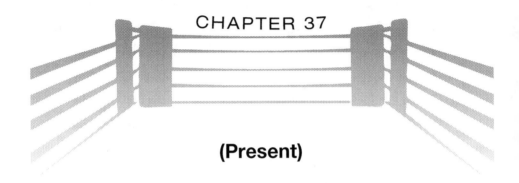

CHAPTER 37

(Present)

Dear Diary,

Sorry, I have not written in such a long it has just been busy but that is a positive thing. Me and Jon are officially girlfriend and boyfriend which I dare say sounds a little childish, but I personally love the labels because it lets me know right where I stand. Jonathan is on the hunt for a house in Miami and he asked me to move with in with him. I said yes which was an easy choice because we have been practically living together the last few months. Plus, I must admit that having a real place to call home again sounded like a daydream coming to life. The houses he showed me had huge bright kitchens, large closets, jacuzzi tubs, two-stories, and a pool right out of my dreams. The only worry I have is these homes are pricy and I want to contribute what I can. Jon is the face of TWE so has a contract over a million whereas Goddesses typically start out at 100,000 a year. I do not want Jon to think I am using him and told him I would be just as happy with him in a small home with a yard, but he was not having it. Drew is not enthused by any of this, but he has made his own bed and he must lie in it. Got to get going! Peace Out!!

"**2**0 minutes baby girl" Jon called out
"Coming" I walked to the front of the bus "We have time"
I smiled and sat on his lap putting my arms around him and nibbled on his neck.

"You are a naughty girl you" he smirked "I love it"

His red-hot lips had my blood sizzling and give me an appetite that only he could fill. My body gets tense awaiting his electrifying touch that charges me all over. He was absolutely intoxicating, and I have felt the rush inside our bodies that covers it with goosebumps. Yet, I knew it was time to go and finish what we started when we get back on our road home.

"I was thinking about when we get back to Miami" Jon said "We can go look at some places"

"Okay I give" I relented "But I am still going to think its way expensive"

"Forget the money" he pleaded "Everyone deserves a home especially you baby girl"

"Our home sweet home" I smiled "with a cute little pug puppy"

"That is a yes woohoo!" he said exuberantly "And I only had to promise a pug"

He picks me up swinging me around in a circle. The joy on his face warmed my heart and I am delighted and appreciative for Jon's warm heart. Love through action I finally understood what that meant. You do not have to give gifts or anything else just give of yourself to the one you love in small ways like opening a door, pulling out a seat, looking in her eyes, and wanting to make them happy forever. It is the things that cost nothing that mean the most.

Walking towards the auditorium we passed a gathering of groupies that followed TWE from location to location. The whole group made googly eyes at us wishing they were one of us or with one of us. It blows my mind to think Drew hooked up with a few of them making their dreams come true as he killed his.

"Do you ever feel like piece of artwork?" I asked Jon "Always being gawked at"

"You are a work of art baby" he responded

"What am I going to do with you" I laughed

"Everything" he said with a sexy tone lifting his eyebrows with that look in his eyes.

Walking through the backdoors Jon gave me a smooch before we parted to go do our own things like two adults should be able to trustingly do. Coming towards me in the hall I saw Sarah who I hugged hello.

"What is the news?" She asked "Never seen you shine so bright"

"I am an officially taken woman" I said showing her my necklace.

"Damn girl" she responded "I am so happy for you and proud of you"

"Thank you, Sarah," I asked, "How is your love life?"

"Steve wants me to move in with him" She informed me "Not mad, are you?"

"No that was our temporary home" I told her "Time to find out where we belong permanently"

The both of us had our make-up done and ring gear on ready to go because I knew it was a busy night tonight. I must escort Drew to the ring for a main match and film a montage. All in a night's work. Me and the rest of The Dog Pound crew came up with different scenarios then we told Dwayne about them, and he puts it together making something creative and entertaining. Dwayne also told me tonight that I was no longer going to be Drews side chick and wrote in the montage that there will be a fight against Drew and Titan winner gets the girl. I must say that I was not at all disappointed because I knew I had grown out of being a ring escort and with Dwayne things were going to happen in my career. He gives you the chance then it is up to you to grab it.

I took pleasure in walking around backstage and of course I love Kraft Services. Yummy. I like talking to my coworkers and the roadies because they work so hard for us, and it is nice making new friends.

"Hey Cams" Clarence one of the roadies called "How you been"

"Hey Clarence, I am good thanks" I responded

I headed to the women's locker room to put the finishing touches on Miss Penny Lane and chat a little with the girls.

"Hello ladies" I said walking in

"Cammie" Barb E Dahl ran over to me giving me a happy hug

"I heard you are in The Dog Pound now" she said

"Yes mam" I admitted "I am quite enlivened"

"You are the first female to make it in" she commented "You have to turn it up and represent for all of us"

"Thanks Barb" I smiled "Promise I will 100%"

"I am proud of you" she responded "Represent!"

Barb hugged me again before leaving the area

I continued talking amongst the Goddesses about different championships, story lines, who is fighting who, men, and a bit of this and that when Tweety walked in clearing the room with her poisonous presence. I no longer allow her the ability to get to me at all.

"So, you think your better than everyone now?" she tried to start with me

"Hell no" I said "There are plenty of talented women here"

"You are a liar" she pushed

"You are a whore" I pushed back

"Maybe so" she said "Maybe I will be Jon's whore"

"He keeps the garbage outside" I left her with those words

I rolled my eyes with a laugh then left the room. I was done with listening to the venom she was spitting. Let her go ahead and embarrass herself which I am sure she will, but Jon is not Drew and it was going to take something more than her to sway Jon away.

Then walking down, the hallway I got a huge surprise when I felt a tap on my shoulder and turned to find a friendly faced Laura standing there.

"Oh my gosh" I said beaming "What are you doing here"

"I wanted to surprise you" she said smiling "I missed my best friend"

"I am so glad you are here" I hugged her tightly

It has been quite a few years since I have seen Laura, so this was completely unexpected and a little odd, but I am pleased to have her here.

"Where is Drew?" she asked "I cannot wait to see him"

"Not sure" I answered "We are not together anymore"

"Why?" she inquired

"Chronic cheating" I said "but we are still friends, I can always find him"

"That would be awesome" she said glowing "I love you Cammie"

Her and Drew were never super close, so it was weird to see her so over the moon about seeing Drew. Could she have had a crush on him this whole time and is now free to unleash it? Anything is possible I suppose. Tonight, has now gotten even more cramped for me so I needed to find Drew asap to drop her off and I can get to work. But Laura has done lots for me over the years and this is the least I can do for her. Laura felt like what home use to be. All the beautiful memories we made growing up, our special spot, and how good she was with Josie. I smiled feeling a warmth wash over me in a fog of happy memories.

"Hey baby" Jon walked up hugging from behind.

"Hello sexy" I replied turning in his arms for a swift kiss

"This is Laura" I introduced them "and this is my boyfriend Jon"

They exchanged pleasantries then Jon ran off since he had a busy one tonight as well.

"Damn Cammie" she smiled "That boy is fine"

"I think he is dreamy" I responded

We both laughed I felt like a teen again with him so many new feelings and emotions I have never felt before but on a mature level. However, I had a mission find Drew and I had a hunch of where he would be which is Kraft Services because he likes to eat and flirt. Bingo I was right there he was at the table with Wendy. I wonder if he is still out there hobbling on one leg or standing on his own two feet.

"Andrew looked who I found" I told him

Drew jumped up hugging Laura

He invited her to join him, and they both looked happy as their conversation flowed. My senses are telling me Laura likes Drew more than friends and who knows maybe she would be good for him. But what is it made her come now is there a hidden agenda or am I just paranoid when it comes to people from my past?

"Are you here to kick me out again?" she asked wearily

"No, I am sorry about that it was important" I explained

"If you and Drew choose to be together, I am cool" I said "It is your lives and has nothing to do with me"

"Thank you" she perked up "I really admire you and your talent"

Wendy was a recruit and seemed like a good girl so I cannot blame her for not understanding all the drama that she is on the outskirts of. And since she is a fangirl, she may be dating Drew only because I did. That would be Karma at its finest.

As me, Drew, and Laura stepped into the not so brightly lit hall I saw a familiar shadow at the other end of the hall. I blinked my eyes trying to clear my sight so I could see what I thought was the appearance of a ghost from the past as if I was not paranoid enough. The presence stood there his gaze not leaving me. I grabbed Drew and showed him what I have seen his face went pale. Was this an illusion? Am I losing it? Could it be?

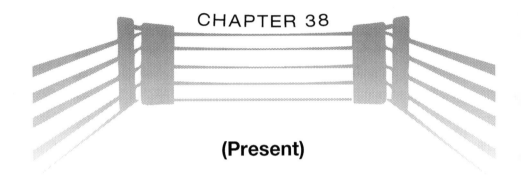

CHAPTER 38

(Present)

As I took a few steps forwards to get a closer look and keeping my distance from this mystery man in whose presence we all felt a little skittish and on edge. The way I see it is we are either in a shared delusion or we are simply making something out of nothing but perhaps its somewhere between the lines. Maybe this whole thing is beyond our understanding, and it is weird why Laura is here? Could she have anything to do with all this? Is her reasoning good or evil? What are her true intentions? It must have something to do with Laura because this is more than just a coincidence.

I thought that when we moved forward, he would back up, but I was totally wrong as he stood there statuesque almost awaiting our arrival.

Me and Drew remained silent as we spoke through our eyes as we have for years. Drew grabbed my hand squeezing tightly as I could feel his trembling. I need to get a grip of myself there is no way this could be true Joseph is dead, in the ground, and buried I was there for the whole thing. It destroyed the life I had then. I could see the wheels turning in Drews head as he pulled me near him. If this is what we think it is, then Laura has something to do with it.

"Friend or foe we must know" I said

"I am with Cammie" Drew backed me

"We should not bother the man" she said sternly with grit in her voice

"What do you know about this?" I accused her tired of playing games

We looked at Laura with discontent awaiting the answer to a question she never planned on answering.

"Wow the dynamic duo rides again" she pouted

"What did you do to him?" I asked angrily

"He was lost I found him and brought him home a long time ago" she answered

We are never going to get answers from her" Drew said furious

I pushed Laura aside as we walked reunited to get some answer to our questions. I got weak in the knees when we stood eye to eye making me woozy as if I was going to pass out. My body turned cold with a shiver we had not been mistaken we were right on point. I had so many questions floating through my head now what, when, were, and most importantly how.

We all stood there with tear filled eyes, but no one seemed to know how to break the ice.

"Hey, Joey, do you remember what we did every time we saw each other" I asked

He smiled a huge grin then waived his hand to say come on.

So, I took a step back ran to him and jumped in his arms hugging him as if we were 16 again.

"Joey babe what happened?" I asked "We were told you were dead"

"She happened to me" he pointed to Laura who joined us

"The evil queen I knew it, it is all been an act all these years" I said emotional

"Come on Joey" Laura barked "It is time to go back home"

My gut reaction was to jump in front of her because I was not going to let her get her grubby hands on my Joey. I will break her arms if she tries that again even though I am missing most of the story.

"Get away from him" I said forcefully pushing her back

"Your pathetic Camille" Lara insulted "holding onto a childhood love affair"

"No, what pathetic is using Joey as a pawn in your sick plan" I ranted "and thinking he could ever fall in love with you PA...THET...IC"

"You better hurry you are going to jail" I told her "And the police are on the way"

And with those magic words, which are a lie, poof she was gone just like that. I am curious to get all the details from Joey later so we can know the entire story and how this went on for so many years. We explained to Joey that the show was nearing the start and explain to Joey that we had to go to work but he was just as important to us. But Joey was cool with it he understood because he has been watching on tv from day one. Drew asked Joey to move in with him and move into the extra bedroom of his apartment which brough a smile to Joeys face. We agreed to meet him there afterwards and sent him with a roadie that would stand guard because you can never underestimate a crazy chick.

A blaze of fireworks went off announcing the beginning of Thursday Night Knockdown.

Drew is doing the second match tonight, so we have a little while to wait and think. I do not understand how every time my life seems to be going smoothly and I am genuinely happy when someone comes by and throws a grenade into my universe. How do I even explain this to Jon? I mean what is to say besides in my life sometimes people come back from the dead. It just all sounds ridiculous it is too much for me so I can only imagine how he will take it. Will this be his breaking point? Please no.

"Ready Drew" I encouraged him "get your head in the game"

I am happy now that Dwayne could not get my escort axed out for tonight, but it would be my last. We walked to the entryway ready to support Drew and root him on I tapped his tattoo and prepared myself to not get one back, but I did and smiled. His music played and we went in giving it our all as we always did. But with all that had happened, which is a lot for anyone to take no matter how tough you are, I felt like I was in a more robotic mode making sure I hit each que and played my part to the tee.

Next, I made my way down to The Dog Pound to wait with them to cut the promo for Hell Bound as I updated John on what I knew so far.

"This gets too much for me" I said "So, if it gets too much for you, I will understand"

"No way baby girl! You cannot get rid of me that easy" he smiled "you can have ghost, zombies, aliens, and vampires to its all good I am a warrior"

He gave me a much-needed laugh. He somehow always knows how to cheer me up. I feel blessed having him as my better half.

As the promo started, we read our lines throwing in a few adlibs. We were clashing against The Misfits who were the arch enemies of our crowd. We were the good guys, the faces, the defenders, and they were the bad guys, heels, destroyers. I was excited to get the last line of the promo it is me holding up a peace sign saying, "Rest in Peace". We would be facing off soon at Hell Bound for the Goddess Championship and I found the whole thing enthralling.

"One thing I am a little nervous and do not know what is going on could you come with me" I asked Jon "I will feel safer" I asked

"Sure, thing baby" he said kissing me

How could we be so wrong, about something so big, for so long. It was baffling. And We had no way of knowing what we were about to hear and if Joey had a decent life or unhappy one.

"I never saw this one coming" Drew said

"Neither of us did" I agreed "I just do not understand"

"That makes two of us" he said "Hopefully we get some answers"

Walking in we saw him sitting on the couch he appeared to be thinking and nervous, so we took a seat beside him.

"Before I begin Bro, I want you to know I missed you "Joey poured his heart out "I felt like I lost a piece of me"

"Cammie my forever love not having you was like being on the verge of drowning it hurt so bad, but was always revived to drown again" Joey told me from his heart

"I felt the exact way" Drew responded

"A part of me died with you that night" I told him

"This is what really eats at me and gets me the angriest is that she hurt the two people I loved by doing all this" He said fiercely "you two"

"What happened to you?" I questioned

When we got in the wreck, there was a John Doe that had just died in the car wreck, I killed him, I was in a coma, but Laura had a hand in it she switched our paperwork. I was a John Doe until she came in a few days later claiming she was my wife Mrs. Boyd, and I was then Bobby Boyd. So, as far as anyone knew Joseph McEnrowe was dead and Bobby Boyd was in a coma. She had devious plans I was in the coma for three months and had the hospital convinced she was the best wife in the world. Once she got me to her home it was like a prison no way to get out without a key. Then she told me both of you had died in the accident it destroyed me. To live with the knowledge that I had killed my twin brother and my forever love was too much for me to bear" He took a deep breath "I became the one thing I swore I never would I became my father"

"The only reason I can think she did this because she thought I would love her because she told me every day about how she loved me and if I would make a life with her, I could be happy and free, but it could never happen I despised her. Not even drunk could I pretend to love her" Joey finished

"Tell me how your lives are going?" he asked

"I have some information that is going to upset you are you prepared to hear it?" I informed Joey

"After we got in the wreck the doctor told me I was pregnant with your daughter. We named her Josephine after you, but she was a sickly child and passed away a few years ago. My parents threw me out as soon as they found out I was with child. And Drew stepped in taking care of me than us. Me and Drew ended up getting married, but we recently separated" I told him everything.

"She really did steal my whole life I would have been your husband and a father" Joey wept

"Yes, I am so sorry babe" I reached out holding his hand crying with him

"How did you find us?" Drew asked

"Television I kept saying that The Crazy Cajun looked just like Drew, but she convinced me otherwise however once I saw Miss Penny Lane, she could fool me no longer I would never forget the face of my girl. So, I came to find you two".

"Cammie, can we talk in private in my room" Joey asked

"Sure" I said following him to his room

"Can I ask you something personal" he inquired

"Yes" I answered "I am an open book"

"Why are you and Drew separated?" he asked

"Because he cheated on me" I admitted "a number of times"

"I am so sorry Cammie" he apologized "He is an idiot to let you go"

"I know you would not have" I agreed "You have an independence that he does not"

Joseph has grown up to be a gentleman and still has that loving and caring vibes that always pulled me to him. I hope being held captive for so long has not messed him up in any way but you cannot go through something like that unscathed. I am angry with Laura for having taken a good man from his family, his daughter, his brother, and me. She has also ruined futures that we will always be second guessing if this was truly supposed to be our futures.

Joey lowers his head into his hands and began crying. I walked toward him and had a seat on his lap giving him a long hug that he needed to get all these emotions out. I gently pushed his hair back revealing his shiny blue eyes I use to get lost in. But even sitting here with Joey I still cannot get Jon far away from my mind.

"I never would have treated you like that" he told me "No one on this planet can touch you"

"I believe you babe" I replied

"Though I did not act like it I loved you the moment I met you" he said sincerely

"Really? Me too," I admitted

"When did you stop loving me?" he asked

"Never" I admitted "but I believed you were gone, I grieved for months, wished they had taken me with you, but I was about to have a child, and I had to move on"

I put my arms around him hugging him with loving and longing putting my forehead against his wanting to kiss him, but I had set my boundaries I am Jon's woman now. Joey always made me feel safe and carefree and I wanted him to feel that again. I wanted to remember how his presence, how he smelled and how he made me feel after I thought I would never see him again. It broke my heart when I thought he passed, and I eventually dealt with that, and this was just our final goodbye to love.

"I have something that should know" I told Joey "I have a boyfriend"

"Who?" he inquired

"Jonathan he came with us" I replied

"Whoa the face of TWE" he looked amazed "Do you love him?" he asked

"I am trying to figure everything out" I answered "A lot has gone on"

Did I just lie by saying I was not in love with Jon or was I worried about hurting Joey further whether I am or not, he should be the first to know? I walked to the front.

"Bye guys" I kissed them on the cheeks "I have to go"

As soon as I got on the other side of the door I jumped straight into his arms.

"Well, that takes the pressure off" he said "I thought you may be dumping me"

"I did figure one thing out" I informed Jon

"What is that?" he asked

"I realized that I am head over heels in love with you baby"

"Good because I am head over heels in love with you too?" He retorted

And there on the twin's doorstep our lips locked as Jon held me deeply in his kiss with hearts in our eyes.

"Let us go home a celebrate" he suggested

"What are you waiting on I am in your arms" I smirked

Getting all hot and bothered I could not wait to get him into our room where I can come in and pop the top off a bottle of wine. But before that I want to get a chance to seduce him and dive into his web of desires. Time to get the leather out. The games have just begun!

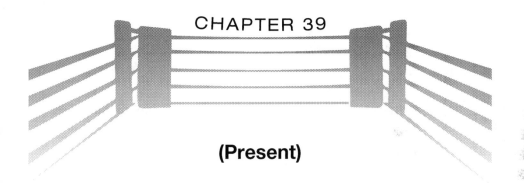

CHAPTER 39

(Present)

Dear Diary,

He loves me he really loves me! When I told Jon I loved him I never expected to hear it back, but I did. For the first time in a long time my heart felt whole, and I thought I would never feel that again. I am also glad to have found out that Joey is alive after being kidnapped and held captive by Laura of all people for years, breaking out, and making his way to find us. Drew and I are in a good place, but I worry about Joey having a hard time considering he has been waiting on me all these years to find me unavailable. Had I been single knowing me I would have given him a fair chance, but it just was not in the cards. I do love him; I am just not in love with him our love has run its course. What is best for Joey now is for him to find what it means to be a free man and get on with his life. I have been hesitant to divorce but I know now is the time. Thanks for the talk. Peace Out!!

"Good morning my love" Jon said "That feels good on my tongue" "Morning baby love" I said back "Your right but that is not all that feels right"

Jon smiled rubbing his fingers across my unclothed body making me squirm.

"You are so beautiful" He commented

"You are the sexiest man I have ever laid eyes on" I told him

I reached over to kiss his bare chest as we lovingly touched, kissed, and enjoyed each discovery.

"I never thought I was the settling down type" he told me "That is until I met you"

"Oh, baby that is so sweet" I replied

"You ready to go see the place?" he asked "if you do not like it, we can move right on"

"I am sure I will love it!" I said jovial

I got dressed and ready to hit the road and see where the car takes me, I am so anxious and excited at the same time. Jon seemed to really love this house he is showing me so I am positive I will love it just as much. The one thing I do know is Jon is a proud Samoan man and will have at least four bedrooms for the big family he may want one day, and I may as well. In my eyes the only thing better than being a Wrestling Goddess is being a mother. We pulled into the driveway of a large two-story grey bricked home with green stucco on the pillars and charming front porch accessorized with a swing on the two-story home. I was in awe at the beauty of the outside it was not too big it was just right for our future, and I have not even seen the inside yet.

"Is the silence good" he asked

I shook my head yes and we both smiled as we walked in the large modern open kitchen with all stainless-steel appliances, gas ovens, and stove top, including a stylish island where we could sit, have meals, or just gather around. There was so much natural light it was hard not to be happy. The Fireplace went all the way up the wall, and I was already thinking how to decorate the mantle, there was a fully finished basement with a kitchenette and bathroom of its own, there were also tons of places where I could put my touch on things in this 4-bedroom 4-bath mini palace in my eyes. The stairs were breath taking like something

I would cherish the kind of steps you watch your daughter walk down with her prom or wedding dress on. And the master bedroom was huge with room for everything, the master bath had a shower and Jacuzzi tub good to soak in, double vanities, a dressing room and big walk-in closet. But the best was outdoors where there was an outdoor kitchen, fire pit, jacuzzi, and a stunning swimming pool with a rock waterfall. This was above perfection to me.

When we were outside, I ran jumping into Jon's arms and kissing his face all over.

"I take it you like it" he laughed seeing my joy

"I love it, but I love you more" I told him "One question because it is important to me"

"Ask me anything baby doll" he responded confidently

Me and Jon have talked about having a life together before, but we never approached the subject of kids directly and such so since were past the serious mark I must ask. So, here goes nothing.

"Do you want a family with me?" I asked, "If yes what timeframe are you looking at?"

"I am so relieved you want a family, and I am ready whenever you are because it will affect your career you should have the say so on when" he said honestly

"The best career in the world is being a mom" I responded "where not ones to play it safe anyhow"

"How did I get lucky enough to find the woman of my dreams "Jon said rhetorically

He pulled me in holding my hips and kissing me with a hunger before leaving me with prickles all over my skin. Then he pulled a keychain out of his pocket holding it up.

"Welcome home lo'u alofa" he said happily

"What does that mean?" I smiled

"Welcome home my love" he answered

"Teach me another word" I posed

"Okay" he agreed "Lo'u fatu my heart"

"Lo'u alofa my love" I repeated "Lo'u fatu my heart"

Jon smiled as he opened a bottle of wine popping the top and pouring me a glass. Always the cavalier.

"You constantly amaze me" he spoke "you are so bold, brave, and strong its quite endearing I have never had such a connection to anyone before"

People have been categorizing me my entire life, but I have never had someone see me in this light. Finally, someone that sees through all the BS and can see the real me. I believed once that Drew saw the real me but now it seems more like he saw through me instead of at me.

"I feel the same way about you" I admitted "And I cannot believe this is really ours"

"I got you a housewarming gift" he told me handing me a present

I opened the box and found an old fashion style sign that said Camille's Kitchen on it. It was just my style and thought it was the perfect first gift.

"I love it" I replied "it is perfect, and I actually have a kitchen now its mind blowing"

I looked over at Jon placing my leg over his and kissed him. I could still see the hunger that he never lost from earlier. He picked me up setting me on the island as he softly pushed up my lime green sundress puling it over my head and to the floor as he was running his hand along my legs and thighs as he kissed me from my collarbone to my cleavage nibbling sensually here and there leaving not a single part of my body untouched. I took his shirt off throwing it to the kitchen floor and trailing my way up chest and back letting him feel my carnal desire. He was like the air that I breathed, and I inhaled him in. He tasted so sweet I hungered for more of his kisses, his touching, his skin bare upon mine. His skin rubbing against mine felt like it was going to set me a blaze. I could feel our soul meshing together as each touch brought us closer to our climax. When we came together, I could swear I felt the house shake because the energy between us was atomic. We both moaned in ecstasy and elation. Now that is how you break-in a home.

"Lo'u fatu" I said placing my hand atop his heart

"Lo'u fatu" Jon said mirroring my movement and shaking his head in agreement

Falling in love is like lightning through your veins, jumping straight into the deep end because you know you will have air and you have nothing left to fear. The more you sink into it the more comfortable and warming it gets. And it is not just saying I love you it is more than words its love in action. I have been in love three times in my life but the first two I fell in love with long ago when I was young and with Jon this third time it is all new to me and I am more mature about the process than I have been before. I came into it with my eyes wide open and want to watch the story as it unfolds in front of me. I think I have found my true soulmate.

"What your plans for today?" Jon questioned

"Joey wants to have an early dinner" I responded "he wants to get some pictures of Josie from me and have me tell him more about her"

"Alright love if you need me call" He told me "I am going to go to hit the gym awhile"

"I will meet you there in a couple hours" I assured him

Jon walked me out to the car opening the door for me then I watched him climb up into his truck before leaving. I love my new house, I love Jon, and I love, love. But love often terrifies me at times. Love has beat me up, bruised me, and left me for dead yet it never hit me hard enough to keep me down. But it does not lesson my first two relationships. Now here I am faced off with love and finally feel that it is becoming one with me instead of fighting me.

Driving up to Aucoin's Seafood Shack I spotted Joey standing outside awaiting my arrival.

"Hi Joey" I greeted him with a wave

"Hey Cammie" he hugged me "you are looking beautiful"

"Awe thanks" I said "you always were the charmer"

We walked into the restaurant dressed casually changed into some jeans, sunflower crop top, and yellow heels. Joey and I sat across the table from one another. It is amazing that even though they were separated for so long how much they still mirrored each other in looks, dress, and demeanor. They were identical twins, so it does not take a rocket scientist to figure out the reason. I do not know why I found it so fascinating, but I did.

I laid out a couple picture on the table of the family and Josie I could look at her little face forever.

"She looks like her mom" he proudly boasted

"But she had her dad's attitude" I laughed

Joey's eyes lit up at my comment as he stared down holding the picture

"I wish I could have met her" he said with eyes watering.

I reached across the table and wiped his tears away.

"I wished that then and I still wish it now" I said "I am sorry"

"Do not blame yourself Cammie" he commented "There is no way you could have known"

"I always told her about you and kept a picture of you and me in the living room and on her bedside table" I told him "She called you her daddy in heaven"

"You kept me alive" he said appreciative "figuratively and literally"

"Did you think about me?" Joey asked

"Every day, I even spoke to you often you hold all my secrets" I admitted "I thought of us as a fairytale that ended way to soon"

When I thought he was passed I would talk to him all the time especially when life got hard, or I need someone to confide in he was the first person who came to mind. But I am glad he was not listening and that he is here with us today.

"Do you still love Drew" he asked

"Yes, but not in a romantic way anymore" I confessed "He caused me a ton of pain, he broke me, for years, and it took a lot of healing"

"I should have been there for you and Josie" he stated "I am sorry"

He reached out to hold my hand which was soothing for both of us. Josephine will always be a connection between us. I started to feel a bit lightheaded must be the wine I thought. Something feels off about this. I pushed the wine aside and grabbed my phone to text Jon.

"Somethings wrong. Please come!"

"Are you okay?" Joey asked

Then he got a crazed smile on his face as he pulled my phone from my hand

"Naughty girl" Joey smirked

His words came through in slow motion as my vision blurred until my memory was gone.

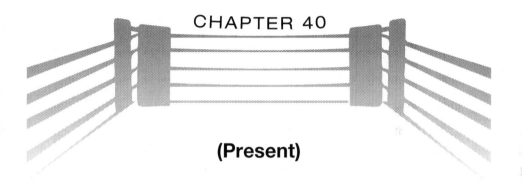

CHAPTER 40

(Present)

As I stirred trying to shake the clouds from yesterday away unable to remember much of anything. I opened my eyes looking at the ceiling confused by the foreign place I found myself in. I spent a few minutes just looking up watching the fan go around scared to look and see who or what I may see beside and around me. I took a breath to compose myself and looked to the side to see Joey beside me. Oh, no have I been taken? If so, I could not freak out I had to keep my wits about me to keep this from getting any worse and see how all this plays out. Although I was freaking out inside, I had to keep it deeply hidden.

I slowly rolled over facing Joey and placed my hand on his chest I steadied myself to keep him from feeling me shake. He covered my hand with his and rubbed his thumb up and down my hand. I did not enjoy playing along with this but at this point it is all I can think to do.

"Did we?" I asked holding my breath

"No babe you drank too much" he answered "So, I brought you to our home"

Thank goodness for that answer I could breathe again knowing he did not violate me in such an intimate way it is every woman's worst nightmare. "Our home" that scares me I am now a caged animal just as I was becoming free as a bird. Why me lord? Why? I must remember that God never gives you more than you can handle so this is just one more situation I will overcome.

"How sweet of you" I lied "Do you want some breakfast?"

"I would never turn down home cooking?" he said happily "but where is my morning kiss"

I leaned down giving him a kiss on the lips that burned like fire. Sitting up I realized I was in a nightgown which creeped me out because I know that I did not change myself. I felt as I had been invaded and was on the verge of tears, but I had to be tough, suck it up, and find a way out. I held my emotions tightly to me and kept collected on the outside. This was just like a horror plot.

We both got out the bed and headed towards the kitchen Joey was in nothing, but his boxers and I was in a dainty nightgown.

"You roll out of bed looking hot" he complimented

"You are pretty sexy yourself" I forced a smile

He gave me a peck on the lips as if we have been doing this for years. I was searching my brain for what to say so I could get a tip on what his intentions were, but my words were failing me. Was this like a hostage situation or just a one-time thing I sure did not feel like I had any freedom at this time and was scared to make the wrong move. Therefore, my actions may not be of someone who has been taken against their will, but it is all I can think of to keep hope and me alive. I hate being controlled but there is nothing that can be done presently. What is Jon thinking? Did he get my message? Does he know I would never runaway? Is anyone looking for me? I had so many questions running through my mind.

I cracked a few eggs, threw some bacon in the pan, and bread in the toaster to get breakfast going and keep my mind preoccupied. Joey came up behind me rubbing my shoulders and softly kissing my neck. It gave me goosebumps over my body like a protective shield. Does he not realize you cannot make someone love you? He knows what it is like to be taken so why would he bring the same fate to me? This feels so cruel.

"It feels so good having you back" he commented

"Yeah, it is nice" I lied again "Good thing I have three days off to spend with you"

I tried to bring him back to reality letting him know I had to go back to work. I then finished the meal, plated our portions, and we sat at the table to eat.

"About the whole wrestling thing" Joey stated "I thought you could put that on the back burner for now"

"I love what I do Joseph" I told him "Do you know how hard I worked to get where I am I would never ask you to give up your dreams"

"My dream is to have a family with you" he said

"That is not possible right now" I urged "I will not allow myself to indulge in infidelity"

"Cannot start something new when I am not even divorced yet" I explained "But I can have a family and a career"

"Maybe I should call Drew" I proposed "to get the ball rolling with the divorce"

"I do not want Drew to know you are here" he said "I do not want to hurt him"

"By now everyone knows were missing" I relented "Does not take much to figure it out"

"True" he replied

At last, I am getting somewhere and all I need is a minute or two because I can drop hints that only Drew would understand. Plus, everyone will know I was not here on my own volition, that I was alright, and to not stop looking. Surprisingly Joey reached out handing me his phone that I quickly dialed.

"Cammie?" Drew said frantically

"Yes" I answered "I need you to start divorce proceedings for me"

"Did he take you?" he questioned

"Yes, me and Joey are getting married" I said "all is okay back at home"

"So, your near home?"

"Pretty sure" I answered "can you say hello to kitty for me?"

"You are going to try to get him to take you to her grave"

"I got to go" I finished "send everyone my love"

Hanging up the phone I found some relief in knowing that Drew got every hint I was giving him and playing along, my heart was still pounding like a kick drum in my chest afraid that Joey could catch on to what I was planning and anxious at not knowing how Joey will react. I am in total worriment wondering what is going to happen next and if he will respect my no infidelity clause even if it was complete bull, he did not know that.

I did the dishes then took the garbage bag out of the bin to take outside thinking this was the perfect way to see if I was legit locked up or not. Joey looked up at me and chuckled.

"I will do that babe" he said kindly "sit back and relax"

I watched him pull the deadbolt key out of his pocket and open the door to bring the trash out but that was not enough time to get away. Well, now I know its official I am kidnapped.

"Do you have something I can change in to?" I asked

"Yes" he replied "look in the closet"

Opening the closet, I found it full of clothes and shoes that were all my style. Now I am even more panicked seeing all the thought he put into this and wondered how long he had been planning this. Will I ever get away? Looks like he is in this for the long haul and that is petrifying. The entire aura of this place feels dangerous making me miss Jon even more wanting to be with him in our home where I know I have safety in his arms. I sat on the corner of the bed and flicked the through the tv and there I was on headline news with a banner running across the bottom of the screen about my kidnapping and pictures of me and Joey plastered on the television set. I quickly changed the channel because I could not let Joey see that the world was looking for us because it may cause him to do something even more irrational. I then turned back to the closet pulling on a tie dye crop top, denim shorts, and heeled Mary Jane Doc Martins. Then walked back to the living room. Seeing all the people that are looking for me did at least give my mind some hope I can get away. They are not giving up on me so I will not give up on myself.

I stood in front of Joey doing a twirl then curtsied towards him bringing a huge grin to his face.

"Thanks babe" I thanked him "I love my new kicks"

"You look smoking" he commented "as always"

"Thank you" I smiled back

Then my eyes were drawn to the table next to the couch where Joey was sitting, and I saw a beer can sitting there.

"What the hell is this?" I asked angrily "Its only 10 in the morning"

"Should I wait until after lunch?" he inquired perplexed

"I would rather you not at all" I demanded "Your dad use to scared me and I will not live with a drunk"

All bets are off now because there is no telling what he is like when he is intoxicated and if he was anything like his father then I was in major danger. I know people change when they drink and that scares the living daylights out of me. Looking in his eyes I can see the pain he has pent up inside from everything he had stolen from him, and I understand that the alcohol numbs the pain he has and the pain he is dishing out because he must know what he is doing to me is deplorable. There are better ways to come to terms with and process all the emotions he is going through instead of saying one more drink and another so many things to deal with it.

"Camille" Joey looked into my eyes "do you still love me?"

"Always have, always will" I admitted "but it is a different love for you, Drew, and Jon"

"Why did you choose Jon?' he asked "is there something else you need from me"

I rubbed my face in my hands knowing I was about to hit him with the truth and the truth can hurt sometimes. I expect this will be one of those times.

"Before I start" I began "I would rather hurt myself than to hurt you"

"I understand it is going to be hard to hear" he replied

"When I lost you, I mourned you and our love but had to let it go, let you go, and your love go or hurt forever. Do you understand?" I began "With the man you are now most importantly lose the booze they are not fun anymore they are there just to get you drunk. You should not be in any relationships until you can fix the relationship with yourself and dry out. It is not your fault for the way things has happened in your life but from right now you are responsible for your own actions no more excuses. Get some mental health help and find yourself because you must learn to love yourself before you can even understand how to love someone else." I finished

"Wow a whole lecture" he smiled "but it does make sense"

"Joseph" I apologized "I am sorry we never had our chance"

"How can you love more than one person?"

This was a hard question to explain in a way that he will understand. I really did love all three of them, but I loved them all in their own way. Let us see what I can put together.

"Love is not like a switch that you can turn on and off" I explained "You were my first love no one can replace that we have so much history between us. Andrew was my second love, and it was beautiful full of great memories, but he broke my trust and I had to move on and let the relationship run its course which it did. Now I have a third love Jonathan, he sees me, and I see him we love each other it is a new mature love, but I believe it will be an enduring one and will be my last love."

"What if I never get over you?" he asked

"I have cried into my pillow asking myself that question many times" I answered "It comes with time when you least expect it trust me"

"I do" he replied

We sat in silence, and I was afraid of the many scenarios going through Joey's mind. I had an idea that if I could get Joey to agree to bring me to Josies gravesite I will be saved because Drew knows that is what I am planning from our short, coded conversation. This is all I have; it is my Hail Mary pass.

"Joey, can we go see Josephine" I asked "I want to introduce her to her daddy"

"That sounds good" he agreed "but as long as there are not too many people around"

"Thank you so much" I kissed him "Thank you babe"

After that confirmation came a well needed exhale and decompression. I was wound so tightly that my lungs were starved for air. I kept up the rouse laying my head in Joeys lap smacked full of exhaustion I feel asleep for a nap. I was wakened in the evening by the sound of glass crashing and Joeys cursing. I heard some cabinet doors being thrown open and closed and cautiously made my way to the kitchen where I was greeted by a cabinet door flying right towards my face, I saw Joey try to stop it as I did not have time to duck and got pummeled right in the face by it.

"Ouch!" I exclaimed in pain "What the hell Joseph"

Joey lowered his head and sat at the table looking very intoxicated.

"I am so sorry Cammie" he apologized though it was barely decipherable "I never meant to hurt you"

"But you did I am going to have a black eye" I fussed furiously "This would not have happened if you were sober"

"Come on babe" he slurred his words "Come here I am sorry"

I walked over to him with a disapproving look on my face. Just until tomorrow, Cammie, you can make it until tomorrow. Joey pulled me into his lap rubbing my legs and arm as he kissed my face that he hurt as the smell of alcohol coming from him turned my stomach. I jumped up quickly running to the bathroom where I puked. I usually have such a strong stomach, but I had been weakened I must admit. I have no patience left for a drunk tonight.

"Are you alright?" he asked seeming concerned

He did appear concerned had this woke him up. Am I giving him too much credit since I am not even sure he knows how to be concerned in his stupor?

"Yes, I will be fine I take bumps and bruises for a living" I said "but you need a shower, teeth brushing, and a good shave if you are sleeping with me tonight"

Joey did as I told then came in wearing nothing but a towel perhaps in a ploy to give me exotic thoughts which usual would have worked not so long ago but there is nothing sexy about being held captive.

"I know I am not built like Drew or Jon" he admitted "but it is all I have to work with"

"I like you the way you are" I told him "Your unspoiled like I always remembered you"

"I took my fingers running them across his chest letting him know I was being genuine. As he went to change into his boxers, I lowered my head to give him some privacy that he did not appear to want. Could he really be trying to seduce me at a time like this and believe it will work? Joey was an unwell man and needed to get the help he certainly needed.

"I see that I am fighting a losing battle" Joey conceded "I cannot force you to love me"

"I wish it could have been different Joseph" I said honestly "but the heart wants what the heart wants"

"I know your weary of me" he said with tear eyes "Just give me tonight one more night"

"What do you mean by that?" I asked

"Look I know your plans do not include me" he came to a rationalization "But I just want to hold you one more time, I will not cross any boundaries, I just need human touch"

"Okay" I said fatigued "It is a deal"

We got in bed I faced the wall as he held me from behind in a warm embrace. He kept our terms and crossed no lines just held me close to share human touch. I had on a pair of pajamas, and he was in his boxers, but he stayed a man of his word. I was uncomfortable in his arms it felt smothering to me as I waited for morning.

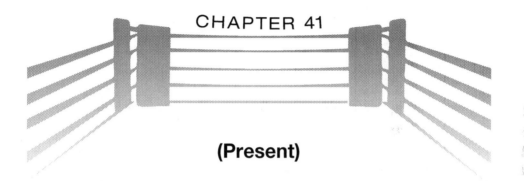

CHAPTER 41

(Present)

Daylight cannot come soon enough as I lie here confound in Joeys arms my skin feeling a blaze in his disturbing presence. Before this I had no discontent for Joey, but he has become someone I do not know, do not recognize. Yet I still feel as if I am in a conundrum because I know what Laura did to him was not right and stole much of his life, which I could image changes someone, but it is not right him doing this to me trying to steal my life that I fancy. I suppose even after what he has done, I still have a soft spot for him because I do not want to see him hurt or in trouble, I want him to get the help he deserves, and I get my freedom.

The clock has never ticked by so slowly as it is tonight which leaves nothing to do but think. How do I always seem to be the one who steps right into a mess every time? This is something that you watch on television or see on the news but it something you never believe will touch your own life. Oh, how wrong I was, and I am proof positive that this can happen to anyone. What is it about me that draws people to me? I never thought of myself as anyone out of the ordinary or anything special. That thought brought me back to a memory from when I first met my manager, Dwayne.

"Hey doll face nice to finally meet you" he greeted me *"I have heard lots about you but seeing you in person make it all so clear"*

"What do you see?" I inquired

"I can see and sense your magnetic axis" he smiled *"I have been doing this a long time and I have to say it is special what you do like you have a superpower"*

"Really" I said a little confused *"but you have not even seen me in the ring"*

"I do my homework and I know that the girl fans want to be you" he replied *"and guys fans want too just be with you because you are unique"*

"Thank you, Dwayne" I said

"Remember this you add to anyone you accompany in or out the ring" he gave me words of wisdom *"Then they get pulled in by the eccentric aura around you"*

Could it be true that I unwittingly pull people into my orbit then leaving them up there floating in the atmosphere. Why am I the one with this I am sure there is many people that can use this "superpower" better with it than me.

"I am a nowhere girl from a nowhere town" I replied *"nothing to special"*

"It works to your advantage" Dwayne praised *"your outlandish and mysterious side make for a great character"*

"Thanks " I replied

"Your special kid, going place, be ready" he smiled before leaving

And now here I am a bird who has had it wings clipped so it could not fly away. I have never been so contented to see the sun begin to peek in through the bedroom window, cars going by, and roster crowing. This quiet moment was so warm, and it was a welcome feeling from the iciness I felt lying next to Joey last night, but he seemed to enjoy it.

I was a bit torn though because on the one hand I cared for him and on the other hand I had nothing but words of venom from what he took me from my job, my friends, love, and Jon. He could have possibly exploded my life and my future, and I would not have even known. But I promised myself never to allow hatred or bitterness impact me and my psyche. I have become a survivor and plan on staying one. Plus, I have the scars and bruises to prove I earned my place in TWE and I tripped into Jon's heart as well. Stuff happens you just must be ready to go where the wind takes you.

"Good morning" I said joyful for the good morning

I was lying on my side facing the wall with my back to Joey. I felt my stomach churn with nausea as he pulled me tightly to him. The heat of his breathing on my neck gave me a barrier of goosebumps. He lightly rubbed his hand and my arm feeling my skins protective blockade.

"It felt good to hold you last night" Joey told me "It was so right"

Was he trying to convince himself or me because it is not working? I decided to keep quite unaware of what to say in response because all my feelings toward him are acrimonious. If you do not have something to say, do not say anything at all.

"Did you sleep well?" he asked stalling for time

"Yes" I lie "I have been dreaming of my sweet girl all night"

Well, I have come this far, I am not going to give up now, here goes nothing. I rolled over facing Joey as I moved the hair from his eyes and caressed his face in my hands while he closed his eyes in satisfaction. I finished with a kiss giving him as much as of the human touch he was craving that I could give him.

"Ready to go see Josephine" I hoped to hear a yes

"If there is to many people there we will not stop" he commanded

"I have a freaking black eye from last night damaging my money maker" I said forcefully "you owe me this"

"Yes, babe your right" he conceded

Thank goodness the plan is still on I sure hope Drew is prepared and passed on the mission instructions. I wish my heart had a steel gate I could close around it in times like this when I must go with my head although I usually follow loves sweet journey. For example, I feel bad for joey who has drugged me and kidnapped me. I feel bad because I played along or stringed him along with it but that was my survival instincts. I never wanted to be that girl. This feels like hell.

I do know I have spent most of my life making sure others were happy which could have been selfish on my part because when everyone was happy was the only time, I could be happy.

I have always been more of a giver than taker. Yet still worried about what people thought of me, did they like me, and was I giving enough of myself to the audience. But Jon soon reminded me there was an in between in which we could escape to. I want to take his advice, live on my terms, and with whomever I chose. I decided too finally live for me.

"I am ready" Joey called out "how about you"

"One more minute" I responded

Now was my turn to stall making sure the guys had time to get here. I dressed especially for my mission with bright green yoga pants, bright pink crop top, and matching bright green sneakers that were good for running. One way or another I will reclaim my freedom today because I would rather die than to live without liberty.

"Okay" I said "all set to go"

My blood pressure rose, and pulse quickened in a state of vigilance as we drove into the graveyard. I had to be on guard and keep my head on a swivel so I will be first to know when the calvary arrives. I directed Joey where to go then we walked hand in hand to Josephine's headstone where I rubbed my hand up and down the marble to make me feel more connected to my precious daughter.

"Josephine Jolee" I called out my voice quivering "its momma"

"Hi Josie, it is your daddy" tears flowed from Joey "I am glad to finally have met you."

Seeing Joey get so chocked up emotionally almost caused me weep, but I could not stop thinking about my escape plan and knowing that if it comes down to it, I will do it all alone.

"I am sorry I did not get to know you" Joey talked to Josephine

"There is plenty of time now Joey" I responded "it will all work itself out its okay"

As he cried, I scoped out my surrounding trying to see if I could catch site of anything, but I logically knew if they had to drive here, I maybe a couple hours which I do not have. Good thing I have on my good running shoes because it seems I may need them.

"Are you alright?" I asked Joey with genuine concern

"Yeah, I am good cause your here with me" he replied

"I am glad you kept your sweetness "I `said "You always played tough but never with me"

"It is okay" I rubbed his hand for comfort since I am not made of ice.

"You honestly think so?" he asked "after everything I have done to you"

"Yes, I do" I replied "we all mess up sometimes"

While we talked, I viewed two figures headed our way and knew my rescue crew had arrived. I turned back to talking with Joey to keep him distracted plus this may be our last conversation. I have no clue how this was going to play out. I pray it is peaceful and nonviolent, but I am prepared for anything.

"Are you ready to go home?" he asked of me

"No, you promised to let me go" I fussed "What changed your mind?"

"I am sorry Cammie" he apologized "but it has to be this way"

It was as if a switch had just pulled in his brain. Now I must compete with a total stranger because I had no idea who he was now. He changes from hot into cold in a second and was a very unpredictable man.

"Joseph" Drew yelled viciously

"What the..." Joey jumped up "I should have known you would set me up"

"What choice did I have" I spit back "I sure cannot trust you"

Joey grabbed my arm yanking me up forcefully pulling me in near him as he took a black Glock 9-millimeter out of his pocket and held it to my side. I was not expecting this!

"What is that for?" I asked tense

"Just in case" he said monotoned

This situation just went from a single flame to a four-alarm fire with seconds. I had not just put myself in jeopardy but also Drew and Jon now their blood will be on my hands.

"Come on bro" Drew pleaded "let her go"

"Stop interrupting me" he shouted "I am talking to Cammie"

"Why did you make me do this?" Joey asked sourly

"Do not put your blame on me" I replied "I was surviving"

"We could have had it all" he suggested

"You could have had it all" I was honest "I would get a loveless life of misery with a full-blown alcoholic that accidently gives the woman he claims to love a black eye"

I was determined to get out of this standoff with Jon and Drew being safe because if something happens to one of them, I will never forgive myself. And I pay very good attention to what people say and do not say so I was positive he was going to gun for Jon even if there is no reason to. Jon is his biggest threat. I have decided that the scenario I formulated in my head had a high likability of happening. My plan may not be the best but right now it is what I got.

"You have been so tender with me" Joey said "I thought you would want to come back"

"You low life look at her in the face" Jon said angrily "Still think that is what she wants?"

"It was a drunken accident she forgave me" he screamed get angrier

"Why did you pretend Camille" Joey asked

"It was not all pretend, but I wanted my freedom back" I snapped "Plus look how you are acting now, you scare me"

I wanted to tear my way from Joey and feel Jon's loving embrace, but I logically know I cannot outrun a bullet.

"Joey please come with me" I suggested "get some help"

"No thanks" he responded coldly

"I am sorry, but you need me" he said "to protect you from these two arrogant fools walking all over you"

"Arrogant at times, fools now and again, but walking on me NEVER" I made it clear

"What does Jon have that I do not have?" he asked

He always brings it back to Jon it is exhausting and this gun in my side is making me sore.

"This is not a competition Joey" I said frustrated

"I need these answers" he begged

"Alright well you asked for it. He has a job, not an alcoholic, never held me against my will, he does not depend on words like I love you to make me feel warm and fuzzy, it is the small things he does that lets me know he loves me, shows how he cares, doing things like just cause its Wednesday, thinks before he acts" I continued "He shows love in action and I love him madly and deeply and there is nothing you can do to change that"

"But I can erase him" he shouted

This was the moment I had been waiting all this time for. *Josie baby its momma, bring me with you or leave me here to live on I love you.*

"I love you Jon" I said just incase

He pointed the gun at Jon as the world around me moved in slow motion I watched as Joey pulled the trigger time to put the doomsday scenario in place. Love in action. I jumped straight in front of Joey as I heard a loud pop with my ears ringing and my left shoulder felt like it was being branded.

Now Finally I was in Jon's arms as he cradled me saying the police and ambulance will be here soon as Drew kept Joey pinned to the ground.

"Your insane you know that?" Jon asked

"Just a little" I managed a smile

"Why did you do that?" he inquired

"He was aiming straight for you" I said "Love through action"

"I am one blessed man" he kissed me "to have an angel like you"

As the paramedics put me in the ambulance, I could see the police putting Joey in handcuffs. A slight tear fell from my eye because I knew he was going to be imprisoned again except this time it will be a whole new world for him.

At the hospital they said I should recover well but rest for a few weeks, I will try but I cannot promise I can sit steal all that time. I also cannot wait to spend lots of time with Jon as he is nursing me back to health then when I get back, I have a Goddess Championship bout ready for me and I cannot wait to put that gold around my waist and hear my fans yelling, jumping, and cheering for "MISS PENNY LANE"

'THE END .

Printed in the United States
by Baker & Taylor Publisher Services